THE HANDYMAN

Julie and Bob Foster are a happily married couple with an adorable five-year-old son. Bob is going from strength to strength in his work, and when Harry, a self-employed do-it-yourself expert, arrives to help out around the home, nothing seems brighter.

But after Harry's arrival, things start to go suspiciously wrong. Harry's cheerfulness and goodwill allow him to be a babysitter as well as helping out around the home and Bob begins to resent Julie's affection for him, suspecting mischief. And then Bob's company goes bankrupt and after a violent struggle with Harry, he finds himself in a near fatal condition.

Handyman Harry has seemingly fixed everything — but in a way no one had ever dared to imagine. For the Fosters, the man who rebuilt their home is subtly, savagely destroying their lives . . .

**Also by the same author,
and available in New English Library:**

STRIKER

The Handyman

Gerald Suster

NEW ENGLISH LIBRARY
Hodder and Stoughton

Copyright © 1985 by Gerald Suster

First published in Great Britain in 1985
by Severn House Publishers Limited.

New English Library Paperback edition 1987

British Library C.I.P.

Suster, Gerald
 The handyman.
 I. Title
 823'.914[F]   PR6069.U/

 ISBN 0–450–37912–X

*The characters and situations in this book are
entirely imaginary and bear no relation to any real
person or actual happening*

This book is sold subject to the condition that
it shall not, by way of trade or otherwise, be
lent, re-sold, hired out, or otherwise circulated
without the publisher's prior consent in any
form of binding or cover other than that in
which it is published and without a similar
condition including this condition being
imposed on the subsequent purchaser.

Printed and bound in Great Britain for
Hodder and Stoughton Paperbacks, a
division of Hodder and Stoughton Ltd.,
Mill Road, Dunton Green, Sevenoaks,
Kent (Editorial Office: 47 Bedford
Square, London WC1B 3DP) by
Cox & Wyman Ltd., Reading

To MAGGIE, whose fears inspired this nightmare and whose love inspired me.
And for MATTHEW and for YAWAR, whose support enabled me to do it.

I and the public know
What all schoolchildren learn,
Those to whom evil is done
Do evil in return.

W. H. Auden

Prologue

ALTHOUGH SHE was thirty, she stood obediently in a corner with her hands behind her back and a dunce's cap upon her head.

There was no one in the room but she never once looked round. She just stood there with her face pressed against the wall, like a little girl in disgrace years and years ago, yet wearing a smart, tailored suit in navy blue with black high heels.

She could not believe this was happening to her, every instinct shrieked out that this was some vile dream. It was impossible that this could be her fate – but the chill of the wall on her nose was real enough, as was the ache in her pressured heels and the excruciating, interminable boredom which tortured her mind into a numbed and catatonic acquiescence on the borderland of sanity.

Time and time again her memory had replayed the sequence of events which had led her to this pitiable state. She saw now all she had missed then. Every incident had been analysed in minute detail and there were moments when she wanted to rend and tear herself for her stupidity – and yet it all had its own horrific and inevitable logic.

Footsteps sounded outside the room. Her body stiffened to attention as her mind went blank.

He was coming.

Part One

1

SOME TIME before the events just described took place, another woman stood alone in the centre of a room and stared fixedly at a photograph. It was just before midnight.

Her face was impassive. One couldn't tell what she was thinking or if she was thinking at all. Judging by the lines around her eyes and the whitening of her blonde curls, she was in her early sixties, though most attractive for her age. The soft flesh of her cheeks had remained smooth and unlined, adding necessary charm to a thin, wide mouth which tightened at the corners. The eyes were clear blue and hard. Her nose was small and straight, with nostrils that were flared and snobbish. The overall expression was prim and smug, suggesting a life of ease with sex appeal lurking behind lace curtains.

The woman wore a smart, tailored suit in navy blue. It graced a body which had grown plump but could still cut a tall figure. Her legs boasted slim calves and she was aware of it, for she wore black leather pumps with high heels.

She gazed steadily down at the gilt-framed photograph held in her white hands with their manicured finger-nails. A sheet of glass separated her stare from the faded black-and-white portrait of a man's face.

He had the sort of features which recalled World War Two newsreels: young, strong and resolute. The wide eyes gazed out of the picture with a joyous innocence. A firm jaw was clamped upon the stem of a briar pipe. The head was crowned by rich, dark hair which had been immaculately brushed back. His broad shoulders were adorned by the uniform of a naval officer.

Behind the woman and the photograph, the thick drapes were drawn. The only light in the bedroom came from a shaded standard lamp in white onyx and gold. The only sound was the woman's even breathing.

Gradually her breathing altered, becoming faster and increasingly shallow. Her ample bosom heaved aggressively with each pant as a crimson flush infused her pale complexion and rose in mottled blotches around her throat. Abruptly her blue eyelids twitched upwards, her stare widened and her eyes blazed with a cold, controlled fury. Her lips puckered as if about to implant a chilly kiss.

There was a sudden, deep intake of breath. The man in the photograph remained innocently confident.

The woman's head rocked once before she spat into his face.

2

JULIE FOSTER had no idea that her nightmare would begin with a strange woman spitting at a photograph and her own desire earlier that day for an extra shelf in the kitchen.

For a long time Bob and Julie had talked about putting up that shelf. Both agreed that the kitchen needed it. Bob had bought the wood, the brackets, the Rawlplugs and the screws. It was obviously a very simple matter. Any fool could do it.

Except Bob and Julie. Julie hated do-it-yourself, it bored her to tears – sometimes literally – and she had no talent for it at all. Unfortunately Bob was the same. There were moments when Julie resented that intensely. She'd been brought up to believe that men always took care of that kind of thing.

Still, they'd had a try at doing it themselves. That started badly and grew worse. Bob didn't have a spirit level so it took half an hour simply to get the measurements right. Then Bob went to work with the hand drill – Julie's father had refused to lend them the power drill because Bob had broken it last time. Forty minutes later he was still drilling – and cursing the drill, the wall, do-it-yourself generally and Julie's father. Next they discovered that he'd bought the wrong screws. Julie lost patience.

'It's all right, love,' she said with cold sarcasm, 'there's no need to scream and shout just because you're not up to it.'

He glared at her and flung down the drill. 'If you're such a goddamn smart ass,' he snarled, 'do it yourself.'

That catapulted them into their first major row in months, though they made it up within an hour and swore they'd never again do it themselves. Bob insisted he'd pay for a handyman – he'd always felt guilty about being an impractical householder. Julie, who went halves on most home expenses, said that she'd take care of finding the handyman. Both were happy with that agreement. They were happy with most of their agreements.

So Julie bought the local paper for the very first time, looked through the classifieds and saw this advertisement: 'HARRY THE HANDYMAN. Cheap and Cheerful. I can fix anything.' A telephone number followed. Julie rang it.

'Good afternoon,' came a woman's shrill, affected voice, which surprised Julie. It was the sort of voice one might expect if one were calling, not Harry the handyman but the madam chairman of some suburban church bazaar.

'Good afternoon, could I speak to Harry the handyman, please?' Julie wondered momentarily if she'd dialled the wrong number, but after a pause a man's voice came down the line. It was ordinary and common and just what she'd originally expected.

Yes, Harry would certainly put up the shelf and as soon as Julie wanted it done. Yes, tomorrow evening at six would be fine. The cost? Well, he couldn't say for certain until he'd had a look at the job but it definitely wouldn't be more than a fiver.

And that was how Harry the handyman came in.

3

'HELLO! HARRY the handyman? Come right in.'

He was of medium height and build and looked extremely fit for a man she judged to be in his mid-forties. His clean-shaven face with its warm brown eyes was open and cheerful as advertised. His appearance was smarter than she'd expected, for he wore a clean white shirt, tightly knotted thin tie, navy blue blazer, grey flannel trousers and highly polished black brogues. His dark brown hair, greying at the edges, was short, oiled, and combed straight back.

''Evening, Mrs Foster,' he sang out as he stepped over her threshold. 'Need a shelf put up then, do you?' He gestured with the canvas bag he was carrying. Julie led him past the living room where her son Michael was watching TV, and into the spacious kitchen.

'Over there.' She pointed to an alcove, its white wall scarred by the holes Bob had drilled. 'We've already had a try ourselves but unfortunately... we didn't really have the right tools.'

'Oh, well, then, you didn't stand a chance,' Harry replied sympathetically. 'There's no doubt about it, you can't do a proper job without the right tools. Just leave it to me,' he assured her proudly. 'I'll have it done for you in no time.'

'Great. If you need anything, just give me a shout. I'll be in the other room.'

Harry called out to her exactly fifteen minutes later. Julie returned to the kitchen to see that the shelf had been put up perfectly. A tieless, shirt-sleeved Harry was packing faded blue overalls into his canvas bag.

'There we are!' he declared. 'Ever seen a straighter shelf than that?'

'No. It's very good.'

'And it's strong. It'll hold. Look.' Harry placed his hands

on the shelf and lifted himself off the ground. 'You can put a lot of weight on that, you can. It's a good, solid wall you've got here.' He rapped it approvingly. 'And you know what the real trick is?'

'No?' Julie tried to appear interested. 'What is the real trick?'

'Number eight screws,' Harry stated dogmatically. 'The long ones. And the reason for that is because you have to penetrate through the plaster into the brickwork by about twenty-five millimetres. So always remember: if it's shelves, it's number eight screws. The long ones.'

'Number eight screws, the long ones,' Julie echoed him dutifully. 'I'll remember that. Thank you.' She stifled a yawn then smiled brightly. 'Well, how much did we agree?'

'For that?' Harry thought briefly. 'Three pounds fifty seems fair to me.'

'That's very reasonable.' Julie gave him the money gladly. 'D'you do anything else?'

'Just about anything around the house,' said Harry. 'Painting, carpentry, plumbing, electrics, washing machines – I'm a dab hand with those – televisions, upholstery... cars too. Jack of all trades, that's me. Oh, and I can do locks as well. Any time you lock yourself out, I'm the man you call. The police always take hours. Other people in the trade'll charge you the earth – and some of them are burglars. Now, I'll get your door open for a fiver. I can fix anything. Harry the handyman, see, that's me.'

'Great,' said Julie, and meant it. She'd suffered terrible experiences with repair men in the past. They were always late, did the job slowly and badly, charged you a small fortune and, six weeks later, whatever they'd done went wrong again and someone else had to be called in. If Harry was as good as he claimed, and so far so good, then he was a godsend. 'Like a cup of tea?' she offered.

'Kind of you, Mrs Foster, but no thanks. I'm expected home for dinner and I don't want to risk spoiling my appetite. She's making roast pork with all the trimmings tonight. Beautiful!'

'Your wife's a good cook, is she?' Julie smiled.

'Oh, it's not my wife,' Harry explained. 'I'm a bachelor as it happens. No, it's my mum who's the marvellous cook. I live with her, you see. Why leave home?' Harry demanded earnestly. 'That's what I want to know. And I don't mind telling you that my mum is the best mum in the world.'

'That's nice.'

'Wonderful mum,' Harry continued relentlessly. 'Everything I am today I owe to her. She's what I call a real lady. Anyway,' he shuffled his feet, 'must be off. Call me any time, Mrs Foster, and a pleasure meeting you.' Julie escorted him to the front door. 'Oh, one thing,' he said, as she opened it, 'couldn't help noticing you've got a little boy.' He glanced back at the living room. 'I do babysitting too.'

'Oh.' Julie nodded. 'Well, thanks, I'll bear that in mind.'

'But don't spread it around,' said Harry. 'It's not a service I advertise because I'll only do it in decent homes, so mum's the word, eh?'

After he left, Julie frowned. There was something odd about a man in his forties offering to babysit and she decided it wouldn't be suitable for Michael. Then she smiled when she recalled Harry looking at her conspiratorially and saying: 'Mum's the word' – an expression she hadn't heard used in ages. Anyway, the shelf was done and done well and if anything went wrong around the house, she had the answer in Harry. Julie poured herself a dry sherry and went on to things she considered more interesting.

After he left Julie Foster's home, an expressionless Harry drove through the suburban streets in his Ford, taking the main road towards Kingston and Surbiton, with the poorer parts of Wimbledon to the north. There was nothing exceptional about the area he passed through. It had begun the century as Surrey countryside and during the Thirties it had been colonised by ribbon development. There were uninspiring but solid brick houses on either side of the road and the only difference between them was the colour of their front doors. The shopping centre through which his car cruised had no individuality either: banks, a post office, a supermarket, an Indian newsagent's next to an Indian restaurant, which had recently added the slogan 'Best Tandoori' next to an elderly sign which proclaimed 'Best Curry', a Chinese take-away which also sold fish and chips, all with façades of unrelieved drabness.

It wasn't an area to which one would go for a life of glamour and excitement. That was precisely what attracted its residents. Young married couples, such as Bob and Julie Foster, saw in it the chance to buy a comfortable house at a reasonable price, where they'd be within easy striking distance of London and could raise children in a cosy environment free from urban violence and decay. Older residents – and those one saw in the street looked as though they'd lived there for a very long time – appreciated the fact that very little ever happened to disturb their settled routine. It was the sort of district where the majority spent their evenings at home or at their friends' homes, and those who went out in search of stimulation had to go elsewhere.

Harry turned into a series of side roads, then stopped when he reached a small public park. It was still light when he left the car and strolled through the gates to a bench, where he sat down contentedly. Above him, there was a mass of low, grey cloud of the type which threatens rain without producing it and some might have found the sultry atmosphere oppressive, but Harry seemed oblivious to the air and to the sky. In front of him, there was an asphalt surface with children yelling and howling and playing and kicking a ball around and he watched them with pleasure.

Some time later, he got back into the car and drove for a mile or so to a leafy avenue, lined with trees and substantial houses of red brick with sloping roofs. Harry parked the vehicle in the garage of one, closed the doors and walked swiftly towards the entrance.

Within the house, a woman watched him from an upstairs window, net curtains veiling her from view. Upon her face was etched an expression of spiteful satisfaction.

4

'I AM not putting my name to this report,' said Bob Foster.

'Don't you think,' Charles Haughey suggested silkily, 'that you're being just a little bit unreasonable?'

'Unreasonable?' His gravelly Chicago voice deepened in pitch. 'Hell, it's flying people in planes that're unsafe that's unreasonable.'

'Oh, for heaven's sake, Bob...' Haughey's finely chiselled features stiffened into lines of condescending disdain. 'Hugh's signed it. Giles has not only signed it but expressed the utmost confidence. Brian Brandreth's happy with it too.'

'Sure,' said Bob, 'they haven't talked to the men who built it.'

'Hugh, Giles and Brian are solid professionals,' Haughey insisted. 'You can't deny that.'

'Have you talked to the men who built it?' Bob retorted. 'I'm telling you they're not happy. They're telling me they weren't given enough time.'

'Enough time? Really! They've taken far too long as it is. Anyway, who's not happy? Parsons tells me he's perfectly happy and he's the chief engineer.'

'Parsons,' Bob answered steadily, 'is a lazy, time-serving yes-man who couldn't give a shit about anything except saving his ass.'

'I say, steady on,' Haughey adjusted his tie. 'I think that's a bit over the top, quite frankly.'

'Then you're not understanding me right, Charles. The company pays me to do something to the best of my ability, which is...'

'I'm perfectly well aware of your job description, Bob, and it would...'

'May I please finish what I was saying?' Bob requested courteously. There was a pause while Haughey sighed softly. 'Thank you. My job is to ensure that every plane we put out

23

meets the required and essential specifications of safety. This plane does not. It almost gets there but it doesn't quite. My name does not go on that report until I am satisfied that it does.'

'I can't help feeling you're quibbling about minor and inessential details.'

'It's the minor and seemingly inessential details,' Bob said, 'which make the difference between a safe flight and a crash with four hundred dead.'

'That's a rather melodramatic scenario, surely,' Haughey commented acidly. 'You seem to be forgetting that I have to talk to the board on Monday. If I can't inform them we're ready to go, I assure you they won't be pleased. You know as well as I do that the company's in trouble. I appreciate your point of view but it pains me that you refuse to see mine. We're way behind schedule as it is.'

'Because the schedule itself was wholly unrealistic.' Bob stared at Haughey, who looked away. 'I told you that at the time.'

'It was perfectly realistic,' Haughey sniffed indignantly. 'It's just that the workers are quite impossibly lazy.'

'That's not my impression. My impression, from spending quite a while with them, is that they're professionals who want to do a good job same as you and me – and they need time in order to do it.'

'Oh, dear,' Haughey sighed again. 'We don't seem to be getting anywhere. And I can't say I care for the intransigence of your attitude. The word "compromise" doesn't seem to exist in your vocabulary.'

'Not where people's lives are concerned, that's true.'

'I think you're being deliberately difficult,' snapped Haughey. 'It's not a good idea, you know, for people to have that impression of you.' He glanced sharply at Bob. 'Think about it over the weekend. The board isn't meeting till midday on Monday, so there's still time for you to change your mind.'

'My decision is final,' Bob returned firmly. 'Until the full specifications are met, I won't be signing.'

'Oh,' said his boss. 'Pity.'

*

As his Audi left the traffic jams of the inner city for the suburbs and the pub where he'd arranged to meet Julie, Bob silently cursed Charles Haughey as the type of Englishman he couldn't bear. The man was inefficient, overbearing to his inferiors and sycophantic to those above him, and seemed to owe his high position entirely to accidents of birth, education and the resulting connections. In the States he wouldn't last a day, Bob reflected.

Not that he disliked the country where he'd lived and worked for the past three years. After all, his father had been English and so was his wife. He'd loved Britain when he'd first visited nine years ago and met Julie. Yet there were certain things about the place which had come to annoy him intensely – like the weather; the class system; the hostility to innovation; the difficulties in the way of becoming rich; and men like Charles Haughey. There were moments when he sighed for sunny California.

He'd first gone there at eighteen, shortly after his mother died. There'd been nothing left for him in the shabby, brownstone neighbourhood in Chicago where he'd grown up. The father he'd adored had been killed in a car crash when Bob was twelve. All his mother's relatives were scattered around Kansas and Missouri. It hadn't been difficult for a youth with his ambitions to say goodbye to the Windy City and go west to Los Angeles. There, he'd worked his way through college, enjoyed the sunshine and the girls while enduring more of the hard times he was used to, qualified as an aeronautical engineer and found a good job with an aircraft company. Within a few years of working furiously hard, he'd attained the California dream and was the proud possessor of a mortgaged Laurel Canyon house with a hot tub, a BMW, membership of the Mulholland tennis club and all the accompanying gadgets and pursuits which prompt Californians to wax enthusiastic about the LA life style. He went surfing, ski-ing and scuba diving, ate in the best restaurants and drank in the bars with the most beautiful girls. He could have had a different woman every night if he'd wanted that and sometimes he did. He owed large sums of money to banks, stores and credit card companies but so did everyone else he knew, and his income took care of his debts. He didn't have a boat but that would certainly come in time – in fact, the one thing he was conscious of lacking was love.

In his experience, Californian women were delightful but superficial. He was too much a native of Chicago to fall for gloss alone, too alert to the detection of mercenary motives. Far too many of the girls he met were out to hook that little gold wedding band with its attached meal ticket for life. They were more interested in what a man had than in who he was, which was fine if the object was sex but not if one wanted a wife. So Bob watched his friends get caught, get married, get miserable, get divorced and get stripped of half their wealth and possessions but wasn't tempted to marry himself.

He travelled. He visited the East Coast, Spain, Italy, France, Germany – and England. That was where he met and fell in love with Julie. She wasn't the most attractive girl he'd known by a long way but she turned him on more and that was what mattered. For him, she was beautiful and all other opinions were irrelevant. He adored her body, respected her mind and was dazzled by her decency.

He'd become so infatuated over just ten days that he'd wanted to buy her a sapphire ring. To his amazement, she wouldn't allow it.

'It's you I care about,' she said. 'I don't want some precious stone to flash around just to impress people. Don't do it, love, it's a waste of money.'

For two years they saw one another at intervals. He came and stayed with her in London, she went and visited him in Los Angeles and once they met up for a glorious week in New York. Julie was going through a period of being fed up with England and at last Bob persuaded her to quit her job and come and live with him in California. Within six months they were married and a year later, Michael was born.

Their marriage was even happier than Bob had envisaged, apart from one important factor. After initial enraptured enthusiasm for a new way of life, Julie grew to dislike living in California. She missed her friends and – to her surprise – her country. She complained about the lack of intellectual stimulation and emotional depth. She called Los Angeles 'a society of surfaces' and found its obsessive materialism crass and boring. Bob suggested that as soon as Michael was old enough, Julie should qualify at the California bar – he'd gladly pay for her studies – and work as the lawyer she was, if that was what she wanted. But Julie was appalled by the legal system in which rhetorical gimmicks counted for more than reasoned argument, in which winning was more important than justice and in which the latter could be bought and sold like any other commodity.

'There're bad judges in England,' she'd said. 'Incompetent judges, perverse judges, stupid judges. But there aren't any corrupt judges owing political favours. You just can't buy an English judge.'

'Aw, c'mon, honey,' Bob had replied, 'who're you kidding?'

'You don't understand.' She shook her head and fell silent.

Bob couldn't endure his wife's visible and increasing misery. He secretly started to explore the possibilities of working in England. One night he took Julie out to dinner and told her he'd landed a job supervising quality control at a British aircraft corporation and how did she feel about moving back to London? She cried with happiness.

They moved to the suburbs of the city which Julie, originally from Lancashire, had come to regard as her own. Bob earned less than he had in LA and credit wasn't as freely available, but when Michael was four Julie went back to her old job and so, by English standards, they lived well. Six months ago they'd bought a large house in a prosperous district, though they couldn't yet afford to do anything with the bare basement. They spent to the limit of their incomes, enjoyed an active social life and were still madly in love. Julie had the joy of being back in her own country among her own kind and her pleasure evoked his.

No, Bob thought as his car neared the friendly brick

building where he'd be meeting Julie before the dinner party, there was little in his life to complain about. It was the weekend now and he should try to forget the sour aftertaste left by his meeting with Charles Haughey. He was looking forward to seeing Julie and hearing all about her day. Was it unusual that he still delighted in her presence after six years of marriage?

'Mum's the word? What does that mean?' Michael asked his mother.

'Well, it's a rather old-fashioned expression,' Julie explained. 'I haven't heard it in years. It means don't say anything. Keep mum. Keep silent.'

'Why does keeping mum mean keeping silent?'

'Don't know.'

'Why don't you know?' Michael demanded accusingly.

'No one's ever told me, love,' Julie responded, and finished her sherry. 'Anyway, I'm going to have a bath. If the babysitter comes, let her in, okay?'

'What's her name?'

'Louise – a student. She seems very nice. And this time,' Julie's voice hardened, 'I don't want *any* bad behaviour.'

'Bad behaviour?' His face became a picture of outraged innocence.

'Listen, you. Don't give me that wide-eyed look because it doesn't fool me for a moment. You were an absolute little horror with poor Liz and it's not surprising she doesn't want to come again. One hint that you've disgraced yourself again and I'll explode. Got it?' He nodded placidly. 'Right. Bath.'

'Mum's the word, all right,' Julie sighed moments later when her firm body sank into the caressing comfort of hot, steaming, scented water. Michael had been quite a handful recently. Last week there'd been the Liz incident and the week before he'd been fighting at school again. It was a pity that Bob had been away twice over the last three weeks. She thought their son needed his father's presence.

God, the bath felt good. She could feel her aches and

tensions dissolving blissfully in its warmth. What a day! Up at seven thirty for her keep fit class. Taking Michael to school. An infuriating traffic jam on the way to work. A tedious day in court. A miserable time shopping for a few essentials in an overcrowded supermarket. Collecting Michael from Angela's. Having the handyman in – at least that had gone well. And at least she could look forward to this evening.

Julie began soaping her body with a big sponge. Although she knew that most men found her attractive, she still lacked real confidence in her looks. Exercise kept her waist trim and her legs were fine but she felt that her hips were too full and her breasts too small. Bob could've told her how he loved her tits and ass every night of the week – he often did – and she still would've been only temporarily reassured.

Even so, she had justifiable confidence in her hair which was blonde, straight and lush. It covered her high forehead with a fringe and curled under her chin, imparting an appealing impishness to her rounded face. Here, her most striking features were her clear blue eyes and her soft mouth with its pouting lower lip. The softness of her skin – the only lines were those of laughter round the eyes – made her look younger than her thirty years.

Stepping out of the bath, Julie rubbed herself down with a rough towel, leaving her skin with a glowing, tingling sensation. She smiled slightly. There were very few things about which Julie felt smug but one of them was her sex life.

She donned a white robe, entered the softly lit bedroom with its king-size double bed, stepped over a copy of *Cosmopolitan* and opened the walk-in wardrobe. Julie didn't think she was obsessed by possessions and had never measured anyone's worth in terms of a bank balance, but she did take pleasure in contrasting her current affluence with her origins.

Her childhood had been spent on the dingy streets of the industrial North. Though she'd never known the grim poverty of which her parents still spoke, she'd been reared in conditions of genteel, working-class respectability, which she thought cramped all expression of style and individuality. Well-heeled London intellectuals who romanticised the warmth and honesty of proletarian Lancashire made her sick. Her first ambition had been to escape.

She'd done that through winning a scholarship to a school in Surrey, then a place at Bristol University. A respectable second-class law degree followed and she moved to London. There she was called to the bar but her fellow barristers alarmed her. Many who had been born to the law sniped at her for being a woman and ridiculed her humble origins. 'Crosby, Lancashire?' the Hon. Cecil Woldringham had remarked once. 'Where on earth is Crosby, Lancashire? Sounds like a clapped-out old music hall star.'

'Isn't that the place,' another mimicked her accent badly, 'where they eat all that bluck pooding an' tripe an' onions?'

Her one concession had been the gradual dropping of her northern accent. But when these assaults with their sexist digs continued, she decided it wasn't very creditable to be at large in such company and left the bar with relief to qualify as a solicitor. She was good at her job – general advocacy in the lower courts and family law, mainly – and content with her salary of sixteen thousand a year.

Selecting an outfit she'd bought recently – a simple white top, a flared pink skirt from Monsoon and black, open-topped shoes – Julie began to dress. It rarely took her long to get ready and fifteen minutes later, she went downstairs to greet Louise, the babysitter, who had just arrived. After introducing the girl to Michael, Julie gave her a drink, phoned for a mini-cab and showed Louise around the kitchen. She switched on the sink's waste disposal unit but nothing happened. For a moment, Julie felt irritated because it wasn't working.

Then she smiled with relief when she remembered there was a perfect solution in Harry the handyman.

As Julie entered the pub, she saw a big, handsome man with a craggy face who looked very clean and who was drinking scotch on the rocks. She was instantly attracted to him – then abruptly shocked into the delightful realisation that he was Bob.

'Hi, honey,' he greeted her with a smile and a kiss, then bought her a gin and tonic and they sat down. 'How was your day?' He looked genuinely interested.

'Pretty dull,' said Julie. 'One of those. Not much one can say about it, really. How was yours?' He told her about Haughey. 'What a creep!' she exclaimed. 'I mean, he's risking people's lives on planes so he can impress the board. That's terrible.'

'Right. That's why I can't sign the report.'

'No, you can't.' Then she added with concern: 'D'you think you've antagonised him again?' Bob nodded.

'Ain't much I can do,' he sighed, 'so I'll forget about it till Monday.' Julie still marvelled at his ability suddenly to switch off a matter entirely. 'Another?' He regarded her empty glass.

'Okay – as long as you're driving.' His fingers brushed the back of her hand as he took the glass and strode over to the bar. 'Thanks,' she said when he returned. 'Oh, one piece of trivial but good news,' she told him. 'The handyman came and the shelf's been put up perfectly.'

'Gee, that's made my day,' Bob returned drily. 'And was he "cheap and cheerful"?'

'Absolutely. And only three pounds fifty. He does other things too. So your days of torment are over, love, and you can forget that life subscription to *Practical Householder*. Remember our row over the shelf?' Julie laughed. 'You know, I sometimes wonder if you're really an engineer at all – I suspect it's all a fraud. Anyway, I don't need you any more. I've got Harry the handyman now. You'd better watch out or he'll be the man around the house.'

'I'm jealous.' Bob smiled. 'You know, I'm really jealous. Boy,' he shook his head regretfully, 'if only I could put up shelves, what a great life I might've had.'

'Don't worry, love,' Julie squeezed his hand in mock consolation. 'It doesn't matter. I forgive you. You're still a man.'

5

'DELICIOUS, EMMA,' George said, and there was a general murmur of warm approval.

'Thank you.' Emma smiled happily. She was the best cook of the three women present and took pride in the fact. 'Would anyone like any more?' The three men and Julie all beamed acceptance of her Peking Duck.

'The light's new, isn't it?' Angela commented. Her pretty, pearly white face framed by dark, wavy hair was lit up by benevolent curiosity and her voice was all sugar and spice as she glanced upwards at the brass lantern.

'Yes – d'you like it?' Emma asked.

'I think it's lovely,' Angela answered, and added brightly: 'We've got one in our kitchen.'

'I think it goes just as well here, really,' said Julie. She did dislike the way in which Angela got in digs at Emma's poorer life style. Julie had respect for Emma. At school she'd always been the brightest of the three. She'd taken first-class honours at London University, she'd gone into magazines and she was now a senior editor. It sounded as though she shone in her job – but it didn't pay especially well.

'It was absolute hell getting that bloody light up,' Emma was saying, then she smiled. 'Max and I nearly got a divorce.'

'Never again,' Max declared with absolute finality, and drank some *sake*. He was tall with short, dark hair and a moustache and beard kept neatly clipped by Emma. His expression was sardonic, his eyes were blue and intensely alive and he smiled a lot. He combined Oxford insouciance with a raffish charm in a way which appealed to Julie. Max was a painter and a good one – everybody agreed on that – and his work sometimes appeared in small public exhibitions and did quite well. Unfortunately, he was often broke too.

Although whenever he had money, Max spent it furiously and mainly on Emma, months sometimes went by when he couldn't sell a picture and didn't earn a penny. Yet he absolutely refused to do anything with his days except paint. So Emma and Max had a small, poorly furnished flat and an ageing car. They didn't have children either, though both said they wanted them 'in time'. Although Julie liked Max, she also resented him for not giving Emma the things Julie knew her friend needed and wanted. Emma was a woman with style, but because Max said he had to be free, her style was cramped. One could see strain on her face and tension tautened her body movements. Julie sometimes felt that Max should be a man and go out and get a job rather than lie about the house painting pictures which nobody wanted. Couldn't he do that in his spare time?

'Max is as bad as Bob when it come to d-i-y,' Julie observed, 'but I think we've solved the problem.' She told them about Harry. 'He says he can fix anything,' she concluded, 'and he's amazingly reasonable.'

'Harry the handyman?!' Angela exclaimed. 'Sort of funny little chap in his forties?' Julie nodded. 'That's unbelievable! I had him round a couple of months ago and we've used him ever since. The absolutely extraordinary thing is – he lives next door to us.'

'What, he has a house?' Emma queried and brushed back her long, blonde hair.

'It's his mother's house,' Angela explained, 'and that's where he lives. He doesn't have a regular job as far as I know. I suppose he earns enough working freelance.'

'Oh, so it must've been his mother who answered the phone when I first called,' Julie commented. 'She didn't sound like him at all. Posh voice.'

'Mrs Parker is rather posh,' Angela replied approvingly. Julie felt irritated. She'd decided some time ago that she had virtually nothing in common with Angela any more. After achieving very little at school, Angela had gone on to temping, secretarial work, frantic socialising and many impassioned love affairs while searching for the husband she now had in George. He'd originally seemed so solid and strong, just the man to stand up to Angela's selfish and irresponsible whims. He could offer her the prospect of security too – he'd just qualified as a chartered accountant and was about to join a multinational corporation. But once he'd fallen in love with Angela, she had him on a string. For eighteen months he'd chased after her while she manipulated his emotions shamelessly, flirting, wining, dining and sleeping with other men. Finally he'd virtually begged her to marry him and she'd graciously consented. 'Extremely stylish woman,' Angela continued. 'Always beautifully dressed and most attractive for her age. Charming woman altogether.'

'And her son's a handyman?' Bob came in. 'That's kind of curious.'

'Yes, he's not like her at all,' said George, who was good looking in a very conventional sort of way and always dressed as though about to be photographed for an advertisement aimed at women. Angela's parents had warmly approved of their prospective son-in-law – George's family was quite well connected socially – and had bought the happy couple a house. George's parents hadn't been quite so enthusiastic initially but Angela had charmed them and they'd given the newly-weds a car. These days, George rose steadily at work and earned well. Angela stayed at home and enjoyed it all. They had a little daughter, Pru, with whom Michael often played. And George was always affable, his manners were flawless, he exuded an aura of dependable capability and he still worshipped the ground on which his wife walked. An able man at work and a kind one at all times, at home he was round his wife's little finger and under her thumb. 'Not like her at all,' George repeated.

'Mrs Parker must be disappointed in her son,' Angela nibbled at a sliver of cucumber, 'though she'd never admit it, and she looks after him really well.'

'Looks after him?' Julie echoed. 'You make it sound as though there's something wrong with him.'

'Well, there is, really,' Angela said, 'or so I gather from one

34

or two things she's let slip. It's nothing very serious. He's just a bit retarded. You know, Simple Simon. But he's extremely nice in spite of it all and wouldn't hurt a fly. Pru simply adores him – he's babysat for us a couple of times.'

Michael stared moodily at his reflection in the looking glass. It wasn't time to go to bed yet but he was bored. Louise was nice enough, he felt, but she was much more interested in her studies than in him. There was nothing exciting on TV, he wasn't in the mood for a story book and none of his toys looked tempting tonight.

It was at times like this that he longed for brothers and sisters. When he'd been much smaller, feelings of loneliness hadn't been a problem because there'd been Juke, an invisible friend who was always on call, had good ideas for games but in the end always did what Michael wanted. But Juke didn't come any more and Michael had forgotten how to call him. Juke no longer seemed real, he was like a tale you made up and now, whenever Michael thought of his old friend or if his parents smilingly mentioned Juke, he felt babyish and embarrassed.

With his parents out and Louise occupied downstairs and Juke long departed, there was no one to keep Michael company and pay attention to him. That made him feel neglected and niggly and so he was naughty. He wanted to misbehave right now. It'd be fun to play aeroplanes, which zoomed loudly around the living room, while Louise was trying to read – but he knew his mother well enough to realise how furious she'd be if there was just one complaint. When Mummy said anything firmly, she always meant it.

He fidgeted in his chair and hoped fitfully that his reflection might do something interesting – like take on a life of its own. Then he breathed on the glass, and on the patch of condensation drew a large M with his finger.

'I wish...' he sighed, then frowned and fell silent. After a pause, he began to breathe on various parts of the mirror, making a pattern like the points of an inverse pentagram and drawing Ms, squiggles and sigils on the surface he'd clouded. Taking a deep breath, he stared fixedly into the eyes of his mirror image, his face screwed up into fierce lines of intense seriousness. 'I wish,' he sighed at last, 'that I could have a friend at night...'

'Yes, I remember that Harry did babysitting too.' Julie allowed Max to refill her glass. 'But only in homes he liked or something, and I wasn't to tell anyone.'

'Did he say "mum's the word", by any chance?' Angela asked knowingly.

'Right.' Julie laughed. 'It must be his catchphrase. But I'm surprised you had him as a babysitter. I just wouldn't feel happy about leaving Michael with a strange, middle-aged man.'

'Yes, but he's not a stranger,' Angela retorted, 'he's my next-door neighbour so I feel perfectly safe. Pru's as good as gold whenever he's there – though unfortunately he couldn't manage it tonight. But I'd recommend him without any hesitation – as long as you promise not to pinch him whenever I need him.'

'A retarded, single, middle-aged man alone in a house at night with my kid,' Bob stated thoughtfully. 'I guess I'm not happy about that prospect. No, wait,' he held up a hand to ward off Angela's imminent protest. 'As you say, he's your neighbour, you know his mother, I'm sure it's all just fine and my attitude's unreasonable. There're some very weird people around and I wouldn't want to take any risks with Michael.'

'Don't be ridiculous, Bob.' Angela shook her head. 'Harry's not one of those at all. Why,' she giggled, 'you should see how Pru bosses him around – it's so funny.'

'But there *is* a dangerous pervert on the loose,' Emma interposed. There was a pause as they all regarded her uneasily. 'Haven't you read about it? It was in this morning's *Guardian*. Police found the sexually abused body of a six-year-old boy in a ditch by Charnley Woods. That's just three miles from where we're sitting.'

*

That same evening, Mrs Mary Parker reclined in an armchair before the fire and was served a gin and tonic by her son. After she'd enjoyed it, she rose, walked slowly into the dining room, sat down at the head of the table and called out: 'Harold! I'm ready.' Harry entered and proceeded to serve her roast pork with all the trimmings and a glass of claret, after which he helped himself, sat down on her right and began to eat.

'Delicious, Mother,' said Harry. 'Absolutely delicious. Especially the crackling.'

'Yes,' said Mrs Parker, 'this time you remembered to rub the salt and oil well into the meat.'

'Oh, yes. Just as you said.' He chewed with enjoyment. 'Mother, you've done it again.'

'Thank you.' She sipped some wine. 'It's a recipe my own mother gave me. If you follow it to the letter, you simply can't go wrong.' For a time they ate in silence. 'You know, I saw something quite extraordinary today,' she said at last, then patted her lips with a napkin. 'I was on my way to the Women's Institute when I saw young Mr Fullerton from across the road going shopping *in his slippers!*' Harry carried on eating. 'Did you hear me, Harold?' she queried sharply. 'I spoke to you just then.'

'Slippers...' said Harry.

'Bedroom slippers. And in the High Street!' Mrs Parker declared indignantly. 'The man's a disgrace to the area.'

'I wouldn't go shopping in slippers myself...'

'I should think not,' she interrupted vehemently. 'I think young Mr Fullerton should be told that this sort of thing simply isn't done here. His wife should take him in hand. Before he gets out of control altogether. Slippers, indeed!' she sniffed. 'Have you nothing to say about it?'

'Well, it's not proper, is it?'

'Quite,' said Mrs Parker. 'Oh, another thing. Dorothy Birkinshaw's been made vice-president of the Catering Committee.' There was a long pause. 'You do know who I'm talking about, don't you?' Harry nodded. 'Are you sure,

Harold?' She stared at him hard and he shifted uncomfortably in his chair.

'She's the very tall one, isn't she?' he said, as though he was trying to get a lesson right. 'You know her from the Conservative Club. Husband's a stockbroker. They went to Madeira last summer.'

'No, that's Barbara Shawcross, dear,' Mrs Parker sighed irritably. 'Don't you ever listen to a word I say? I sometimes wonder why I bother telling you anything. Dorothy Birkinshaw's married to Clive the architect, as I've told you countless times. Well, I supported her today,' Mrs Parker continued animatedly, 'and she's agreed to nominate me for madam chairman of next year's Charity Committee.'

'That's very good. Congratulations, Mother.'

'It's not definite, of course. But if it does happen, I just can't wait to see Jane Henderson's face. It'll be positively bright green with envy!'

For the remainder of the meal Mrs Parker, who requested and was poured a second glass of wine, spoke at intervals about 'scruffy, unemployed louts' she'd seen in the street and who should be put in the army; a waiter in the restaurant where she'd lunched, who'd been extremely polite to her and earned her warm approval and an extra five-pence tip; and Mrs Margaret Thatcher, whose policies she praised and whom she'd met once at the local Conservative Club, an encounter she'd often described as 'the proudest moment of my life'. When she'd finished her meal, she rose majestically and her long, mauve evening gown flared out behind her as she stepped, in her high-heeled silver sandals, into the living room.

While his mother relaxed over a large, illustrated book about Edwardian high society, Harry was busy. He brought her coffee, stoked up the fire and then, donning a little white apron, he cleared the table, washed the plates, pans and cutlery, dried them up and put them away. There was a fair amount of hard scrubbing to be done and the mahogany dining table had a few spots which required his attention but after a time, the rooms in which he'd worked were gleaming and immaculate again. Taking off his apron, Harry spread newspaper on the floor, picked up a pair of black court shoes Mrs Parker had left by the freezer and proceeded to polish them until they shone brilliantly. Then he went and stood in front of his mother.

'D'you need anything more?' he asked.

'No, thank you.' She shook her head once. 'You won't forget to clean the oven tomorrow, will you?'

'Of course not.'

'All right, you can go now. Good night, Harold.'

'Good night, Mother.'

He went upstairs to his room. This was an extraordinary contrast to the rest of the house, for the bed was half-made, a chaos of objects littered every available surface, there were crumbs on the carpet, and pictures torn from newspapers and magazines were stuck haphazardly on the walls – Elvis Presley and Rocky Marciano, Clint Eastwood and Sylvester Stallone, Gene Vincent and Charles Bronson.

One shelf housed luridly covered paperbacks by James Herbert and George Scarman, Nick Carter and James Hadley Chase, Ian Fleming and Mickey Spillane and there was also a stack of *Superman* and *Conan the Barbarian* comics. The contents of another shelf included a bullworker, wrist strengtheners, chest expanders and a replica model of a Colt .45 revolver. But tonight Harry ignored these and neglected the stereo and its headphones in favour of the video, which he switched on to show Donald Duck cartoons. In no time at all, he was wholly absorbed and chuckling away.

His mother went to bed ninety minutes later. Passing Harry's room, she noticed that he was still up but it didn't seem to bother her. Passing into her bedroom, she kicked off her sandals, then opened a drawer and extracted a large buff envelope. From the envelope she took a framed photograph of a man and held it up before her eyes.

As she gazed, her irises seemed to harden into ice-blue stones which blazed with frozen fury, her mouth tightened to a thin red line, her nostrils quivered and her voice came out

of her taut throat in a harsh whisper of hatred.
 '*How do you like what I've done?*' she hissed.

6

ONE SATURDAY morning, a woman sat on a park bench and read a newspaper while her little boy, who'd tried the roundabouts and swings, sat glumly on the end of a see-saw and wished there was someone else he could play with. When his mother finally looked up, she noticed that Neil had been joined by a middle-aged man and they seemed to be having a wonderful time going up and down on that see-saw.

'Up and hey! And down and wheee!' the man kept shouting and Neil was loving it and laughing and giggling. The man was respectably dressed and his face was open and pleasant, but although the woman was glad that her son was enjoying himself so much, she couldn't help thinking of the child murderer they hadn't caught yet and the sight of the stranger having such fun with Neil made her feel uneasy. She folded her paper, didn't take her eyes off them for an instant but kept smiling all the while, gave it exactly five minutes, then overruled Neil's protests, thanked the man for entertaining him and took her boy away.

Afterwards, Harry sat on a swing and looked disappointed and slightly hurt.

But meanwhile, Julie was delighted with her discovery of Harry. He repaired the waste disposal unit after which the spin drier went wrong so he fixed that too. Over the ensuing weeks, the electric carving knife broke down; a speaker wouldn't work; and a curtain rail needed to be put up in the spare bedroom. Each time Julie sent for Harry and each time his work was done immaculately and cheaply.

Julie decided that she quite liked him. He seemed completely open and inoffensive. He radiated cheerfulness and always had a good word for everyone, including Julie's friend Angela. 'That's another lady,' he declared approvingly, 'and her Pru's a very nice little girl.' But his warmest praise was always for his mother. 'Brought me up herself, all on her own,' he told Julie.

'What happened to your father?'

'Died when I was young,' Harry said sadly. 'Never knew him. Not properly. Only got the dimmest of memories...' and then he winced slightly and changed the subject back to his mother. 'I'm so proud of her, you know. Real lady.'

'Have you got a lady of your own?' Julie enquired genially.

'No.' He shook his head as though the thought hadn't occurred to him in years. 'Don't need one.'

Although she thought that was sad, Julie initially didn't spend that much time chatting to Harry. He was, after all, a bit dull. He didn't seem to think much. 'I do most of my thinking with my hands,' he explained. The truth of this was revealed in the excellence of his handiwork and the affable banality of his views.

However, his work was fenced around with one prohibition on which he insisted: no one could watch him at it. Julie complied with the rule, made sure Michael observed it and thought nothing of it. Lots of people loathe being watched while they're working, she reasoned, and she had no desire to watch Harry anyway.

Bob met the handyman one evening when he came home in a foul temper after another row with Charles Haughey followed by a knocking in the Audi's engine on the way home. Harry asked politely if he could take a look at the car and half an hour later, the engine was purring sweetly. Bob offered Harry a drink and took the trouble to talk to him.

It proved quite difficult to shut Harry up, once he'd got going. After rhapsodising once again about his mother, he went on to his likes, which included Fifties pop, televised wrestling, table-tennis – 'Oh, we must have a game some time,' Bob said – comics, *Practical Householder* magazine, Walt Disney cartoons and Charles Atlas courses (Bob had to feel his biceps, which were like steel cables), and his dislikes, such as 'boring, intellectual discussions', travel, wines and spirits – 'Give me a decent bottle of brown ale any time,' said Harry – and indecency, obscenity and blue language. He climaxed a monologue on politics by saying: 'There're all these people trying to pull society down. But what I'd like to ask them is: what're you going to put in its place, then, eh?'

Julie thought that Bob would scream from boredom, but after the handyman had gone, he just laughed and said: 'Harry's okay. He's totally banal but he's okay.'

But perhaps the person who got most out of Harry's visits was Michael. The two seemed to strike up an instantaneous rapport. One evening, fairly early on, Julie came into the kitchen to see Harry doing card tricks, to Michael's enormous and noisy delight. Since she liked a little peace and quiet just after work, she was happy for Harry to entertain her son after he'd done whatever needed doing. Occasionally Julie eavesdropped – just as a safety precaution. Everything she overheard seemed harmless enough – conjuring tricks and jokes and rhymes and stories – clearly Harry had a talent for enthralling children, just as Angela had said. Michael loved it whenever Harry came. That meant fun and frolics and things he didn't know, stories and laughter – and Harry always listened to him. 'Harry's funny,' he said, more and more, 'and he's nice. He's my new friend. When's he coming again?'

'Don't know, love,' Julie usually responded. 'When something goes wrong, I suppose.'

Michael started hoping that things would go wrong.

There was a particular Friday evening which to most residents of the neighbourhood seemed ordinary enough. Bob and Julie went out to dinner in London's West End and afterwards danced at a night club; Max and Emma saw an arty film in a half-empty Richmond cinema; Angela watched television while George told bedtime stories to Pru and then attended to the household accounts; Mrs Mary Parker was driven by her son to wine and cheese at the local tennis club, of which she was a non-playing member; and Harry, who had not been invited, consoled himself with a glass of brown ale at a nearby pub. He had two hours to kill before collecting his mother but it appeared that he was content to be alone.

The interior of the pub was light and spacious, and painted and furnished in various shades of brown. The decorators had tried to impart the flavour of a lounge in some old-fashioned seaside hotel. There were prints of nineteenth-century Surrey hanging on the walls and in one corner, a tank of goldfish. Little notices by the bar enticed the customers to try 'Real Ale', which was in fact drawn up by gas pressure from kegs of metal, and to "Taste the Tang of the Sea with our Scampi in a Basket' though, of course, the seafood was frozen. The attempt at period charm had also been marred somewhat by two slot machines which coughed and clanked continually, a video game which emitted a constant series of loud squeaks, and a juke box which Harry approached the moment he saw it.

He smiled happily when he perceived that the playlist included Golden Greats of the Fifties and instantly inserted two fifty-pence pieces for a selection of seven hits. His choices included Bobby Darin's 'Dream Lover', The Everly Brothers' 'All I Have to Do Is Dream', Tommy Steele's 'Singing the Blues' and 'Big Man' by the Four Preps. Returning to his seat, Harry sipped his ale and nodded his head in time to the music as his eyes took on a wistful, faraway gaze.

Trade was steady in the pub that evening. There were plenty of young couples and also groups of well-dressed men in their forties and fifties, most of whom were telling stories and laughing loudly. However, here and there were dotted a number of solitary men who, like Harry, were drinking in silence.

There was one individual of Harry's age who, up until the latter's entry, had been looking morose as he drank his way steadily through double whiskies with beer chasers. He had thinning hair, a hard, coarse face with a broken nose, a low forehead and dark, cold eyes. He'd been staring at the beige carpet while occasionally muttering to himself when Harry's first selection – 'Chantilly Lace' by the Big Bopper – came on the juke box. Suddenly he raised his head and smiled a broad, lazy smile – his first of the evening – and turned to stare approvingly at whoever was responsible for the choice of music. That was when he saw Harry, and his smile slowly faded to be replaced by an intensely puzzled frown. He shook his head twice, as though he was a wet dog, then continued to gaze at Harry while his mouth tightened.

At first, Harry didn't notice him. He carried on drinking ale slowly and his left foot began to tap the floor in time to the beat. It was only when the record ended that he became aware of the other man's close scrutiny from another table. Harry looked back, his expression bland and pleasant, as if to say, Glad you're enjoying the record I chose. But abruptly, something struck him about the other, causing him also to frown. Seconds later, Harry's eyes widened in surprise and his head rocked backwards as though he'd been hit.

His hand shot out to grasp his glass but the movement was clumsy and the glass went over, flooding the table with foam and beer that dripped onto the carpet. As the second record came on the juke box, Harry sprang to his feet and made for the door, his face crumpling in confusion and bewilderment. Instantly the other man was out of his seat and after him.

Outside, the car park was dark and deserted as Harry sprinted for his car.

'Hoi!' his pursuer shouted. Two pairs of leather soles came slamming down on the concrete. 'Hoi!' There were five yards between them. Harry's hand was in his jacket pocket and fumbling for his car keys as he ran. He failed to find them – and he reached the Ford at the instant the other man seized his shoulder and pulled him round, leaving them with six inches between their faces.

'What d'you want . . . ?' Harry's voice was thin and his tone quavered. In answer, the other man pulled out a lighter and flicked on the flame.

'Harry Parker . . .' he said slowly, as though he still couldn't quite believe it. 'Thought so.'

'No...' Harry returned hoarsely, 'no, that's not me. Never heard of him.'

'Don't you fucking dare deny it.' The voice was a growl and the words exhaled in a cloud of alcoholic vapour. 'Just don't you fucking dare.'

'You're wrong. Honest.'

'If I'm wrong, how come you ran the moment you saw me?' He grinned unpleasantly, revealing large, stained teeth. 'Eh? 'Cos you remember me. You remember what you did to me, you dirty bastard. Been a long time, hasn't it?' The flame was extinguished. Harry was silent. 'Whassa matter? Lost yer voice?'

'All right,' Harry said at last, his voice very small and quiet. 'All right, Phil.'

'That's better. That's a bleeding sight better. So you do remember me after all. 'Course, that means you remember what you did to me, me and the others.'

'*I couldn't help it!*' Harry burst out. 'You don't understand what it was like! I had no choice, I...' His voice cracked into a helpless squeal. 'But I'm sorry, Phil,' he whispered, 'I'm really, truly sorry.'

'Not half as sorry as we were, mate. We thought you was a friend. We treated you right. And what did you do, you disgusting little piece of dog shit? You know, I reckon the only thing that got me through was thinking of what I'd do to you when I finally caught up with you. Well, it's taken me years, hasn't it? Years and years. And I find that after all these years, you're just the same and as disgusting as ever. First you deny it all. And then,' he was spitting his words, 'then all you've got to say for yourself is "sorry". Well... you're going to be sorry, just like you said. Really, truly sorry.'

'Phil, please, I've gotta fetch my Mum...' but Harry's plea was answered by a vicious backhand cracked across his face. As Harry's head was flung backwards by the impact of the blow, Phil laughed and grabbed him by the lapels.

He wasn't prepared for the roar of rage which seemed to erupt from Harry's stomach, for the left fist which thudded against his ribcage and sent him staggering back, flinging out his hands in an effort to keep his balance, or for the right fist which smashed against his unprotected jaw. Phil hit the concrete in a sprawling heap. Harry emitted a small shriek and kicked him in the face. Phil rolled over, sobbing, his tears of pain mingling with his blood.

Harry stood over him. His chest was heaving too.

'You always was a coward,' he breathed. 'Come looking for me again and I'll kill you.' More sobs came out of the grovelling body on the ground. Harry extracted his keys from his pocket, walked over to the car, climbed in and drove away fast.

And as he drove, it was his turn to sob, until he was crying so uncontrollably that the car was swerving all over the road. Eventually, he stopped in a side road, wound down the window and wept with his face in his hands, moaning and wailing in an agony of grief as if he had lost all he loved.

But some time later, when he collected his mother from wine and cheese at the local tennis club, he seemed fully recovered and said nothing about his evening at all.

That Saturday was bright and fresh and sunny and Mrs Parker decided to go shopping in Richmond. Harry drove her there and they left the Ford in the multistorey car park, then proceeded up the busy High Street where Mrs Parker stopped frequently to gaze into shop windows and make purchases. She was wearing an elegant suit in light brown, with matching hat, gloves, handbag and high heels and walked with her nose slightly uptilted and a proprietorial sway of her hips. The pavement was crowded and it was difficult to go two abreast: Harry trotted obediently behind her, carrying her shopping bags.

Eventually, Mrs Parker swept into Dickins & Jones department store where she bought perfume and eyeshadow before visiting Lingerie, where she took her time selecting several pairs of old-fashioned, baggy white knickers trimmed with lace. Harry stood and watched silently. She did not speak to him. When she'd paid, she handed him the package, he slipped it into a bag, she walked away swiftly in the direction of Skirts and he followed behind her.

For a time he stood and watched again as his mother took skirts off the rack, held them against herself and smiled into a mirror. Then she took one which was soft and pink and pleated, and with a light laugh held it up against Harry.

He stiffened, winced and sprang back as though she'd burned him. She laughed twice, and there was a sneer in that laugh, and a high clear voice from behind them exclaimed: 'How funny!'

Mother and son turned to see a smartly dressed Angela – and George, who was carrying bags and standing behind her. Harry's face flushed furiously.

'Mrs Parker! How lovely to see you!' Angela gushed. 'Hello, Harry, how are you?' He smiled and nodded nervously, as if too embarrassed to speak. 'What a pretty skirt!' Angela continued merrily. 'I wonder if they've got it in my size. And what a lovely outfit you're wearing, Mrs Parker, I've always admired your taste. What a super surprise running into you like this!'

'It's very nice seeing you and George, dear,' Mrs Parker responded pleasantly. 'Everything all right?'

'Oh, yes, thanks,' Angela said with a sweet little smile, while George muttered: 'Fine, thank you.'

'Oh, good, I am pleased.' Mrs Parker smiled back as her slim, manicured hand patted her curls just beneath her hat. 'We're choosing a few things for autumn.'

'So're we,' said Angela, 'and George is helping me choose them, aren't you, darling?'

'Well, yes.' George glanced down and shuffled his feet awkwardly. 'I feel it's important to choose the right thing,' he added.

'I simply adore the current fashion, don't you?' Angela looked at the mannequin ten feet away. It displayed a short black jacket with a skirt that was tight at the hips and sheathed the legs before flaring at the calves.

'Yes,' said Mrs Parker, 'it's very attractive indeed and if I were your age, dear, I'd buy it instantly. You've got exactly the right figure for it.' Her hand touched her own hips, around which her skirt was perhaps just one size too tight. 'Of course, at my age one has to be a little more conservative.'

'But I loved what you were looking at just now.' Angela sprang at the rack where the skirts were a few sizes smaller and plucked out Mrs Parker's choice of design. 'George, look!' she squealed delightedly, as she held it before the mirror, then twirled around. 'Don't you think it would suit me, darling?'

'Looks very nice, darling,' said George.

'Oh, yes, I rather think I'll try it on.' Suddenly Angela turned on her husband and with a shrill giggle, swung the skirt through the air so its pink pleats fluttered in a flowery flirtation of frivolous femininity just before she seized his belt and draped it from his waist. 'New autumn fashions for men,' she teased, as George smiled weakly and blushed.

'And why not?' Mrs Parker joined in gleefully. 'George, dear, it really suits you.' She sniggered spitefully at his discomfiture. 'Oh, Angela, do make him try it on.'

No one was watching Harry, who'd twisted his back and his head away from them and was staring at the floor, shopping bags trailing forlornly from his strong, hairy hands. That was just as well, for at that instant his features were contorted into a tortured, dumb contraction which mingled misery and blind hatred.

'Harold!' his mother shrilled, 'you're daydreaming again. Where're your manners?' and at once he turned to face her, a picture of bland pleasantry and filial submission.

That night, Bob and Julie were lying naked on the bed and caressing one another softly. It was shortly after midnight and they had just made love. A bedside lamp gave out a soft and friendly illumination to the interior. Outside, there was a storm. Pellets of rain drummed a mad tattoo upon the window-panes and the trees hissed as the wind soughed through them, howling its ode to autumn.

'I love thunderstorms at night when I'm in bed,' Julie murmured. Lightning flashed and seconds later, there was a clap of thunder, succeeded by a low, menacing rumble. She closed her eyes dreamily, her skin still tingling from the embraces of her man, her blood suffused by a warm glow of well-being. The wild autumn weather heightened her feeling of delicious languor and every blast of wind against the solid brick walls of her home emphasised her sense of security.

'Yeah,' Bob murmured back, as his brawny arm held his woman close to him, 'yeah.' He ran his hand down her back and patted her bottom. 'I've got an idea,' he announced softly. 'How about me making us a hot toddy?'

'That's a good idea,' said Julie. 'With brandy?'

'Brandy, honey, cinnamon, cloves,' he said, 'and a couple of extra ingredients.'

'Okay, love.' She sighed contentedly as he rose, threw on a towelling robe and padded out of the room. While he was away, she rejoiced in the fact that it was the weekend and they had no plans at all for Sunday. No people to see, no work to do, just a quiet day in which they could enjoy one another and Michael. She smiled lazily as Bob came back into the room with two mugs exuding steam and an aroma in which were mingled brandy and spices. 'Thanks,' she took hers and tasted it. 'Mmm, good.'

'Hey, not bad. But you know something? The kettle's not working.'

'What?'

'Yeah, I had to use the cooker. I tried both plugs. Nothing doing on either. Could be the plug or the socket, I guess. Maybe it's the fuse. Or it could be...' He stopped because Julie was laughing. 'What's so funny?'

'You,' she chuckled. 'You looked so puzzled and helpless just then. You always do whenever anything like that goes wrong. "The kettle's not working",' she mimicked him. '"Could be the plug or the socket, I guess".'

He smiled ruefully: 'Maybe it's the fuse.'

Julie laughed harder. 'Remember when it took you half an hour to wire a plug? Well, we've got the answer to that one now.'

'Harry,' said Bob.

'Harry,' said Julie. 'I'll call him on Monday.'

'You know something?' Bob stretched out on the bed beside her. 'It's just a little thing I've noticed. I know Harry's a real find – but ever since we've found him, things keep going wrong. Sure he fixes them and does a great job, but I've never known so many things around the house go wrong.'

'What're you suggesting?'

'It's all a plot,' Bob said with mock-seriousness. 'No question about it. Every time Harry comes to fix something, he screws up something else so he can come again. That's why no one can watch him working. See, underneath it all, he's a really smart guy.'

'Silly thing.' Julie laughed again and ruffled his hair affectionately.

They finished their drinks, then switched out the light and cuddled up to one another beneath the duvet. Within minutes, Julie was asleep.

Bob lay awake. He listened calmly to the raging of the elements outside, trying to concentrate on that and not on thoughts thrown up to nag him by the preceding week. Although Julie admired his ability to switch off from problems at work, in fact this was more of an appearance than reality. He just didn't see the point of boring Julie with his worries and not talking about them was one way of trying to forget them.

Again an image of Charles Haughey intruded upon his peace of mind and again his boss's prissy voice echoed in his head. Bob told himself to switch off, to concentrate entirely on the gales and the rain. With winter approaching, perhaps he should take up some indoor hobby, he reflected. That'd be another way of relaxing his mind.

For instance, there was that book in the box down in the basement they used as a store room. He hadn't looked at it in ages. It concerned his father's secret shame and Bob had always intended to take the matter up and research it – yet there'd been some curious psychological block over doing it. Maybe he didn't really want to find out more because it might alter the image he had created of his father. Anyway, it had all happened so long ago.

Julie had sometimes suggested he pursued the matter whenever he seemed bored and restless. She was familiar with the story but it didn't mean that much to her. After all, she'd never met Bob's father. He wasn't a person in her life. Bob thought her attitude was fair enough – he took little interest in relatives Julie described and whom he'd never met. Yet it was – yes – sad that his father hadn't lived. Bob was sure that she would've really liked him and he would've taken to her.

Images of the man came back into his mind, all of them associated with strength and tenderness – except for that one bad time when Bob was nine. Then his father had lost his job and it had taken him several months to find another. During that miserable period, he'd become a changed man: brooding and sullen and bad tempered... and drunk and resentful. Thank God he'd found work again and in no time he'd gone back to being his old self, but Bob had never forgotten that nightmare and the sound of his mother's desperate pleading as whisky splashed into a glass. 'A man is not a man without work,' his father had said. Bob agreed. Maybe that was why he found it so difficult to switch off entirely...

That thought vanished and was succeeded by another and then another, but Bob would never recall them for he was passing into sleep and into dream.

Now he was in a car, roaring down a Californian freeway. Julie and Michael were next to him. They were all happy and laughing. He was confident that nothing could go wrong – and then the engine began spluttering as the car slowed to a halt.

He climbed out. The surrounding scene had become an English suburban side road. He couldn't repair the car so he had to walk somewhere and fetch help. As he walked, there was a cloudburst and rain came down, drenching him. The wind hit him with an icy blast and he shivered. It became harder and harder to keep going.

Up ahead, there was a house and its front door was open. He was sure he'd find help there, but the wind was so strong and his limbs had become so weak that every step cost him a mighty effort of will. He had the impression that hours were passing as he tried to cover the few yards to the door.

At last he reached it and went inside, finding himself in a dark, narrow passage. On his left, there were bars of steel and beyond them a cage. Within that cage, a man lay chained. At times he cried out and writhed within his bonds. Bob screamed. The prisoner was his father.

He had to help him. Bob ran down the passageway, searching for an entrance to the cage. There were no doors but at the end he was confronted by a thick sheet of glass. He peered through the pane and recoiled in horror.

His car stood outside and inside it, Julie and Michael were crying out in terror and beating vainly on the doors and windows. Bob tried to smash the glass before him, but all strokes slipped on the polished surface. He screamed out his helpless fury as his wife and child implored his aid – for there, standing by the car, was Harry. In one hand, he held the car keys. In the other, he held a spanner from which blood was dripping.

'I can fix anything,' he said, and laughed.

The kettle – or rather, the defective plug – was repaired by Harry on Monday, but a few days later, the sink was blocked in the bathroom so Julie called him again. To her immense relief, he said he could come over right away – for the blockage couldn't've happened at a more inconvenient time. It had been a hard day and Julie needed the bathroom as she and Bob were due for dinner at Angela's at eight o'clock.

But Harry fixed the plumbing fast, and as she shot into the bathroom, Julie was grateful. When she emerged she could hear Harry entertaining Michael, as usual. He was telling him rhymes:

> 'Mrs White
> Had a fright
> In the middle of the night.
> She saw a ghost
> Eating toast
> Halfway up a lamp post.'

'Great!' Michael laughed and clapped his hands. 'D'you know any more?'

> 'Early in the morning, late one night,
> Two dead men got up to fight.
> Back to back they faced each other,
> Drew their swords and shot each other.
> Paralysed donkey riding by,
> Kicked the blind man in the eye.
> Deaf policeman heard the noise
> And went and spanked those two dead boys...

'How about that, then?' Harry demanded.
'Even better,' Michael gurgled, 'even better.'
Julie smiled to herself as childhood memories came flooding back, then frowned as the phone rang. She frowned even harder when she realised it was Louise calling to say she was very sorry but something crucial had come up and she couldn't make babysitting tonight.

As Julie slammed down the receiver, she realised there were two alternatives. She could call Angela and cancel dinner – or she could ask Harry if he was free to babysit. And given Angela's strong recommendation of a man she'd employed herself, it would cause great offence if Julie's friend found out that, although Harry had been there at the time, Julie hadn't even bothered to ask him.

Julie asked. Michael pleaded. Harry considered the matter, said he'd like to but had to phone his mother first though he was pretty sure it'd be all right – and so it was. When Bob came home and Julie told him what had happened, he said: 'Hell, we kind of know the guy and he's okay,' and assured her she'd done the right thing.

So Harry got paid for babysitting too that night – and anyone in Julie's shoes would've thought it a stroke of luck.

7

'GUESS WHO'S joined us for drinks,' gushed Angela, as she welcomed Bob and Julie into a living room which could have featured in *Interiors* magazine. Julie saw that an elegant, elderly lady was seated on the sofa next to Max and Emma. 'My next-door neighbour, Mrs Parker.'

'Pleased to meet you,' Julie smiled, and Bob squeezed the woman's bony, white hand. 'How extraordinary,' she continued, 'we've just come from seeing your son.'

'Yes, he told me he was babysitting for you tonight,' Mrs Parker said pleasantly.

'When did this happen?' Angela demanded. 'I had no idea until Mrs Parker told me.' Julie explained. 'Small world!' exclaimed Angela, as George offered peanuts to the guests.

'Yes, I'm always asking Harry for help these days, it seems,' Julie observed. 'He's very good.'

'I'm delighted to hear it,' said Mrs Parker. 'I've always thought that Harold had genuine talent for things around the house. His father was the same, of course. Personally, I've always been hopeless at that sort of thing.' She laughed, and it sounded like a nice laugh. 'Let's face it, when things need fixing, it's a man's job.'

'I quite agree,' said Angela. 'George is marvellous.'

'Pass,' said Julie. George, who was still standing, offered Angela another Cinzano. His wife nodded curtly and extended her glass.

'But why the hell should men be any good at that sort of thing?' Max objected. 'I'm useless around the house and proud of it.'

'Yes, Max,' retorted Angela, 'but who else is impressed?' Mrs Parker laughed merrily. 'It just means that poor Emma has to do it all.'

'I'm not poor Emma,' Emma protested irritably, 'and if

Max is completely useless at d-i-y, it doesn't bother me at all.' She looked sharply at her husband. 'You do your fair share in other ways, don't you, darling?'

'That's right,' Max said blandly, and exhaled cigarette smoke.

'But it must be nice for you, Mrs Parker, having Harry around,' Julie put in. 'I'm starting to believe he really can fix anything.'

'Yes, he's very good at that,' the woman answered somewhat sadly.

'I hope you don't mind my asking,' said Bob, 'but has Harry never left home?'

'He left once.' Mrs Parker looked even more regretful. 'It wasn't a good idea. You see,' she frowned, 'Harold's basically a fine boy, a very fine boy but...' she sighed, 'at times it's all been a bit of a burden. It was when his father died that the difficulties began, really. A growing boy needs his father, don't you think?'

'Very much so,' Bob agreed. 'When my dad died, it took me a very long time to get over it. My head was screwed up for quite a while.'

'You were a delinquent for a time, you told me,' Julie commented good-humouredly – but Mrs Parker extracted a small white handkerchief from her black bag and wiped an eye.

'In the end, I'm afraid something very similar happened to Harold,' she began, then checked herself abruptly. 'Sorry, this must be boring for you. No? Well, just stop me if you do get bored – it's so good of you to listen and sometimes, well, one can get lonely with no one to talk to.'

'Please go on,' Angela urged her. 'And I see your glass needs refreshing. George!' Her husband sprang up and attended to it.

'Thank you, dear.' Mrs Parker smiled at George. 'You see,' she resumed, 'it really wasn't Harold's fault. There's much in him that's very noble indeed but... he was young and immature and confused, and got into the wrong sort of company. He's not aggressive at all, you see, but being of a sweet, rather passive nature, he's a bit too easily influenced. That really was a most distressing period for me, when he left home...' Her face was a picture of melancholy. 'It did my health – unfortunately I've always suffered from a variety of annoying ailments – it did my health no good at all.'

'I'm sorry,' said Angela.

'But you said your son came back,' Emma prompted.

'Yes, he had a breakdown. And very depressing though it was, in a way it was a godsend and rescued him from much worse things. He couldn't look after himself, you see, he needed his mother no matter how many foolish things he'd said, and that was why the breakdown happened. And although I was hurt and dismayed by some of the things he'd done, when I saw that he felt guilty and sorry, naturally I took him back again and I've looked after him ever since. I don't regret it. It's a mother's duty to shelter her child against the world. And Harold is very nice and kind and there's lots to console me, really, though at times I can't help thinking how different it would have been if only his father had lived.'

'I'm surprised you haven't chosen to marry again, Mrs Parker,' Max said with a flirtatious smile, and she looked pleased.

'Oh, I'm much too old to think about that,' she sighed, and extended a long, slim, stockinged leg, balancing her foot on a black high heel.

'Not at all.' Max was enjoying drawing her out. He had an extraordinary curiosity about people. 'You must've toyed with the idea in the past.'

'Oh...' Mrs Parker giggled, and as she crossed her thighs, she tossed her black skirt hem and Bob was flashed by her white knickers. For an instant he was aroused, then shocked by what she'd done, and then astonished by his reaction to a woman old enough to mother him. He started watching her intently and hoping she'd do it again. Next to him, Julie had seen the flash too and found the action unbecoming to age and distasteful. 'There have been some very fine, kind men who...' Mrs Parker smiled ruefully. 'No, what with Harold to look after and so on, it just hasn't been possible, really. I admit there've been times when I've thought, wouldn't it be wonderful if a man could take care of me, for a change?' Angela smiled happily here, 'but then I have been in love, very much in love,' she mournfully lowered her blue-shadowed lids, 'and perhaps one true love is enough for a lifetime.'

'Oh...' Angela breathed sympathetically. 'Why are women's lives sometimes so sad? Mrs Parker, I do hope you can stay to dinner. It's really no trouble at all.'

'Thank you, dear, that's really so very kind of you,' Mrs Parker put her glass down, 'but I simply must be on my way.' She rose, smoothing the shiny black dress over her plump buttocks and arresting Bob's thoughtful attention. 'There's a little something in the oven which I made just for me – and in any case the doctor says I need to rest more. Well,' she smiled brightly, 'thank you all so much for being so patient with me. It can be very helpful when people take the trouble to listen. And Angela, and you too, Mrs Foster,' she looked directly at Julie, 'you can't imagine how much I appreciate your kindness to Harold. It's so good for him to feel wanted, you know, and he's also frightfully good with children. Boy or girl, Mrs Foster?'

'Boy. Six years old.'

'What a handful!'

'You can say that again,' laughed Julie. 'Takes after his dad, the little horror. Going through this phase where he's got so much energy, if it's not directed anywhere, he gets naughty.'

'Only one way to deal with that,' Mrs Parker declared briskly. 'Smack his bottom and stand him in a corner.'

'That's a bit strict and old-fashioned,' Julie commented.,

'But it's the only thing that works, my dear,' Mrs Parker returned. 'No, no,' she shook her head wisely, 'anything else is all too likely to produce a spoiled brat – and I should know because I was much too indulgent. Take an old mother's advice, Mrs Foster – one can never be too strict with boys.'

*

'Let's play a game,' said Michael.

'All right,' said Harry, 'what d'you want to play?'

'Wrestling!'

'But we've just had that.'

'Again!'

'Give us a rest,' Harry pleaded. 'Uncle's tired.'

'I want something you can play in the whole house,' Michael declared. 'How about Follow My Leader?'

'Give over,' said Harry. 'That's boring.'

'Well, it is a bit,' Michael admitted thoughtfully, 'but it's the only one like that I know.'

'Don't know many games, do you?'

'I know some,' Michael objected. 'I mean, there're loads I know from school but you need lots of people. And I know a lot of others but you have to be by yourself. There's some I play with Pru but they're a bit soppy. D'you know anything for just the two of us?'

'Yeah,' said Harry, 'Murder In The Dark.'

'What?' Michael's eyes lit up.

'But it's probably a bit too grown up for you.'

'No way,' said Michael.

'You have to have all the lights out and I bet you'd be scared.'

'I'm not frightened of the dark,' said Michael. 'Never have been,' he lied.

'It's a rough game,' Harry told him. 'Your mother might not like it.'

'But I like rough games. Mummy knows that. So does Daddy and he doesn't mind at all. How d'you play it?'

'Well, it's a very frightening game. One of us has to murder the other one.'

'Sounds great.'

'In the dark.'

'Cor!'

'But you have to find him first.'

'Like Hide and Seek...?'

'Yes,' said Harry, 'only this is better.'

'How d'you murder him?'

'You stick a knife in his guts.'

'Wow!' Michael's eyes widened. 'Really?'

'Well, it's more fun if you use a real knife but be careful with it and don't plunge it in. I mean, have a heart, Michael, it's only a game.'

'Let's play it now. You hide, I'll seek and then I'll find and kill you.'

'All right,' said Harry. 'Is there a knife we can use?'

'Mum's big one. The one she uses for cutting the meat.'

'Then you take that and I'll disappear and turn all the lights out. You stay here in the kitchen and count to a hundred before you come and look for me – that's if you can count to a hundred. Five, wasn't it, last time?'

'Oh, shut up and hide,' said Michael.

'It works better if we're both very quiet. So once we start, shush, okay?' Harry winked at him. 'Mum's the word, then.' He left the kitchen.

Michael opened a drawer and took out the big, sharp, shiny blade and squeezed the chunky wooden handle. He held it tightly while he counted to a hundred, then extinguished the kitchen light and went out into the darkness.

At first, he couldn't see a thing. All was dark and silent and he was afraid to move in case he bumped himself on something. The thick darkness amplified all sounds – stairs creaked, a clock ticked and plumbing burped threateningly. He tried to remember the exact position of the hall table as, to his relief, he realised he could now perceive it dimly as a square, squat mass. Holding the knife out before him, Michael advanced cautiously, his heart thumping so hard he was sure Harry could hear him. The living room and the dining room were eerily illuminated by a low, sickly moon – and the tired, dingy light showed there was nowhere for Harry to hide.

Michael drew a deep breath and slowly ascended the stairs. His brain whirled with calculations. He'd check the bathroom, though that was an unlikely place because Harry would be in the bath or nowhere. His own bedroom?

Michael felt comfortable about exploring there. Or would it be the spare bedroom and bathroom on the top floor?

There was a tight cough. Michael started. It came from his parents' bedroom. He halted at the top of the stairs. That was the room which awed him. Sometimes he was welcomed there and got into bed with Mummy and Daddy. That was great and usually happened on Sunday mornings. But sometimes the door was locked and he'd learned long ago that if he knocked, they just went quiet and didn't answer. They'd both told him to go away whenever that happened – unless it was fantastically urgent – because Mummy and Daddy were very busy and not to be interrupted even if it was the phone. Naturally he was curious and went away noisily and came back silently – to hear gasps and groans, animal grunts and whispered endearments, his father's roar and his mother's cry.

It had frightened him at first but as he'd grown up, he'd realised that whatever they were doing, they were having great fun. They were always so happy and nice to him afterwards. That made his curiosity itch even more. Some great mystery was celebrated in that bedroom – 'I'll tell you when you're older,' Mum always said – and some inner certainty told him that he was here because of it.

But would Mum and Dad like him playing games with Harry in their bedroom? No. So after he'd killed Harry, he'd have to tell him that they couldn't play in there any more. Michael entered the room, stood by the door and stared around him hard. There was no sign of Harry. He checked behind the curtains, the sofa, round the other side of the bed and then, with a cry of anticipated triumph, flung open the door of the walk-in wardrobe and stabbed at the dresses and coats. There was nobody there.

That left one, and only one, place. Michael knelt by his mother's side of the bed, whipped up the cover and peered beneath the mattress. It was too dark to make out much but of course Harry was there – you could tell by his wheezing. That meant his chest had to be opposite Michael's face.

'Gotcha!' Michael shouted and thrust downwards.

'Aargh!' Harry screamed. 'Aargh! Please! Don't!' Michael jabbed the blade into what felt like trousers and gurgled with delight at his victim's yells of terror. 'Aargh! give up! Done for! MURDERED!'

'Lights!' cried Michael. 'I've won, I've murdered Harry!'

'Delicious, Angela,' George led the chorus of praise, 'absolutely delicious.'

'Oh, it's just an old recipe of my mother's,' Angela told them modestly. 'Anyone for any more?' There was plenty but everyone said it had all been so marvellous, there just wasn't room for any more – apart from George, who looked full but still asked for a small second helping. 'I'm so glad you enjoyed it,' Angela enthused, as she piled his plate. 'I like to think that if there's one thing I don't need to be modest about, it's my cooking.'

Oh leave it out, love, Julie thought wearily, as George bent reluctantly over his overcooked pasta with tinned sauce. Opposite her, Emma was masking her irritation over the fact that Angela, who had money and all day to prepare dinner, always gave the poorest hospitality.

Bob wondered why Julie and Emma bothered with Angela at all. He himself had little respect for the woman though on occasion he fancied her voluptuous figure intensely. 'The trouble is, though,' he'd told Julie, 'she just loses her appeal whenever she opens her mouth.' He knew just how much Angela could annoy Julie – he'd spent many hours listening to his wife's emotional outbursts against Angela, followed by her searching analysis of the relationship – and he was sick of hearing it. 'If you don't like her,' he'd been telling Julie for a year, 'don't see her.'

'It's not that simple. It's not quite that I don't like her...'

'Sure, and you're old school buddies – so don't see her so often.'

'It's not that easy.'

'Why? What's the problem?'

'Well, for a start there's all her help with Michael.' That

was undeniable. Every weekday, Angela made sure that Julie could do her job by collecting Michael from school, along with her own Pru. She gave the children something nice to eat at home and minded them until Julie came. She said it was no trouble at all and she thoroughly enjoyed doing it. Julie wasn't sure how she'd manage without Angela's help – it had always been a bit like that – and if Angela wanted to see her often, well, she supposed she should be pleased and she couldn't very well refuse without giving offence.

Bob had noticed that Emma couldn't tear herself away from Angela either, even though she was always bitching about her. 'Why do *you* go on seeing her?' he'd demanded once. 'Because she's loyal,' Emma had replied instantly, 'despite everything, she's loyal.' Obviously, growing up together had tied the three girls in bonds which even hatred would never break. It was curious that without any conscious calculation, they'd all come to live in the same area.

'Poor Mrs Parker,' Angela was saying, as George uncorked another bottle of burgundy, turning the Spanish label towards him so no one could see it. 'I wonder why she never found another man?'

'She could still do it,' Emma commented.

'I think she should've done it years ago,' Angela declared, 'instead of wearing herself out, coping with Harry. I know Max'll disagree but I'm afraid I'm rather old-fashioned. A woman needs a man,' she smiled graciously at George, 'whatever anyone says. Frankly, you can keep Women's Lib. Give me a man who'll keep me.'

'Quite so,' said George. 'I don't understand all this fuss about feminism. I mean, equality for women is all very well in theory but in practice – sorry, darling?' he inclined his head attentively. 'Ah, yes, the wine, of course.' George attended to the hostess and her guests.

'Well, I disagree.' Max lit a cigarette. 'I'm totally pro absolute equality for women. Just as long as they realise there's no women's lib without men's lib.'

'But I like the present system,' Angela objected. 'I don't want to be liberated.'

'You're missing out,' Emma put in sharply.

'What am I missing?' Angela shrugged. 'I think the so-called women's movement is just a ploy to make women go out to work in addition to everything else they do. Of course, there are a few remarkable individuals like you, Emma, and you, Julie, who actually thrive on it – but what's the average woman's fantasy? I bet you it's like mine – being absolutely swept off my feet by some rich, dashing, wicked, handsome brute of a man and pampered.'

'Shall I bring the coffee in, darling?' George asked.

'What're your fantasies about, George?' Julie queried.

'They're all about me,' Angela said smugly.

Heavy footsteps sounded on the stairs.

'Right!' barked a man's voice. 'The Sandman's coming.'

'Sandman?' Michael giggled in his bed as Harry entered. 'Who's he?'

'Haven't you met him?' Michael shook his head and Harry looked shocked. 'Well, I never! What? Never met the Sandman? Dear, oh dear, this is disgraceful.' Michael laughed harder. 'The Sandman's the one who comes and chucks sand in your eyes so you have to close 'em and go off to sleep.'

'Oh, I get. A pretend.'

'He's not a pretend,' Harry retorted indignantly. 'He's as real as Father Christmas.'

'Oh, he knows Father Christmas, does he?'

'They're very good friends,' said Harry.

'Tell us another, you.' Michael clapped his hands. 'You're super. I'll tell my mum you're the best ever. You will come again, won't you?'

'What? And have to look after you again? You must be joking. Have you murdering me all over again?' He chuckled. 'That's more than my life's worth. No. Never again!'

'Aw, c'mon...' Michael pleaded, 'I didn't kill you really. Next time you can kill me.'

'Oh, yeah? Kill you, can I? Might do that if you don't go to sleep nice and quiet. Your mum said you had to be in bed early and it's way past your time.'

'Yeah,' Michael considered the matter, 'I suppose I am a bit tired. Oh, well,' he snuggled into the folds of the duvet, 'thanks for playing with me. Good night, Uncle Harry.'

''Night, 'night, son.' Harry gazed at him tenderly then switched out the light.

After Mrs Parker had finished the quiche Harry had prepared for her, she left the plates for him to wash and went up to her bedroom. Everything was as it should be. The ironing had been done and lay neatly folded on the bed, and he'd also sewn up the loose frill on her petticoat. She inspected the garments with satisfaction before putting them away, then proceeded to her private ritual.

There was hatred etched on her face as she strode over to the drawer and wrenched it open. As she glared down at the buff envelope, a thought struck her suddenly, for her hand froze in the air like the poised claw of a carrion bird.

Her bosom heaved, her chest twitched and she clapped her hands to her heart. Abruptly she grunted as her body was wrenched around and racked by a fierce, stabbing pain. She swayed and staggered back several steps, her lungs gasping, her face suffused by a mottled purple, her lips a hideous blue and her features contorted.

'Harold...!' she sobbed, then her body was jolted by a spasm and she collapsed unconscious on the carpet.

8

KNOCK! KNOCK!

'Have you finished yet?' Michael demanded.

'Not yet,' Harry called back from within the kitchen. 'Be done in a jiffy. Give me a moment.' There was a pause during which Michael fidgeted impatiently. 'Okay, you can come in.' The boy went through. 'All done,' the man announced cheerfully. 'I reckon your mum'll be pleased with that spice rack.'

'Yeah.' Michael helped Harry pull off his overalls. 'Now you can play with me.'

'All right. What shall we play?'

'Murder In The Dark!'

'But it's morning,' Harry protested. 'Where's the dark?'

'We can draw all the curtains...'

'Sorry, but it'll have to be another time,' said Bob, who'd just come in. 'You and me,' he put his hand on Michael's shoulder, 'have got a date at the zoo and it's time we were getting along. Hey, that's neat,' he glanced at the new spice rack. 'Julie'll be pleased when she gets back. How much is that?'

'Cost you two pound exactly.'

'Worth every penny.' Bob peeled two pound notes off a wad and gave them to Harry. 'Thanks.' He paused momentarily. 'I heard about your mother and I'm sorry. How is she?'

'Recovering,' said Harry. 'Thank heavens. At least, she seems to be making a good recovery. Always had trouble with her heart, unfortunately, but I'm not saying it hasn't been a bit of a shock.'

'Sure. Wish her well from all of us,' Bob said, 'when you see her. Is she still in hospital?'

'Yes. I'm off there now, in fact.' Harry held up his canvas

bag. A bunch of flowers nestled within the open zip.

'Ah.' Bob shifted his gaze to Michael. 'Get your coat on.'

'Sure, Dad.' Michael left the room, and Harry shook hands with Bob and left. Just as he left the house, the handyman looked lonely, bitterly lonely.

Julie had been invited to Angela's for Saturday morning coffee. In the fireplace, gas flames licked at asbestos logs, taking the chill off the October air outside.

'And that's why I don't go out to work,' Angela was saying, in that high, delicate voice which recalled the chinking of china cups. 'I think being a mother's a full-time occupation, really.' She sipped coffee. 'And that's why I admire you, Julie. It's amazing the way in which you go out to work and look after Michael, especially,' her tone dripped syrup, 'since Bob has to be away so often these days. You must be feeling exhausted.'

'Not at all.' Julie spoke calmly but felt like snapping. 'Michael doesn't need me all the time any more – and I like my job.'

'There's more than enough to do at home, I find.' Angela glanced at the order and cleanliness of the room, for which she had a daily help to thank. 'And that's why I'm so proud of George. He does so well, I don't need to earn money.' Outside, her husband raked leaves in the garden.

'It's the same with Bob,' Julie returned. 'I don't need to earn money either' – yes I do, she thought, the way we spend – 'but I prefer to have a career.' She finished her coffee and plonked the cup defiantly on the saucer. 'It makes life much more interesting. If I had to stay at home all the time, I'd go mad from boredom. I don't know how you manage it, Angela.'

'All done!' George sang out heartily, as he came into the room. 'Just the car to wax and shine and I'll be right with you, darling,' he told Angela.

'Good. Then we'll go off and buy me some knickers,' she replied matter-of-factly. 'You know,' she confided to Julie,

'George just loves being there when I'm selecting knickers. Funny, isn't it?' George blushed and shifted his feet awkwardly, Angela tittered and Julie wished she hadn't mentioned the matter. 'Run along, pet, and get the car nice and shiny and then we'll be ready. Have you heard,' she changed the subject as George left the room, 'about poor Mrs Parker? It's awful!'

'I know – heart attack,' Julie replied. 'Harry told me when he came round this morning. Happened the night we were here. He's obviously very upset, though he's taking it well. I hope his mum gets better soon.'

'So do I.' Angela smoothed down the pleats of her smart new skirt, which was oatmeal coloured as if in tribute to a recent photograph of the Princess of Wales. 'You know, just before this dreadful thing happened, Mrs Parker proposed me for membership on the WI Charity Committee. I'm not sure if I'm up to it, but I was really rather flattered.'

'That's kind of her,' said Julie. 'You must be thrilled.'

'I thought it was a wonderful gesture. She's been ever so good to me – and I can't help feeling sorry for her. Why don't we go and visit her in hospital?'

'Maybe.' Julie's tone was neutral. She hadn't actually liked Mrs Parker much at all. 'If I can find the time. Harry's going there every day, he tells me, and that must be nice for her. Let's hope she can come home soon.'

'Absolutely,' said Angela. 'And he really will have to look after her properly this time. Let's face it, like most men, he'd be lost without her.'

Harry sat stolidly by the hospital bed and gazed impassively at the mass of dry blonde curls and grey roots which surmounted a skull over which skin had been stretched. His own breathing was as wheezing and constricted as hers.

'Have you...' she croaked, 'have you brought it?'

'The envelope?' He took it from his canvas bag and held it up before her eyes, which glittered with a cold, hard and final fever.

'Give...' Ragged claws scuttled out from under the bedclothes and snatched the object. Harry watched as an emaciated hand darted within the envelope and pulled out a frame, holding it so that her son couldn't see the picture.
'Mother, d'you need a hand?'
'No,' she whispered fiercely. Her talons scratched greedily at the back of the frame. Her expression was fixed in a twisted smirk of malevolent triumph as she plucked out the picture and cast the frame aside.
'Mother...' Harry began, but Mrs Parker moaned softly and tore the photograph in half.
'He's dead now,' she sighed, and lay back peacefully on the pillow. Seconds later, her body quivered as if in anticipation of a lover, her limbs twitched and she was dead.
It happened so suddenly and unexpectedly that at first Harry didn't react at all. He just stared dully at his dead mother. After a time, his chest began to wheeze audibly and heavily. He coughed drily and picked up the halves of the torn photograph. As he matched them, he went into a fit of wheezing and coughing. A cry of pure pain came out of his throat. Still clutching the photograph, he slumped at the feet of his dead mother and sobbed out his heart.

Part Two

9

'YOU GET over it,' said Harry, 'in the end you get over it. But it's painful. Long as I live, I'll always miss my mum. She was everything to me.'

'I'm sorry,' Julie murmured.

'I'll be selling the house,' Harry continued. 'Can't live there any more. Too many memories.' He looked forlorn. 'I've been looking for a place to buy. Trouble is,' he scratched his nose, 'I don't like anything I've seen. Mind you, I'd like to go on living in this area. I've made quite a lot of friends locally.'

'Another cup of tea?' Julie offered.

'Don't mind if I do.' He held out his cup. Michael, who was lounging against the spin drier Harry had just repaired, clicked his tongue impatiently. 'All right, all right,' Harry admonished him genially, 'I'll be with you in a moment.

A key turned in a lock, there was the sound of a heavy, masculine tread and Bob came into the room. Julie looked up with a smile which faded fast as she noticed his angry expression.

'Hi,' he said curtly, and she could smell whisky on his breath. He glanced at Harry and didn't look pleased to see him, though the handyman just smiled blandly.

'Hello.' Julie watched concernedly as Bob took a glass from the kitchen cupboard, left the room momentarily and returned with a bottle of scotch and a tumbler of neat whisky. 'You okay?' she asked anxiously.

'I'll tell you later.' Bob drank, coughed, sat down – and suddenly glared at Michael, who had clambered onto the washing machine. 'Get off there!' he snapped.

Michael looked up, startled by his tone. His face flushed as he jumped down, he gave his father a hurt look and then he left the room very quickly.

What's eating him? thought Julie.

'Now there's a father's authority,' Harry commented cheerfully, as if blithely unaware of the tension in the room. 'But you love him really, don't you?'

'Yeah,' Bob said morosely.

'Wish my dad had been around when I was Michael's age,' Harry continued. He regarded Bob pleasantly. 'Did you have a good father?'

'Yeah.' Bob finished his drink, swallowing the scotch as though it was water. 'But he was dead when I needed him too.'

'Tragic,' said Harry.

Bob poured himself another drink.

'Bob!' Julie exclaimed.

'Yeah, what is it?' he growled.

'Go easy, love,' Julie urged him.

'If a man wants a drink,' he stared hard at her, 'he has a drink, right, Harry?'

'If he wants one,' said Harry.

'Have a scotch,' Bob said.

'Oh, not for me, but thanks for the offer.' Harry finished his tea and put down his cup. 'Tell you what I wouldn't mind, though, seeing as I'm still thirsty,' he turned to Julie, 'and that's a glass of Michael's Ribena. That's if there's enough.'

Bob drank and stared sullenly ahead as Julie gave him a look which mingled anger, pain and bewilderment, then complied with Harry's request as noisily as she could.

'Thank you.' Harry drank gratefully and there was a long, awkward silence. 'You know something,' he spoke at last, 'I've been thinking. I dunno if you two will agree with me, but I can't help feeling that the trouble with this country is that too many people don't work hard enough. It's not right, that. Now, I've always believed that fair's fair. You work hard and do a good job and you should be paid well for it.'

Bob scowled at his shoes, then poured himself more whisky. Julie took a glass of water from the tap and sipped nervously. Harry surveyed the kitchen contentedly.

'By contrast,' he resumed, 'if you don't pull your finger out and get stuck in, well, I mean, that's what I call throwing a spanner in the works, ennit? I don't care what people say, when you get down to the grass roots, it's none of this pie-in-the-sky lark for me – I like to keep my feet firmly on the ground. And people who just won't pull up their socks and get on with it, well, no jam for them as far as I'm concerned. You see, if only we could all put our noses to the grindstone...'

'Stop,' said Bob.

'Eh?'

'Just stop,' Bob told him, 'and would you please leave.'

'Bob!' Julie exclaimed.

'Now,' Bob told Harry.

'Gosh, I'm sorry...' Harry rose to his feet looking like a worried retriever, 'I'm really sorry, I didn't mean to upset you otherwise I wouldn't've been so outspoken, but believe me, Mr Foster, I didn't mean any offence and...'

'I mean no offence either,' Bob cut him short, 'but I have to talk to Julie. We'll talk again another time.'

'Oh, of course, I'll go right away.' Harry picked up his canvas bag. 'No offence intended, no offence taken.' He hovered in the doorway.

'Bye,' said Bob.

Julie glared at her husband, shocked by his drinking and his rudeness, as Harry gave her a half-hearted wave and departed. She was too tense to follow up an impulse to run after Harry and apologise on Bob's behalf. Instead she continued to stare at Bob while her lower lip trembled and she had to keep swallowing.

'What's wrong?' she asked at last.

'I've lost my job,' said Bob.

10

OF COURSE there'd be no problem about Bob bouncing back with a better job soon but in the meantime there was some embarrassment and inconvenience. For example, he lost the company Audi he'd liked and had to make do with public transport and Julie's little Fiat whenever she wasn't using it. Then their mortgage payments were steep and he had no savings other than his redundancy payment. There were plenty of regular bills too. 'Don't worry, love,' said Julie, 'we'll just have to draw in our horns for a bit. Let's face it, you'll be back on your feet in no time.'

And Bob went at it with a will after just a few days of alternating anger and despondency. He passed his time in writing letters and career summaries, going through the classifieds, making phone calls and attending interviews. Everyone he saw was polite and pleasant and showed him the door.

He refused to sign on for unemployment benefit. Weeks passed with him dashing out for promising appointments, returning in an optimistic glow, then biting his lip when a letter arrived a few days later, informing him that the meeting had been a pleasure, that his name would be kept on file and wishing him every success elsewhere.

A few weeks became two months and Bob's assault slowed down. He started hearing the same story from more and more people. He was a specialist, they told him, there were only a limited number of jobs going for those in his position and at present, there were no vacancies. It was also faintly rumoured that Charles Haughey's reference had rather damned Bob with faint praise.

As time went by, there was less and less for Bob to do with his days. He responded begrudgingly to Julie's suggestions that he should consider other, temporary, work alternatives, signed on at various executive employment agencies and went to more interviews without any result. Time hung heavy on him. He mooched about the house and read plenty of newspapers. He watched TV and he listened to the radio. He went out for strolls, visited the public library and went on to the pub. He often smelled of drink when Julie came home from work.

She could sense his frustration, his contained rage – and it upset Julie and disturbed her. She had been shaken by his sudden sacking but she blamed it on that scheming bastard, Haughey. She was astonished that Bob hadn't yet found a job but she blamed that on the recession. No, it wasn't Bob's fault and he was doing all he could – but there were times when he seemed to be sinking into a stagnant swamp of negativity.

And now that he was at home most of the time, she found herself resenting the fact that he did nothing around the house, not even the hoovering or washing up. 'Even Max does the hoovering,' she'd protested. 'All the more fool Max,' said Bob.

He sat there doing less and less, it seemed. He was no longer making much effort to be stimulating. His appearance was gradually slipping. He washed his hair less often and sometimes he didn't shave until Julie asked him on arriving home in the evening. She knew it was hard and she wanted to help him in any way she could – yet Bob was disappointing her for the first time ever.

Originally, she'd consoled herself with the thought that at least Bob would be spending more time with Michael. At first, that had happened, and Julie thought she'd seen tears in Bob's eyes when he hugged his son one night. But as his morale sagged, his veins of tenderness ran dry. He became irritable with Michael and shouted at him. He didn't feel like playing with him or taking him out. It was as though his emotional resources were draining away along with his cash reserves. He made love to Julie less often and without much consideration or enthusiasm. One night he couldn't make it and that lasted for a week – but when he finally succeeded in overcoming his impotence, it was not with the granite hard-on she adored, but with a limp dick.

In Julie's view, he was becoming unreasonable too. 'Why don't you collect Michael from school?' she'd suggested. 'It's not fair on Angela having to do it all the time.'

'No.'

'No? Why not?'

'Because the only fathers who wait at the school gates are out of work. The kids know that. D'you think that'd make Michael proud?' he rasped. 'And besides, where's the fucking car?'

Julie didn't know what to do. She hoped and prayed that he would find a job soon. Meanwhile, it didn't help to learn that George had been promoted again, and Max's recent sale of a dozen paintings gave Julie less pleasure than Emma had expected her to show.

True, there were moments when it initially seemed as though everything would be all right again and soon. Occasionally, after an interview which he felt had gone particularly well, Bob had his hair styled in the West End, bought a new suit, took Julie out to an expensive restaurant where he ordered the best of everything and radiated controlled energy and calm confidence in the future. Unfortunately, however, he always drank too much and by his fourth post-prandial brandy, his energy ran wild and his confidence grew manic. Nor, in bed afterwards, did his body perform what his eyes had originally promised – and sure enough, within a week there'd be another letter of apologetic rejection. Julie grew to dread these occasions, which raised her hopes so high then disappointed them so bitterly.

One day she came home with Michael to see a brand new BMW parked in the driveway. Entering the house, she saw a smartly dressed Bob, shining with high spirits and drinking whisky cheerfully.

'Hi, honey!' he cried. 'We're hitting the town tonight and hard.' Julie felt a chilly sense of apprehension spread through her belly. 'How d'you like the car?'

'You mean, the one...?'

'Sure.' He grinned at her. 'Pretty neat, huh?'

'Is it yours, Dad?' Michael burst out excitedly.

'Bought it today.'

'Great!' shouted Michael. 'When can I have a ride in it?'

'He likes it,' Bob said, as he regarded a glum Julie. 'What's your problem, honey?'

'Nothing,' Julie sighed, 'nothing at all.' She added dully: 'It's a nice car.'

'What's the matter with you?' Bob asked irritably, then noticed that Michael was watching them intently. 'Michael, your mother and I want to talk privately.' Their son reluctantly withdrew to his room. Julie turned her back on Bob and went into the living room, where she sat down, still wearing her coat and with her bag on her lap. 'Michael!' she heard Bob shouting from the bottom of the stairs, 'on Saturday Daddy's taking you to the latest Walt Disney, okay?'

'Thanks,' Michael called back from his room. Now Bob came in, walked over to the centre of the room, regarded her with bright, glazed eyes and took a deep, celebratory swallow of his drink.

'I've got the job,' he declared proudly, 'this time I know I've got it.' Julie winced inwardly. He'd said that last time.

'What, you mean you've signed with them?' she queried.

'He's as good as told me I've got it.' Bob smiled with triumph. 'Quality control like before, only this time it's for twenty-five grand and I'm responsible directly to the board. There's no car – the salary reflects that – so I've taken care of that little problem.' His free hand waved in the direction of the drive and he began to pace the room excitedly. 'Hell, it feels good to be back where I belong.' He rounded on her. 'What's with you, Julie, aren't you glad?'

'Is it definite?' Julie asked.

'As good as.'

'What does "as good as" mean?'

'What is this?' he demanded. 'An interrogation? The guy in charge actually said: "You're the best candidate we've seen." He promised they'd be in touch tomorrow.'

'But did he actually offer you the job?'

'Boy!' Bob exclaimed bitterly, 'you're a real downer!'

'I don't mean to be.' Julie's finger gripped her bag-strap hard. 'Honestly, I'd love nothing more than for you to get that job and I'm really proud of what you've achieved so far – but I just don't feel like celebrating until it's absolutely certain. I mean, wouldn't it be a better idea to leave off buying a big, new car till then?'

'Listen.' His finger prodded the air forcefully. 'This time I've got this gut feeling that tells me I've got it for certain.'

'Sure,' she retorted bitterly, 'just like last time and the time before.' Instantly she regretted her words.

'Fuck you,' said Bob. 'I bust my ass to win and all you can do is sit there being negative.'

'No,' she protested, 'no, that's not right. I just can't bear it when you tell me something's certain and it isn't. You used to say that nothing's ever certain until the signature goes on the bottom line. Believe me, I'll be ecstatic when that happens – but it's not there yet. Suppose something goes wrong?' Her shoulders were hunched as she leaned forward urgently, her eyes imploring him to listen to reason. 'Then we're stuck with that car and where's your money?'

In answer, he left the room and came back seconds later with an exquisitely wrapped bunch of beautiful red roses, which he held tightly by the stems as though he was wielding a truncheon.

'I bought these,' his voice choked, 'for you. I thought you'd be pleased with my news. I thought you'd be glad. Well, thanks a heap for trying so hard to make me feel terrible – here's some appreciation.' He tossed the flowers into a corner. 'Thanks a million for your great belief in me.' His words were thudding into her heart. 'Now let me tell you something. I'm getting that job. And I'm also going out tonight and you can stay at home and bitch.' He glared at her. 'I'll be back whenever.'

'Bob...' she faltered, but he stormed from the room and the front door slammed. Julie stood quite still, her face blank and listened to the car departing. After a time, she started to cry.

He didn't come back until some time in the early hours. By then, Julie had long gone to bed and was sleeping fitfully. She drew away from him instinctively as he slumped into bed and her senses were assaulted by blasts of his breath – whisky, heavy wine and ill-digested garlic.

The next morning, he lay in a stupor punctuated by abrupt snores as she dressed. Julie left the bedroom as soon as she could and drove to work with tears streaming down her face.

The evening of the Fosters' row was when Harry finally decided that he'd have to face The Room. For years it had been referred to just as the lumber room. For him, though, it possessed some special significance. He hadn't entered it in over a decade. Yet since his mother's death, every room in the house other than this one and his own had been stripped bare and all the furniture sold. Judging by the tea-chests and suitcases which now dominated the living room, Harry was ready to depart.

He sat in the kitchen, mournfully munching a jam sandwich and drinking a glass of brown ale. After finishing his sandwich, he licked his fingers, then drank some more. Gradually, his soft, sad expression lifted and his features were etched with lines of fierce determination as he rose, went up the stairs and confronted the door of The Room.

His hand reached out, as if to knock, then he checked himself abruptly and bit his lip. Taking a deep breath, he grasped the door handle and flung the door open, rather as though he was playing a US marshal.

Light blazed. At first sight, there was nothing unusual in the room at all – just cases, boxes and old furniture. In one corner, there was a wind-up gramophone and next to it, several piles of 78s with deep blue, dark green and dull red labels. Harry looked uneasily at that corner before turning his attention to the cases and boxes.

For a while, he went through their contents – clothes, plates, cutlery and assorted papers, mainly to do with money. He barely glanced at these. After a time, he pulled towards him a bulky, brown leather case which looked as though it had been manufactured some time before World War Two. It was covered with stickers – British Overseas Airways Corporation, British European Airways, Cunard and P & O. Harry opened it up.

The first thing he saw was a little girl's dress in bright pink. He screamed.

Then a cry of rage came out of his throat, he seized the dress and he ripped it in half, tossing it aside as his breath came in great heaving sobs.

'Control yourself,' he said aloud. Making a deliberate effort to quieten his breathing, Harry regarded the next object, a woman's suit. His knuckles went white as his hands gripped the material. He bit his lip. It seemed as though a monumental effort was required if he wasn't to explode – then the garment was thrown contemptuously aside and followed by a pair of high-heeled shoes.

There wasn't much left in the case. A Zippo lighter. A faded pocket of Player's Navy Cut cigarettes, with ships and a bearded sailor on the front of the packet. An old photograph album, which Harry picked up and opened – only to scream once again and hurl it aside. For a few moments, his fists pounded the floor. Rage, pain and shame ruled his face in quick succession before he clenched his fists and forced himself to look at the last object which had lain in the case for so long. It was a large, leather-bound blue book. On it, the word DIARY was stamped in gold letters. Harry snatched it up and, as if fearful of the contents, scrambled out into the hall. There he opened it – and gasped. The first page showed a photograph of his mother when young. Anyone would've said that she was beautiful.

He flicked through the pages, which were covered with elegant handwriting. Suddenly a sentence caught his eye. He read it, frowned, read on, drew back, then, closing the diary firmly, took it down to the kitchen for further study.

The book so engrossed him that he left the remains of his brown ale untouched. As he read, his eyes widened in shock and astonishment. At times he sighed and his body twitched with anguish; at moments he grunted hoarsely and angrily.

And at one point he turned a page to see something which

made him drop the book in stunned amazement. For a full five minutes, he failed to retrieve it. He just sat with his mouth open and stared blankly into space.

'No,' he breathed at last, all the while shaking his head, 'it can't be.'

Julie drove home feeling angry and miserable. Bob had called her secretary earlier that day and left a message that he was picking Michael up from school. At any other time, Julie would've been pleased, but his action today was irritating her intensely. Arriving home, she saw that the driveway was unoccupied. That meant that Bob would be out in his stupid new car. He'd probably taken Michael with him too.

Yet on entering the house, the first thing she heard was Michael laughing in the kitchen.

'How do elephants get up cherry trees?' came Harry's voice. Julie felt bewildered. 'Sit on a seed and wait till spring.' Michael laughed again as she entered the kitchen.

'Hi, Mum.'

'Hallo, Mrs Foster,' Harry sang out. 'Your husband called me this afternoon. Said a ring needed replacing on the Hoover.' Julie frowned crossly. Even she could do that. Why couldn't Bob? 'All done.' He gestured proudly at the vacuum cleaner. 'There's not a speck of dust that machine won't pick up now.'

'Thanks,' Julie muttered. She looked at Michael. 'Where's Daddy?'

'Said he had to go out,' Michael and Harry responded in chorus.

'But he'll be back in time for dinner,' Harry assured her.

'I had a ride in the BMW today,' Michael announced.

'Ah.' A tight-lipped Julie returned to the hall and took her coat off. On the hall table there were letters from American Express, Diners Club, Barclaycard, Access and the gas board – all bills. Next to them was a note scrawled in Bob's untidy handwriting: You were right, I heard today. I didn't get the job. Happy now? See you later. Bob.

He was obviously drinking somewhere, Julie reflected. She needed one herself. Her guts tight with tension, she went back into the kitchen and towards the fridge.

'How do elephants get down from cherry trees?' Harry demanded. Michael looked blank and shook his head. 'Sit on a leaf and wait till autumn.' Michael giggled as Harry turned to Julie and suddenly enquired concernedly: 'You're looking a bit down in the dumps, Mrs Foster. You all right?'

'Oh, fine.' Julie nodded mechanically as she mixed herself a generous gin and tonic.

'Just the usual problems, then,' he commented.

Julie was about to nod again but checked herself.

'I wish it was just the usual,' she replied, this time with feeling.

'I know how you feel,' Harry said kindly. 'I've got quite an unusual problem myself.'

'Oh?' She wasn't really that interested but reminded herself that listening to someone else's troubles usually took one's mind off one's own. 'Why? What's happening?'

'Well, as I was telling Michael here...'

'He's sold his house,' said Michael, 'and he's got nowhere to go.'

'Found nothing,' Harry continued. 'Nothing I liked. No place I could call a home.'

'And he's got to move out next week,' Michael said.

'Have to be a hotel, I suppose,' Harry scratched his head, 'not that money's a problem but I do hate wasting it. Or else I'll find a room somewhere till I get settled. You don't know anyone who's got a nice room to let for, say, fifty quid a week?'

'Um – not off hand,' Julie answered. 'I'll ask around, though.'

'Why can't Uncle Harry stay here?' Michael demanded. 'Till he finds somewhere.'

'I wasn't suggesting that...' Harry faltered.

'There's the room at the top,' Michael went on relentlessly, 'and it's never used. What's the point of a spare room that's always spare?'

84

'Hmmm.' Suddenly Julie was thinking hard. She was furious with Bob. What he needed was a good kick up the arse. She knew he didn't like people staying. But perhaps if Harry moved in – for just a week – it would bring him back to reality. She wouldn't even bother to ask Bob's permission. If he didn't like it, they could have a row – Julie was spoiling for one tonight. 'Well, you can certainly stay for a week,' she told Harry, 'and you're welcome.'

'Why, that's extraordinarily kind of you, Mrs Foster. Much appreciated.' Michael cheered loudly. 'And in your lovely home! What a compliment! I'll be quiet as a mouse, I promise you, and thank you very...'

'Harry's coming to stay!' Michael drowned his effusive thanks. 'Harry's coming to stay! Harry's coming to stay!'

'And don't worry, I'll sort myself out,' said Harry. 'A week is all I need.'

Bob tossed back his double scotch and ordered another. The drab, sparsely peopled pub in which he stood reflected his mood. His thwarted ambition was curdling into rage and self-hatred. He wasn't used to situations he couldn't control. His fate depended on the decisions of other people and he could do nothing about it other than sell himself hard. He had tried – and nobody wanted him. He itched to be at work, to be exercising his abilities, making decisions and mastering events. His fists clenched when he thought of all he could do – if anyone let him.

God, how he hated that double-dealing bastard of yesterday! So smooth, so polite, so reassuring – then that terse letter of today, complimenting Bob on his abilities and wishing him luck elsewhere. It must've been written and posted immediately after the interview, perhaps even before it. What a slimy son-of-a-bitch Richard Spinks had been! The interview had meant nothing, it was just a formality before they promoted someone from within the corporation. Then why interview Bob at all? Why waste his time, raise his hopes and let him down? Why pump him full of sweetly scented bullshit? Richard Spinks needed a good, hard all-American punch in the mouth.

As a result, hadn't yesterday evening been just great? He had to face the horrible fact that he'd behaved abominably and made a total fool of himself. He could barely bring himself to face Julie.

How could this be happening to him? He'd never been out of work before. It was as though he'd accidentally stumbled into someone else's nightmare – the way he was feeling and acting just wasn't the Bob he knew. He should be master of his fate, not the victim of it. Yet here he was, neglecting Julie, snapping at Michael, drowning in drink and screwing up at interviews. He felt heartily ashamed of himself as he ordered another scotch.

He knew he was slipping in Julie's esteem yet somehow he couldn't control the slide. Being jobless made him feel vulnerable, so he had to project a hard front simply to protect himself from slights. He could not allow his state to diminish his manhood. That meant no to being a househusband; no to drawing the dole – he'd never taken a handout in his life; no to taking some crummy job just to bring in a few bucks; and no to being Julie's junior partner because she was winning the bread. All the same, Bob had to admit he'd become very touchy about that lately.

He'd say sorry to Julie and try to make it up to her, Bob decided. But he would stand firm on one issue. She'd want him to take the BMW back, Bob knew, and that simply couldn't be done. He needed his own car, he felt powerless without one, and any car he drove had to be good. That BMW was his and its loss would be yet another blow to his self-respect, so he'd have to keep it. (How Michael had loved it when Bob drove up at school today!) And buying that new car, Bob told himself, had been good positive thinking. You had to believe you'd make it, and that meant you had to act as though you were making it. Once he had a job, the car and all the other expenses wouldn't exactly be a problem. If he started counting the pennies and planning for prolonged unemployment, why, he'd get to thinking that way too, and would lose the confidence he needed to bounce back.

Even so, there were those horrible mornings when he rose feeling empty, useless, tired and vacuous, thinking in treacle and unable to move into gear. On those days, there was nothing to do except go through the classifieds, write and mail a few letters, then sit around hoping that the phone might ring. When it didn't, he'd be shaken by alternating bursts of burning anger and cold rage. His guts would feel as though an army of ants was nibbling on them. Five minutes would crawl by like an hour, until Bob wanted to smash something in his agony of boredom and frustration. By midday, he'd be drinking.

It killed time he didn't want, eased the pain and banished the boredom. Instead of smouldering with resentment all day, he could burn up all his anger in an hour. After a few glasses, life became interesting again and he could once more feel optimism and make positive resolutions for tomorrow. Unfortunately, the booze was upsetting Julie.

In fact, Bob decided as he took another drink, it was getting out of control and had to stop. Today's disaster had to be faced bravely. It was time he got a tight grip on his life again. Tomorrow he would rewrite his career summary and investigate jobs outside London – yes, anywhere in England. As for the drinking, he knew just how to combat that. He'd fight the tedium of being out of work by employing himself.

There was something he'd meant to look into for many years now. It was that mystery involving his own father's secret shame. The moment had come to delve deeper, as he'd always intended. Before, he'd never had the time. At present, that was hardly a problem.

Self-discipline, Bob thought approvingly, that was the key here. Well, since there might be a heavy scene coming with Julie, and since tomorrow would see the commencement of a cleaner life, there were two good reasons for one last drink. Besides, someone had just put 'Satisfaction' on the juke box.

He smiled slightly as he bought the whisky, and silently drank the health of Harry. Bob had forgotten to go to the bank today and found himself out of cash, but the handyman had gladly obliged with a ten-pound loan. Pity it was all gone.

11

'YOU'VE MADE this room much more interesting,' Michael remarked. He regarded the surrounding chaos happily. 'What're these?'

'My books,' said Harry, who was sitting on the bed.

'*I, The Jury*,' Michael read out slowly. '*My Gun is Quick, Vengeance is Mine, One Lonely Night, The Long Wait, The Big Kill, Kiss Me Deadly*...'

'They don't come any tougher than Mickey Spillane,' Harry declared. 'See, it says that on the back.'

'Funny pictures on the front. Look, that woman's showing her boobs.'

'But what about him?' Harry pointed at the man in the picture. 'See the way he's holding that gun? No messing about with Mike Hammer, I can tell you.'

'And who's that?' Michael pointed at a poster Harry had spread over the bedside table.

'That's Rocky Marciano,' Harry answered proudly. 'Greatest fighter who ever donned a glove. World heavyweight champion 1952-6. Forty-nine fights, forty-nine wins, forty-three of 'em by knockout. What a man he was!'

'And this?' Michael picked up a grip strengthener.

'Go on. Close it if you can. Use both hands.' The boy's small fists tightened around the handles of the object and he squeezed with all his might but nothing happened.

'Can't budge it,' he grumbled. 'Not possible.'

'It takes practice, I'll give you that.' Harry took the grip in one hand and effortlessly squeezed it shut. 'And it helps to have a bit of strength.'

'God, you are strong,' Michael said admiringly, 'though my dad's incredibly strong too.'

'Harry!' Julie called up from the first floor landing. 'Sorry to trouble you – but d'you think you could just give me a hand with something?'

'Your mum's calling me.' Harry jumped up. "Scuse me a moment.'

'It's this window in the bathroom,' Julie said, as he came down the stairs from the spare room. 'I can't seem to get it shut. Must be stuck.'

'No trouble at all.' Harry strolled into the bathroom and shut the window with ease.

'Thanks.' Julie smiled at him. There was a loud buzz from downstairs. 'Oh, hell, the washing machine...'

'I'll do that.' He bounded down the stairs and turned towards the kitchen.

'No, please...' Julie called out after him, 'the stuff needs to go in the drier and it's quite complicated.'

'Used that model for years,' Harry called back. 'Not to worry. I'll have it done for you in a jiffy.'

Julie thought of insisting – after all, he was under no obligation at all to help with the washing – but restrained herself. If he really wanted to take care of a tedious task, why stop him? It seemed that he just loved helping with every household chore Julie hated – even the loathsome duty of ironing – and he always did it better than Julie herself. Harry had been here for three days now and she had to admit that she was glad of it.

He'd insisted on giving her fifty pounds in cash, brushing aside all her attempts to refuse it. 'As I see it, Mrs Foster,' he told her, 'I'm honoured to be in your lovely home as your paying guest. And that means – no arguments please – that I pay. That's the paying part. Of course, anything that goes wrong or needs fixing while I'm here – that's the guest part.'

He couldn't've been a better guest. Julie got up in the morning to find a pot of strong tea brewing in the kitchen – he'd made it five minutes before. When she came home dying for a break, he took Michael off her hands and made him happy. Harry leapt at every chance of lifting the domestic burden off her shoulders. Then, every evening so far, the moment it became apparent that he wasn't needed, he went out for a couple of hours, then retired unobtrusively to his room. At times it was just like having a servant. Julie couldn't help bossing him around.

And perhaps Harry was responsible for the improvement in Bob, who'd amazed her by agreeing readily to a week of Harry staying. Julie had been hard on him that night but he'd taken it without a murmur and it looked as though he was really trying once again. He was drinking less. His eyes were clearer, his face more determined. He gave the impression of harsh effort. He'd even admitted that he'd developed a drink problem – and his idea of fighting it by using slack hours to research something personal, struck Julie as being very sensible.

She vaguely recalled the story – he'd told it to her years ago – and was quite curious about the solution to that particular enigma, but doubted if anyone would ever discover it. Still, researching that would be infinitely better for Bob than brooding sullenly with a bottle for company. He'd rescued that old file from the mess in the basement and was re-reading the contents, his face glowing with fascination.

'All in the drier!' Harry cried, as he trotted back up the stairs. She smiled at him again. 'That's what I like to see!' he assured her, 'a nice, big, cheerful smile. Life ain't much but it's all you got, Mrs Foster, so stick a geranium in yer 'at and be 'appy!'

A day later, the Fosters gave a dinner party, returning the hospitality of Max and Emma and Angela and George. Julie felt she had to invite Harry too. After all, he was more than just a lodger and he did know Angela. In fact, at the time she thought she'd made a wise decision, for she returned from work to discover that Harry had laid the table and was working on the meal. 'Least I can do,' he said.

The occasion was a success and Harry's cooking proved excellent. True, Angela irritated Julie and Emma as usual. Wearing a new outfit – her jacket, blouse, skirt, stockings, shoes and handbag were all in varying shades of rust – she kept praising George for his recent promotion. Her husband sat there and looked smug. Max played down his recent success, though he did mention that he'd just been interviewed by *Time Out*. Emma looked proud of him and toyed with her new gold bracelet, a present from Max. Bob had little to say but managed to play the part of genial host and refused to be riled by Angela's persistent questioning about the progress he'd made in securing a new job. As for Harry, he was a model of correct behaviour. He spoke only when spoken to and, to Julie's relief, never talked for long.

'You must have a fair bit of time on your hands, Bob,' Angela remarked over the coffee. 'Don't you find that just a little bit frustrating?'

'It could be,' Bob answered evenly, 'but I'm not allowing it to upset me. Any spare time I have gets taken up by a little research into family history.'

'That must be very interesting for you,' Angela commented with a patronising smile.

'It is,' Bob returned blandly.

"Scuse my asking,' Harry came in suddenly, 'but is that anything to do with that old file I've seen you studying?'

'That's right,' said Bob. 'It belonged to my dad.'

'Wish I had something from my dad,' Harry murmured wistfully. 'He died when I was so young I can barely remember him – but that wasn't what I was meaning to say. What I meant to say was...' everyone looked at him and he paused, '... was, I'd like to propose a toast.' He raised the glass of wine he'd hardly touched. 'It's been marvellous, the hospitality I've had here, and I'd like all the guests to raise their glasses and join me in wishing health and happiness to two wonderful people – Bob and Julie Foster!'

Everyone complied with his wish, though Bob and Julie looked slightly embarrassed, and Harry then fell silent until the two visiting couples had left.

'No washing up for you,' Harry declared with absolute finality. 'You're to leave that to me. No, Julie, no arguments,' he waved aside her protests. 'Listen, today I found a place and I'll be moving out just like I said, so you might as well make use of old Harry here 'cos you won't be having him for long.'

'Okay,' said Bob, and slipped an arm around Julie's waist,

'then we'll be off to bed and many thanks.'

'My pleasure.' Harry beamed at them and Bob smiled back. As he squeezed Julie's waist, he knew it would be all right tonight.

'C'mon, honey.' He led his wife up the stairs.

Harry set about the task of clearing up with speed and efficiency and within half an hour, everything was done. Yet instead of going to bed, he helped himself to a glass of Ribena and took it into the living room, where his eyes darted to where Bob had been sitting earlier that day.

A thick file had been carelessly deposited on top of the TV. Harry picked it up and extracted a large notebook of American manufacture. His breathing came fast and shallow as he flicked through the pages. He looked guilty and furtive as he read the odd extract – penned in an untidy, masculine scrawl – and he started at every sudden sound and glanced anxiously behind him.

Suddenly he saw something which made him catch his breath, hold it and exhale it in a gasp. He swayed groggily as he read it through again, then sank into an armchair where he sprawled like a man of straw.

For a long time he did nothing except stare blankly at the notebook. Gradually, a frown etched itself upon his face, as though for the first time in years he was making an effort to think very hard.

And as he thought, slowly – very slowly – his warm brown eyes darkened and hardened into hatred.

12

AS MICHAEL watched his father and Harry playing table-tennis at the local leisure centre that Saturday, he felt pleased that the man he sometimes called 'uncle' was staying for another week. Harry's new place had suddenly fallen through, it seemed, which was fine as far as Michael was concerned.

Take today, for instance. When Dad had suggested one of their ping-pong mornings, Michael had reminded him that Harry loved the game, so couldn't he come too? After all, Dad was always complaining he didn't know anyone who could give him a good, hard match.

So, Dad had given Michael half an hour's tuition – 'Push the ball over the net, push the ball, push the ball!' – and was now knocking up with Harry. It looked as though Harry would go the same way as Mr Thomas and Mr MacDonald and all the other men Dad had slaughtered here. Yes, Harry could play all right, but he just wasn't as good as Dad. Dad had this exciting, slam-bam style. When he hit the ball with his forehand smash, there wasn't a man in the world who could return it, except maybe those champions on television. There it was again now and poor, old Harry was just standing there and looking stupid as the ball whizzed by.

'Good one,' he commented admiringly. 'Beautiful smash you've got there, Bob.' Michael was glad that Harry had taken to calling his parents by their Christian names. It made things friendlier.

'How about a game?' Bob suggested.

'Oh, yes, have a proper game,' Michael urged them. 'I'll keep score.'

'All right, then,' said Harry. 'Play for service.' He threw the ball in, it passed over the net several times, then Bob slammed it past his opponent.

'Dad's service.'

Bob threw the ball up and hit it hard, sending it rocketing over the net. Harry's wrist flicked in response and the ball shot back and past Bob.

'Love one,' said Michael, regarding Harry with as much surprise as his father.

Bob executed his heavy top-spin serve. This usually struck his opponent's bat and flew out, but Harry chopped it. The ball hit the net and trickled over, bouncing twice before Bob could reach it.

'Love two.'

This time Bob sliced the ball with back-spin. To his amazement, Harry returned it with a fast and wristy forehand slam that left him gawking helplessly.

'Love three...' Michael was bewildered.

The fourth serve was Bob's famous googly, which had always fooled opponents, but Harry merely flicked it at Bob's backhand and the ball died on the latter's bat.

'Love four...?'

Bob's next serve was a low backhand. Harry returned it and Bob flung himself into a vicious forehand slam. Harry smashed it right back and it bounced and struck Bob's chest.

'Love five,' Michael murmured faintly, 'five love. Change service.'

He watched with growing stupefaction as his father's game went completely to pieces. Harry treated his deadliest deliveries with apologetic contempt. The best Bob could do was sneak a point here and there with uncharacteristically pawky play. As the game went on, he swore frequently under his breath and tried to slam impossible balls – all of which missed the table by a yard and hit the back wall. He lost both his concentration and his temper. Harry handled Bob's slipshod play as easily as Bob handled Michael's, even, it seemed, giving him a point here and there out of charity. The final score was a devastating 21-6 to Harry.

'Lovely game,' declared the victor. 'I had no idea you were this good, Bob.'

'Good?' Bob snorted indignantly and glowered at him.

'Good? Hell, I was terrible! The fact is, I'm totally out of practice.'

'Well, I thought you played jolly well,' Harry assured him pleasantly, 'though there's no denying that practice makes perfect. How about another game? You'll probably beat me this time.'

'No, thanks,' Bob muttered irritably, and added: 'I seem to have pulled a thigh muscle.'

'Oh, sorry to hear it. But many thanks, anyway.' Harry grinned and extended his hand. Bob shook it reluctantly. 'How about you, then, Michael? Reckon you can beat Uncle Harry?'

'You're good,' Michael declared reverently. 'I've never seen anybody beat Daddy before.'

'C'mon, then,' said Harry. 'Let's go.' Michael rushed forward eagerly and picked up a bat as Bob sat down heavily. It hurt getting beaten by a guy like Harry at a favourite game and in front of his son. Somehow he'd have to get even and restore the respect he felt he'd lost. He watched gloomily as Harry now threw away point after point to his excited son, clowned, praised Michael's play, and after allowing him to build up a solid lead, took control again to win 21-14.

'Brilliant play, Michael!' Harry exclaimed enthusiastically. 'Brilliant play.'

'I did better than you, Dad,' Michael announced gleefully.

'Sure,' said Bob, and winced inwardly.

'Right!' Harry declared. 'Another.'

'Uh, uh.' Bob felt that if he didn't get out of the leisure centre this minute, he'd go crazy. 'It's time for lunch.'

'All right, then, lunch,' Harry responded, 'and I know just the place. Round the corner from here. They do beautiful egg and chips.'

'Great,' Michael concurred, 'let's go there.'

'Eggs and chips are okay,' Bob said, 'but I know a better place.'

'But I fancy eggs and chips,' Michael objected.

'Wait till you see where I'm taking you,' Bob retorted

somewhat sharply. 'They do absolutely unbelievable hamburgers.'

'But I don't fancy hamburgers. I'd much rather go to Harry's...'

'C'mon,' Bob cut him short, 'we're going.'

Unfortunately for Bob, the restaurant he'd suggested was closed for redecoration and three doors away from the one recommended by Harry, so they ended up there after all. Michael and Harry thoroughly enjoyed their eggs and chips and chattered non-stop about nothing. Bob sulked and ate little. He knew that Julie would think it childish of him to be such a sore loser, but then there was that American saying that the only good losers are losers.

It was fast becoming a damn nuisance having Harry for another week. Originally Bob had agreed with Julie that there was nothing much else they could do. It wasn't Harry's fault that his place had fallen through, the man had nowhere to go, he was being incredibly helpful – they couldn't just turn him out onto the street. But the lack of privacy was getting on Bob's nerves; so was the way in which Harry did everything around the house, making Bob feel doubly redundant; and so was the fascination Harry seemed to exercise over Michael, which had clearly been strengthened by his triumph at table-tennis. What man would be happy at seeing his son so impressed by Harry? The guy had to go and soon – and meanwhile something had to be done about his growing influence.

'You've got to stand up for yourself,' Harry was telling Michael, with his mouth full of chips. 'Otherwise you've got no chance.'

'But he's bigger than me,' Michael objected.

'The bigger they come, the harder they fall,' Harry returned. 'Know who said that? Bob Fitzsimmons, England's last world heavyweight champion, 1897–99. He only weighed in at about twelve stone but he said it just before his fight with Ed "Freight Train" Dunkhorst, who was all of twenty-two stone – nearly twice his size.'

'What happened?' Michael's fork had paused halfway to his open mouth.

'Fitz knocked him out in the first round,' said Harry. 'Flattened the Freight Train. See? No need to be scared by size. The bigger they come, the harder they fall.'

Michael put a large, soggy chip in his mouth and chewed thoughtfully.

'But Pete's a really good fighter,' he said at last.

'Who's this?' Bob queried abruptly.

'Peter Gallagher,' his son replied nervously. 'This bloke at school who's in the form above me. He smashed up Bill Stevens and Bill Stevens is really tough.

'And you've got a problem with him?' asked Bob.

'He says he's going to get me.'

'And what I'm saying is,' Harry explained, 'that this Pete is a bully and bullies are cowards. They run away if you stand up to them.'

'That's true enough.' Bob put his elbows on the table. 'But first you have to know how to fight them. Michael,' he fixed the boy with his eyes, 'when we get home I'll be teaching you some boxing.'

'Boxer, are you?' Harry said. 'I never knew that.'

'A long time ago I used to go to this gym in Chicago. That's where I really learned how to fight.'

'Wish I'd done some boxing,' Harry said wistfully. 'Trouble is, my mum wouldn't let me. Boxing,' he pronounced the word reverently, 'real man's sport. Closest I ever got to that was pretty tame, I have to admit. I used to be quite a dab hand at arm-wrestling, not that I'm comparing them.'

'Oh, yeah?' Bob smiled slightly. 'I did a little myself, ages and ages ago. Why don't we give it a try?'

'What, now?' Harry queried.

'Why not?' Bob returned easily.

'Wow!' exclaimed Michael. 'You're both really strong. Bet you Dad's stronger, though.'

'Probably,' said Harry, 'but there's no disgrace in losing to the best.'

'Let's go,' Bob murmured.

Harry put his right elbow on the table and stretched out his hand. Bob grasped it – it was dry, large and firm, so this wouldn't be an easy contest – while Michael regarded them with awe.

Bob's eyes hardened as he put pressure on Harry. Very little pressure came back. Instantly Bob had his opponent's strategy sussed. Harry was the type who held up his arm like a ramrod and defied your strength. The way to beat a man like that, Bob thought, was to keep your own power coming and coming and coming until his biceps slackened with the strain and his will collapsed along with his muscle. Harry was evidently no weakling and wouldn't fold for at least a few minutes, but there was no way a mummy's boy could take Bob's uncoiled strength for long.

Time passed while Harry, his face impassive, held his arm upright without budging one fraction of an inch. Bob began to grit his teeth. His biceps started to ache. He grunted twice as he redoubled his effort – with no visible effect whatsoever. It was like trying to shift a boulder. Surely that extra ounce of pressure would do it? No – and a bead of sweat broke out on Bob's forehead.

That was the instant when Harry made his move. An unexpected burst of strength forced Bob's arm back three inches. Now Bob had lost leverage. His mouth tightened and he screwed up his eyes as he tried to fight back. Harry relaxed the pressure and contented himself with holding Bob right where he was. Pain stabbed Bob's muscles in two separate places as he struggled to recover – then Harry sensed the draining of his strength and commenced his second assault, pressing Bob's hand relentlessly towards the table. With his white knuckles a mere inch from the plastic surface, Bob fought back with a fevered desperation, forcing Harry's hand up by half an inch – but that effort exhausted his reserves. Harry looked at him once before pinning Bob's hand flat upon the table.

'Phew!' Harry exclaimed, released Bob's hand and wiped imaginary perspiration from his brow. 'Quite a contest!'

'God!' Michael looked dazed. 'You beat Dad!'

'Don't know how I did it,' Harry told him. 'I mean, your dad's a really strong bloke. For a bit, he had me worried,' he looked kindly at Bob, 'but like I said, I'm not too bad when it comes to arm wrestling.'

'You're very good at it,' Bob muttered. His biceps felt as though it had been pounded with a steel hammer. 'I had no idea you were so strong. Although strength isn't the only thing which counts in fighting. Speed, timing, bodily coordination, that's what makes for real punching power...' He stopped, because Michael wasn't listening. He was staring admiringly at Harry as he felt his muscles. 'Okay, let's go,' Bob sighed wearily. He was suddenly feeling horribly tired.

In the car, Michael sat in the back with Harry and listened to his stories about famous strong men while Bob drove in silence.

'What fun!' Harry cried out on their arrival. 'What an excellent day it's been so far, eh? You know, we must do this again. Well, Bob,' he clapped him patronisingly on the shoulder, 'thanks for everything and I mustn't intrude any further. I'm off to my room, if you'll excuse me. Going to watch some Walt Disney on my video.'

'Okay.' Bob scowled at the carpet. 'Michael, it's time for your boxing lesson.'

'Later, Dad,' Michael answered casually. 'I'm going to watch Walt Disney with Harry.'

'No, you're –' Bob nearly said 'fucking' – 'not.' He seized his son by the wrist.

'Ow!' Michael squealed. 'Stop it! You're hurting!' Bob relaxed his grip and was shocked by his loss of control.

'Listen.' His voice sounded grating and unnatural even to his own ears. 'D'you wanna get beat up in school on Monday?'

'Bob's right.' Harry made it sound as though he was handing down a fatherly judgement. 'You listen to him, Michael. He knows.' Bob's toes curled within his shoes in impotent anger. 'And when you've finished, then you can come on up and I'll rerun the film.'

'Promise?' Michael pleaded.

'Promise.' Harry left the room. Michael watched him go.

'Okay,' Bob declared with unconvincing heartiness. 'This

is going to make you unbeatable. Now, first of all show me how you throw a punch. C'mon, hit my hand.'

Michael came forward reluctantly and punched Bob's hand listlessly. His mind was elsewhere.

'At first it seemed fine,' Julie was telling Emma at the local wine bar that lunch-time. 'All right, so he could stay another week. I mean, at that point, another nine days didn't seem like much. But somehow it's started to get to me all of a sudden.'

'Meaning?' Emma poured more wine for both of them.

'Well, there's the privacy thing, obviously, though initially Harry seemed very unobtrusive. But these last few days, he's been around the whole time and it's as though we can't get away from him. For example, the other day, there was this TV programme I wanted to see, and when I went into the room, there was Harry watching something else with Michael – just like one of the family.'

'I hope you switched channels instantly.' Emma lit a cigarette.

'Well, no.' Julie looked unhappy.

'Why not?' Emma demanded. 'It's your house. He's only renting a room for a few days. Frankly, I think it's sheer cheek for him to plonk himself down in your living room like that.'

'I know,' Julie sighed, 'but the trouble is that Harry's always so kind and helpful and obliging, it's dead difficult to say no to him.'

'You mean, you feel in his debt?'

'Yes, I suppose so.'

'Oldest trick in the world,' Emma commented. 'Put someone in your debt and then do what the hell you like.'

'You think so?' Julie frowned. 'But I can't believe he's that calculating. He's so innocent, so childlike...'

'What? A man in his forties? Don't you believe it – oh, hi, darling,' she greeted Max, who'd just come in. He wore an old leather jacket with paint-splattered jeans, and though his face was relaxed and his mouth was smiling, his eyes were slightly glassy.

'Hi,' he greeted them affably.

'You're stoned,' said Emma.

'Guilty,' he agreed cheerfully. 'Good Lebanese red which I scored at Murray's.' Taking a glass, he helped himself to the wine. 'Just dropped by to say hello,' he continued. 'Don't let me spoil your conversation. Soon as I've had a glass, I'm off to buy some brushes. Mmm, that look's nice. May I?' Picking up a strip of ham from Emma's plate, he popped it in his mouth and chewed with enjoyment.

'Julie's just telling me about Harry.' Emma repeated the gist of what she'd heard. 'And let's face it, we've both met him, we agree he's a nice, inoffensive little chap – but quite honestly, I suspect he's pushing his luck.'

'Hmm, I wonder.' Julie accepted more wine from Max. 'Take this, for instance,' she said. 'Harry used to keep to himself in the evenings – but he's spent the last three playing with Michael. Not that there's anything wrong in that – except that there's this gut feeling Bob and I have that Harry's intruding just a little bit too much. And I know it's only a passing phase, but it's sometimes as though Michael would rather be with Harry than with us.'

'It sounds,' Max drawled, 'as though he's taking over your space.'

'Yes, that's quite a good way of putting it.' Julie's fingers drummed nervously on the table. 'And his platitudes are getting on my nerves. Doesn't he ever say anything that's original? I know that sounds unfair but... and another thing. He's at home the whole sodding day. Now he's inherited money from his mum, he's given up being a professional handyman. But even though that's annoying Bob, what with never having the place to himself, he feels he can't really object because Harry helps me such a lot.'

'Putting you further in his debt.' Emma stubbed out her cigarette.

'You could be right.' Julie spread the last of her Brie on a hunk of French bread. 'He doesn't seem to be looking for anywhere else to stay.'

'Oh, *I* see his game.' Emma brushed crumbs off her floppy, flower-patterned dress. 'Well, the solution's perfectly simple. You've got to talk to him, Julie. You've got to talk to him today. And you've got to tell him as nicely as possible but in no uncertain terms, that he's leaving next week.'

'Yes, but suppose he's got nowhere to go?' said Julie.

'That's his problem,' Max replied.

'Yes, but he's been so extraordinarily helpful.'

'Julie,' Emma regarded her sternly, 'you're playing Yes But. And if you keep on answering, "Yes, but" to everything we say, we'll all be here till midnight and you'll be stuck with Harry for Christmas.'

'Which isn't far away,' Max added.

'So tell him straight,' Emma urged.

'Or invent a relative who's coming to stay,' Max suggested.

'He's got to go,' Emma insisted. 'He's upsetting you, that's obvious. And for heaven's sake, Julie, is it your home or his? So tell him.'

'You're right,' said Julie. 'I will.'

Knock! knock!

'Come in!' called Harry. Julie entered his room to see him playing some video game with Michael.

'Hi, Mum!' her boy shouted. 'We've been having an absolutely fantastic day. And you know something? Harry beat Daddy at table-tennis *and* arm wrestling! Then Daddy gave me a boxing lesson and taught me how to throw a left hook.'

'Sounds great.' Julie smiled. Inwardly, she was quite surprised at Harry's victories, knowing full well how much her husband prided himself on his physical strength and sporting skills. 'Where is Daddy?'

'He must've gone out,' Michael answered. 'He's in a terrible mood. He kept losing his temper during the boxing, just like he did in the table-tennis match. But he said my left hook was good. Look.' Michael punched the air.

'That's enough Clint Eastwood for now, love. I came up here for a quick chat with Harry.'

'Oh. D'you want me to go, Mum?' Julie shook her head.

'I'm very pleased you've come for a chat,' Harry said, 'because I've been wanting a word with you too. Go on,' he indicated the edge of the bed, 'sit down and make yourself at home.'

'It's okay, thanks.' Julie smiled and remained standing. Her gaze took in the video and stereo, the books, posters and body building equipment. He's settled in very, very comfortably, she thought. Emma was right. She was just about to begin the little speech she'd prepared when Michael spoke up suddenly.

'Harry's got this great idea,' he said.

'You know your basement?' Harry came in fast.

'Yes...?' What's coming now? thought Julie.

'Just a dark, damp room for storing things, isn't it?' Harry continued. 'Not much use to you at all.'

'Well, the storage space is useful...'

'But that's all.' Harry looked directly at her. 'See, I've been down there, Julie – hope you don't mind but Michael kindly took me – and I was thinking. And what I was thinking is: if it could be renovated properly, you could have a whole separate flat down there. Sort of bed-sitting room with cooking facilities and a bathroom. That'd increase the value of your property no end, and if it took your fancy, you could have a separate entrance and let it out.'

'Bob and I have often talked about that,' Julie answered truthfully. 'The trouble is that it'd cost a small fortune to have it done up.'

'And that's where *I* come in,' said Harry. 'You see, I love working with my hands. Be a joy to transform that place.'

'I'm sure it'd be a beautiful job and you could do it more reasonably than anyone else, but at present we're not in a position to make any financial commitments, unfortunately,' Julie returned.

'No, no, Julie, you misunderstand me entirely,' Harry

responded with fervour. 'You and your husband and young Michael here have been so extraordinarily kind to me, it's the least I can do to make some form of reparation. See, I don't need the money. I've got as much money as I'll ever need. I don't have to work again ever – but a man needs to work, I say. You know,' he smiled benevolently, 'it'd give me such joy if that could be my Christmas present to you.'

'But we couldn't possibly accept it...'

''Course you could,' said Harry. 'And if you refuse my gift, you'll be depriving me of a joy.'

'But...' Julie faltered while her mind calculated. Suppose her fears came true. Suppose Bob couldn't find a job, or could only find one hundreds of miles away and they had to sell the house. What Harry was proposing would add, and add substantially, to its capital value.

'But me no buts,' Harry interrupted. 'You see before you a man who thrives on hard work and challenge. And I'd like to start tomorrow, if that's okay with you.'

'I'll have to talk to Bob first,' Julie demurred.

'Please try and persuade him,' Harry pleaded. 'You'd make me so terribly happy.'

She would recall those words often in the months to come.

13

'SHIT,' BOB hissed through clenched teeth as the BMW encountered another red light and yet another traffic jam. 'Aw, shit,' he sighed wearily as the car slowed to a halt, 'can't even get to school on time.'

Nothing I do seems any good, he thought, as his body sweated with frustration. He'd sent out two hundred job applications, cut down on his drinking and adopted a positive attitude – but nothing had happened. He had very little cash left. Bloody Christmas was coming, which meant buying presents he couldn't afford and faking a happiness he didn't feel. Another month of this and he'd be on pocket money from Julie.

Until he'd investigated public records, he couldn't take his research any further – yet he kept sitting at home and hoping for the phone call which would put him back in business. Today, once again, that hadn't happened. There hadn't been any letters either.

Growing desperation had made him seize on an outside chance to turn his situation around. If it worked – and it was a very long shot – he was still pretty sure that Julie wouldn't like it. But what was the alternative? That campaign had commenced today and there wasn't much he could do now except wait.

Waiting – that was the story of his life at present, Bob reflected as the lights went green, five cars made it over the cross-roads, he crawled forward hopefully – and the lights went back to red again. Around lunch-time, he'd sunk into a state of abject misery and despair. The craving for a drink had been almost insupportable – but he no longer kept any in the house, he didn't have any money on him and he'd somehow resisted the temptation to go to the bank.

The continuing presence of Harry wasn't making things

any easier. This morning, the man had started work on the basement, which had meant hours of banging and crashing. It also meant that Harry would be staying until it was finished – but as he and Julie had agreed, Harry's offer was like being handed ten thousand pounds or more. Given the current, dismal position, it simply couldn't be refused. Even so, Harry was starting to drive him crazy.

It took twenty minutes to cover the two remaining miles to Michael's school. A group of boys hung around outside the gates, talking and laughing. His son for once wasn't among them. Bob's eyes roamed the pavement and finally picked out Michael lounging in solitary misery on the street corner. Bob drove up to him and opened the car door. As Michael climbed in, the boys by the gates shouted something and he blushed.

'Hi,' said Bob.

'Hi.' Michael stared glumly at his shoes.

'Okay day?' Bob enquired, as the car moved away from the kerb. Michael didn't answer. 'I asked if your day was okay.'

'Yeah.'

'Something bad happen?' Michael shrugged. The car slowed as they encountered another traffic jam. Bob turned to regard the boy closely. It looked as though he'd been crying and there was a small blue bruise just under his right eye. 'How'd you get that?'

His son turned to stare accusingly at him.

'Your left hook didn't work,' he said bitterly. 'I got beaten up in front of everyone.' He sniffed and wiped away a budding tear.

There was a depressing silence. Bob was about to reach out and grasp his son's hand in consolation when the light's went green.

'I'm sorry,' he said.

'He rubbed my face in the dirt.'

'Jesus!' Bob growled, and felt sick. What could he say? 'I guess you can't win 'em all. But – uh – if you lose one, you can always make a comeback.' Like me? he thought.

'Yeah.' Michael sounded utterly unconvinced.

'When we get home, you and me, we'll work out something.'

'Sure.' His tone was sullen. They didn't speak for the rest of the journey.

'I'll fix you something to eat,' Bob announced, as they entered the house. He went into the kitchen to discover Harry having tea.

"Afternoon, Bob,' he sang out, then as Michael slouched in, he added: 'Hey, what's up with you?'

'He lost a fight,' Bob explained, when Michael didn't answer. His son immediately glared at him as though he'd betrayed a confidence.

'Got beaten, did you?' Harry chuckled.

'It's not funny,' Michael snapped.

'But it's not the end of the world,' said Harry.

'That's what I'm trying to tell him,' said Bob. 'C'mon, son, have a pizza and let's talk about it.'

'I'm not hungry,' Michael muttered, 'and I don't want to talk about it.'

'Oh, I reckon you should,' Harry replied. 'You know, analyse the fight, go through the moves again, see where you went wrong.'

'Everything went wrong!' Michael burst out. 'He was too big and strong. I hit him with a left hook just like Daddy said and he just laughed at me and called me... he said I punched like a sissy...' he gasped, in between the sobs which shook his body. 'He... he squeezed me in a bear hug, he threw me on the ground and then he... he...'

'I know,' Bob said, as his son collapsed into a chair and wept. 'Hey, take it easy, Michael.' He put an arm round his shoulder. Michael twisted his body and shoved it away. God, I need a drink, Bob thought.

'Here,' said Harry, 'here.' He knelt down in front of Michael and to Bob's surprise, put a hand over his face.

'Go away!' Michael shouted.

'Get a load of this,' Harry retorted, and squeezed Michael's cheeks between his thumb and fingers. The boy squealed in shock and pain.

'Goddamnit, what're you doing?' Bob snarled, as Harry released his grip.

'Hurt, that, didn't it?' Harry told Michael pleasantly. 'Now do it to me.'

'Huh?' Michael blinked at him.

'Go on. Do that to me.'

Bob observed that the boy had stopped crying as Michael's hand reached out for Harry's face, grasped the cheeks and feebly squeezed.

'Aargh!!!' Harry screamed, and fell to the floor. 'God, I had no idea you were that strong.' Suddenly Michael was fascinated and his tears forgotten. 'That's Uncle Harry's Secret Grip, you see. Been known to make strong men weep. I mean, he wrestled you, didn't he? Now, wrestling is grips. So what you have to do is wrestle him – and I've got lots more where that came from. Look.' Harry's hand snaked out for Michael's face and the latter shrank away. 'That's what he'll be doing.'

'Teach me,' Michael begged.

'All right,' said Harry, 'how about now – up in my room.'

'Oh, yes, please!'

'And afterwards,' Bob put in, 'you come down here and show your daddy what you learned.' Michael didn't seem to hear him. Bob gritted his teeth as his guts writhed.

'Right,' Harry declared, 'a wrestling lesson straight away and then you have your tea. I tell you, you'll be making mincemeat out of Pete Gallagher. Yeah, Mincemeat Gallagher's what he'll be by the time you've finished with him.'

Michael laughed and ran out of the room without once looking at Bob. His father squirmed inwardly. The thought of sitting here like some useless wimp while Harry taught Michael how to fight properly was too much to bear.

'Harry,' he said in a strangled voice, 'you know that twenty pounds I owe you?' It choked Bob to say this but hanging around would choke him even more. 'Make it up to thirty and I'll pay you back tomorrow.' A drink, a drink, a drink, oh God, I'm dying for a drink.

'No problem.' Harry took a roll of ten-pound notes from the pocket of his grey flannels, peeled one off and proffered it to him. 'Pleasure to help.'

'Thanks.' Bob took it. 'I – uh – have to get something from the shops but I'll be back in time to fix something for Michael.' Just like a woman.

'Oh, I can take care of that.'

'Har–ry!' Michael called from upstairs.

'Okay,' said Bob. The pub was calling him. 'Oh, and one thing. These little loans I always repay are just between the two of us, right?'

'Oh, right,' Harry assured him, 'I won't go telling anyone. Far as I'm concerned, mum's the word.'

For Julie, the period leading up to Christmas was a nightmare. Buying expensive gifts in shops overcrowded by bad-tempered people had always been trying enough, but this particular December seemed imbued with a malice directed specifically against her.

Bob was once more degenerating into a leaden depression, dominated by drink. There were no job offers, no interviews even. She'd ask: 'How was your day?' and he'd answer: 'Whaddo you think?' Then he'd enquire: 'How was yours?' and his eyes would glaze over as she told him.

'For Christ's sake,' she blew up at him once, 'if nothing's bloody happening, why don't you go to the Public Record Office and follow up your research?' But he just shrugged and poured himself another drink and mumbled something about maybe tomorrow, as though he'd lost all interest in the idea.

It no longer bothered her that his libido had declined again, for his look and his touch had ceased to arouse her. She wanted Bob – not this stranger who slurred his words, talked nonsense and did little except stare at the TV in a semi-stupor. On the occasions when he railed against his fate, his bad temper was frightening, but in a way, the good temper which sometimes accompanied his bloodshot eyes, sweaty forehead and reddened face was even more tyrannical and distressing.

'Great acting!' he'd roar at some forgettable TV programme. 'Hey, Julie, ain't this great? Okay, girl, so we got our problems – but we'll soon be through that shit, I tell you – and now, right now, what's so bad about the two of us here now, huh? Hey, honey, give us a smile!'

Something was also very wrong between Bob and Michael. As Julie understood it, Michael had trouble with a bully at school, Bob had taught him some boxing and the result had been disastrous. Then Harry – of all people, Julie thought – had had a session with him and Michael came home crowing as though he'd just won the world heavyweight championship.

'It worked, Mum, it worked!' he kept telling Julie triumphantly. 'Pete Gallagher got me in this bear hug again with everyone watching and I gave him Uncle Harry's Secret Grip across his chops. He couldn't believe it. Nobody could. And then he started squealing and his eyes went all watery and he let me go and fell over with me still on top of him and I squeezed and I squeezed and he was crying by then and no longer fighting and I said: "Say, submit" so he said "submit", and I rubbed his face in the dirt just like he does with us and everyone was cheering me and laughing at him...' Michael paused for breath.

'Well done, love,' said Julie, as she tucked him into bed. 'Now eat your apple.'

'I was the hero of the school today.' His teeth went *scrunch* on the fruit's green skin. 'Nobody ever beaten Pete Gallagher before. Colin Evans went and congratulated me, and he's nine and the toughest bloke around. And Susie Simms,' suddenly he looked shy, 'gave me a kiss.'

'Good for you,' said Julie.

'He won't be bullying any of us again,' Michael declared defiantly. 'If he tries anything, I'll soon sort him out. And Jackie Hargreaves and Nicole White and Linda Dawson and all the other girls in my form came and asked me to be their protector.'

'Well, you be their protector,' Julie told him encouragingly. 'Daddy must be proud of you,' she added.

'Dad?' His expression altered to one of profound disappointment.

'Have you told him?'

'Yeah.'

'And what did he say?'

'Not much.' Michael looked hurt. 'He was drunk again.' Julie swallowed. 'I think he's just jealous because he didn't teach me anything. I learned it all from Uncle Harry. He's really strong – much stronger than Dad – and he knows all about fighting. Dad's useless.'

'You mustn't say that,' Julie admonished him sharply. There was a fierce, stabbing pain in her heart. 'That's just not true.'

'Daddy's gone funny,' Michael observed sadly. 'He doesn't play with me like he used to. He doesn't do anything. He's become like Frank Meacher's dad – and Simon Crowther's – sitting around the house all day doing nothing except drinking. I don't like it when he's like that.'

'No...' Julie took him in her arms and held him tight. 'You must try and understand. I know it's difficult now but it won't be for long. In the end, it'll be all right. We've got to be strong, love.' She held her voice steady as she fought back the tears. 'Daddy's not well but it *will* work out in the end.'

But Michael still shied away from Bob. The occasions when Bob grabbed him and demanded his attention only frightened him and made matters worse. Meanwhile he was coming to hero-worship Harry. That was bothering Julie more and more.

Even so, what could she say? She could understand why Bob resented it – but why couldn't he make more of an effort? What sort of example was he setting? And what real complaints could she openly level at their paying guest? He was still as helpful as he'd ever been, in spite of all his work on the basement. That, he said, was going very well. Just how well it was going, Julie couldn't discover – for Harry's first action down there had been to build double doors he kept padlocked.

'Sorry, Julie,' he told her amiably, 'but you must know me by now. I won't have anyone down there inspecting my progress – makes me nervous, you know what I mean? I mean, I want it to be a really nice surprise for you. I want you to see it when everything's done. And, I tell you, I'm doing such a beautiful job, you just won't believe it.'

There wasn't much Julie could do except comply with his wishes. Meanwhile Harry sometimes went out in a van he'd rented and returned with sacks, bags, pipes, tubes, wires, bricks, panels, wood, tiles, pots of paint and other appurtenances of the interior decorator's trade. Twice Julie demanded a serious talk and vehemently insisted on paying for the raw materials. Always she received the same answer.

'No. No. Absolutely not,' said Harry, 'and if you suggest it again, I promise you I'm going on strike. I mean that. Now, you wouldn't want to spoil old Harry's little treat, would you? That'd be cruel – and somehow I don't think you're like that.'

'Why worry?' asked Angela, when Julie put the matter to her. 'If he's prepared to do it and it gives him pleasure, you'd be a fool to offend him – and he's such a dear, sweet, kind man. After all,' she fingered her new gold necklace, 'Harry's adding so much to the value of your house. That might come in useful if things don't work out for Bob.'

'I know it must be bloody awkward,' was Emma's response, 'and Harry *is* putting you further in his debt – but if I were in your shoes, I think I'd do the same thing. It's too good a chance to miss, really.'

So Julie's dreary life went on – and on and on and on. She rose and went to work, where she did her job competently and without taking the slightest pleasure in it. Then she came home tired to a drunken husband, a son who avoided him and a chirpy bore to whom she was indebted. Evenings passed slowly and forgettably. There was no style in her life, no glamour any more, and even the genuine warmth between Michael and herself was chilled by anxieties he recognised but about which they dared not speak.

Harry seemed omnipresent. Even when he went out, one

felt he was still there. Julie soldiered on because she had to, yet each day she awoke and retired with misery. She started to see her life as a box whose dimensions were inexorably shrinking.

Christmas was coming. The thought filled her with dread.

It was morning on Boxing Day when Angela received an unexpected phone call from Julie, who sounded distraught.

'Come over right away,' Angela said decisively, and immediately told her husband to make some good coffee. Judging by Julie's tone, her Christmas had been as wretched as Angela's had been wonderful. 'Poor Julie,' she murmured to herself.

Her friend arrived ten minutes later. Angela gave her a short, warm hug and a long, cold look. What she saw concerned her. Julie had come out without putting on any makeup and it was clear she'd been crying. There were dark pouches under her eyes and the lines which had recently appeared on her face had aged her.

'Take it easy, it's all right,' Angela said gently, as she helped Julie into a chair. 'George has put some coffee on for us.'

'Thanks,' Julie answered tiredly. She'd rung Emma first but there was no reply, and in her desperation for someone to talk to, she felt relieved to be with Angela. 'Oh God,' she sighed.

'Coffee's ready!' George announced brightly, as he entered the room bearing a tray, then greeted Julie enthusiastically. 'Merry Christmas!' he beamed. 'And a happy new year!'

'Thanks, same to you.' Julie managed a pained smile.

'Something wrong?' George enquired politely.

'Darling, why don't you take Pru out for a walk or something?' Angela came in. 'Julie and I have to talk privately.'

'Oh, all right.' George served the coffee, then picked up his own cup.

'Can't you have that later, pet?' asked Angela.

'Well – um...' George glanced down at his coffee. 'But it'll be cold by then.'

'You can always reheat it.'

'I suppose so,' George murmured. 'Oh, well.' He put down his cup regretfully. 'Better leave you to it, then. See you later.' He edged out of the room. ''Bye for now.'

'Mmm. It's good coffee.' Julie drank gratefully, relieved that George had gone but marvelling at Angela's ability to send him away with a snap of her fingers.

'Thanks. Blue Mountain.' Angela put down her cup and regarded her friend sympathetically. 'What's wrong?' she asked. 'You can tell me.'

'Oh, God, everything. Christmas, the whole bit. I hate Christmas!' Julie burst out. 'The tension and the shopping and the crowds and the money spent and that sickly false joviality...'

'Sounds like you're having an absolutely rotten time of it.'

'I am.' Julie returned aggrievedly. 'And why me? What have I done to deserve all this shit? I mean, there's Bob with no job after hundreds of applications, and let's face it, being American over here doesn't help in a recession and he's not familiar with the English style of interview game – and so he's boozing heavily as I'm sure you've noticed.' Angela nodded. 'All the same, I thought I'd still do my best and try and make it a nice, family Christmas. I thought, on Christmas Day, we'll just have the three of us.'

'No Harry?'

'No, thank God. I've told you how that's got to me.'

'But he's so sweet,' Angela protested.

'Yes, but would you like him living with you? Anyhow, I was very relieved when he told me he'd be staying with friends over Christmas.'

'Friends?' Angela raised a neatly pencilled eyebrow. 'I didn't know he had any.'

'That's what he said. But on the afternoon of Christmas Eve when I was decorating the tree, he came in with all these big, wrapped presents and said they were for us.'

'What's wrong with that? Sounds lovely to me.'

'Well, I thought it was a very nice gesture – and thank heavens I remembered to buy him a present. Unfortunately, the next thing he said was that his friend had fallen ill and so he had nowhere to go. I felt like going round and shooting his sick friend, but what could I do except invite Harry to join us? So,' Julie rolled her eyes, 'we're stuck with Harry for Christmas.

'Christmas Eve's pretty miserable,' Julie continued, 'and we don't do much except wrap presents and watch TV. Meanwhile, Harry's insisted on taking over the cooking for tomorrow. I let him. I'm feeling so wiped out, I no longer feel like cooking ever again. But I keep on getting these irrational waves of paranoia over Harry taking over my home. Anyway, the Big Day comes and it's all right at first. Michael's happy with his stocking, breakfast's okay and then it's time to gather round the tree and have our presents. That's when it starts.

'First, what's really just a minor thing,' Julie went on, 'Bob's presents to me are all wrong.'

'Wrong?' Angela frowned.

'Well-intentioned but wrong. I didn't want anything expensive. I know how difficult it is for him at present. So I said I wanted an umbrella. Just an ordinary, straightforward women's umbrella. He goes and gets me this gaily coloured, twee little parasol. It's not me at all. I'd be ashamed to be seen using it. It's as though he's lost both his understanding of me and his sense of taste. Then there's a year's subscription to *Cosmopolitan* – but I did that for myself last month. Finally there's a small bottle of this cologne he bought me last year and which I told him didn't suit me. I'm not pleased...'

'I'd be dreadfully disappointed,' said Angela.

'... but I want to keep it all nice so I try and pretend I am. He keeps asking me what's wrong and then he has his first drink. Then Harry goes and gives me a beautiful, bone china tea service which must've cost a bomb. It's really lovely and surprisingly tasteful, but I'm embarrassed by his extravagance and it puts Bob in a bad light. I wish he hadn't bothered. But it gets worse when it comes to Michael.

'Bob's gone and got him this huge teddy bear. It's an extremely nice teddy bear and most kids would be delighted, but perhaps Bob hasn't noticed that Michael hasn't been into teddy bears for a while. Like me, Michael acts pleased and once again Bob notices and starts brooding. Then Harry goes and gives Michael his own bloody video with games.'

'Must've cost him an absolute fortune,' Angela observed. 'He must be terribly fond of Michael.'

'And I wish he wasn't. Because, of course, Michael's straight into playing Space Battle or whatever it is, the teddy bear's lying neglected in a corner and Bob's really pissed off. We go on to our Christmas dinner. The food's good, there's crackers and so on, but I don't feel like saying very much, Michael's got this fixation on Harry and Bob keeps trying to attract his attention and failing.

'The Christmas pudding comes and at first it doesn't light. Bob promptly goes and sloshes half a bottle of brandy over it, the damn thing flares up, burns the table-cloth and ends up looking all black and scorched and Michael says he doesn't want any. There's quite a bit of tension by now as we munch our way through brandy-sodden suet. Harry and Michael keep reading out those awful jokes you get in crackers and finding them hilarious. I've got a headache.

'Then everybody slumps in front of the TV. I absolutely insist on doing the washing up because I can't bear it and want to get away. When I come back, Harry and Michael are playing Space Battle and Bob's having scotch. Harry suggests a game of Charades, which I like and so we give it a go. Michael and Harry have obviously had plenty of practice. Bob's never played it before and he just looks ridiculous. Michael's laughing at him.

'Then Bob says he wants a sleep and vanishes upstairs. I feel everything's hopeless, but after the Queen's speech, I go up to our bedroom and there's Bob boozing from a bottle he's hidden. Before I can say anything, he tells me he's had this really promising phone call. I don't want to hear about things that're just "promising": that's happened too many times before. I try to go away and he grips my arm so hard, it frightens me. He's just not the man I know. Finally, he lets me go and I return downstairs to nothing very much, thank you.

'By the time Bob comes down, he's pie-eyed and legless. Then Harry puts on Paul McCartney's "Simply Having a Wonderful Christmas Time" and I'm ready to scream. There's a glint in Bob's eye I don't like as I bring in some sandwiches. Harry goes upstairs to the loo. Suddenly Bob gets up and follows him. They're away for a bit and I start worrying. Then I hear they're talking on the landing – and raising their voices.

'I tell Michael to stay where he is and as I go towards the stairs, I overhear Bob saying: 'You're leaving tomorrow." I stop and listen.

'"Just calm down," Harry tells him.

'"I said, you're leaving tomorrow." It's said with that menacing growl Bob gets when he's really annoyed. And Harry's saying: "How have I upset you?"

'"Never mind that shit," Bob says. "It's my house. You're going."

'"But what about the basement I'm doing up..."' Julie mimicked Harry.

'"Fuck that. You're going."'

'Charming,' Angela commented.

'I should've intervened there and then,' said Julie. 'I should've gone up, interrupted, calmed them down, got Harry alone, apologised for Bob – but I just couldn't think straight. And the next thing I hear is Harry saying: "I take exception to this. I think this is out of order."

'"I don't give a shit what you think," Bob shouts at him. "Who the fuck are you anyway?"

'"I'm a guest in your house," Harry says. "And what's more, I'm a paying guest."

'And Bob replies: "Big deal. I don't want a bum like you spending time with my son."

'That's too much. That's totally insulting. I start up the stairs, and Michael has crept into the hall behind me as

Harry says: "Me a bum? What about you? What about all the money I've lent you so you can go boozing? You're just good for nothing."'

'Jesus!' exclaimed Angela.

'And Bob hit him,' said Julie.

'*What?*'

'Oh, yes. Bob hit him hard. Harry wasn't expecting it. It was a great big punch in the mouth. Harry's head went crack against the wall and he fell down the stairs. Michael saw it and started screaming. Harry was out cold.'

'Oh, my God,' breathed Angela.

'So that was my Christmas Day,' said Julie. 'Bob drunk and violent and then remorseful, Harry unconscious and Michael bawling his head off. We had to carry Harry up to bed. I was in a terrible state, phoning around and trying to get a doctor, which I couldn't. And suppose Harry wanted to call the police and have Bob done for assault. Or he might want to sue. Thank God, he came round and said there was nothing broken, though he'd lost a tooth, and he'd be all right. By that time Bob had passed out.

'He's still out of it,' Julie told Angela, 'and Harry's in bed too. That's why I had to phone you. That's why I had to come over and talk. Oh, Christ, Angela,' Julie shook her head, 'I can't stand it. I just can't *stand* it!'

14

IT WAS a day later. Harry lay in bed. A plate of half-eaten food which Julie had brought him reposed on the bedside table, but Harry paid it no attention. He was engrossed in the study of a thick set of photostats, each sheet of which was covered in untidy handwriting.

Heavy footsteps sounded on the stairs. Harry sat up, momentarily startled, then quickly hid the papers beneath the bed.

Knock! knock!

'Come in,' Harry called out, then drew back slightly in surprise as Bob entered. He looked much better than he had in a long while. His hair was newly washed and glossy, he'd had a very close shave and his face was unusually relaxed, even if his grin was slightly sheepish.

'Hi.' He smiled. Then: 'How're you feeling?'

'Oh – er – not too bad, thanks.' Harry looked uneasy. 'Be up and about in a day or two.'

'Good,' Bob said quietly, then took a deep breath. 'I'm sorry, Harry. I'm very sorry indeed about what happened.'

'Oh. Thank you.' Harry's face lit up with pleasure. 'Really kind of you. Much appreciated.'

'I've been going through a really rough patch lately, and I guess I just got upset and snapped and lost my cool.'

'Understood,' said Harry, 'and it's all right. No hard feelings at all. Let's face it, these things happen.'

'And I take back what I said. I didn't mean it.'

'Oh, what did you say?' Harry scratched his head and looked puzzled. 'Can't remember. Oh, well, thanks, and not to worry and don't mention it. And what's more, not another word more. All forgotten and forgiven.' Harry smiled and held out his open hand. 'Shake.'

'Sure.' Bob stooped to shake Harry's hand.

'Here's to friendship,' said Harry.

'Sure. You know,' Bob told him pleasantly, 'I had some excellent news today. Things're going to work out. I'll tell you the good news after I've told Julie.'

'Marvellous!' Harry replied warmly. 'I shall look forward to it. Congratulations, Bob, on whatever it is and I'm very well pleased for you.'

'Thanks. Be seeing you.' Bob turned to go. Two dark, malevolent eyes glared with hatred at his back.

'It's not what you think,' said Bob, as Julie regarded him apprehensively, 'and sure,' he smiled ruefully, 'I know what you're thinking.'

Why's he dressed up? thought Julie. Is this another manic state, oh God? Is he about to announce a victory before he's won it? She took a deep breath. If he says we're going out to dinner, I shall scream.

That was when Bob took a sheaf of documents out of his suit pocket.

'This time, the good news really is definite,' he smiled into her eyes, just the way he used to. 'Read the letter. And here's the contract. All that's missing is my own signature.' Vitality vibrated around his body once more as he passed the papers over.

Her hands trembled as she read the letter, realised that the offer was definite, grasped that the job was ideal for Bob and took in the superb salary. Her heart bounded for joy – then she noticed something which made her catch her breath.

'The money...' she faltered, 'it's amazing... but it's in dollars.'

'I know,' Bob returned calmly, 'that's the problem. The job's back home in California. They want me even if nobody does over here. But the prospect must be quite a shock for you, and there's no way I'm signing until we've talked it through and you're happy with it.'

'It's all too much.' Julie shook her head. 'Oh, Bob...' she took him in her arms and hugged him, 'I'm so proud of you, love, landing a job like that...' His own hug was strong and loving. 'It's wonderful news but...'

'I know.' He stroked her back. 'Can you face a move back to California again? You don't need to decide right now, honey. Think about it.'

'I'll have to. It's just so sudden.' She hugged him hard again.

'How about dinner out tonight?' Bob suggested. 'Somewhere good.'

'Yes,' said Julie, 'yes.'

Several hours later, when they were both having a second brandy with their coffee, Julie had made her decision. There were plenty of things to be said against it. She hadn't liked California the first time, it would mean another disruption of their lives, Michael would be uprooted once again and there was no guarantee it would work out long term. But it was a relief from the nightmare which Julie's life had become. Right now, what was so wonderful? What would she be missing? She was getting less and less satisfaction out of her job. Were the friends she'd missed so much in the past really nourishing her? What was she getting out of her life here at present?

And of course, in the end, the deciding factor was Bob. When he was so alive and radiating confidence and strength, as he was now, all her old love returned and all the bad memories and wretched resentments were forgotten. If she agreed to his proposal, he'd once more be a man, a strong man and her man. He'd take care of her, as he'd always done, until he lost his job.

But if she put herself first, remembered all the bad times in California and said no, then she could see the immediate future all too clearly. He'd feel brought down and defeated again. He'd go back to being the unhappy creature whom she tried to look after but for whose inner pain she could do nothing. Bob and Michael would grow further apart and the drab misery of her life would continue. In any case, she just couldn't go on watching her man degenerate into a sullen wreck.

'Just think of it,' he was saying, his features glowing with delight as he pictured his homeland, 'sunshine all the year round.' Outside, a shrill wind whipped pellets of hail against the restaurant window. 'The sea. The beach,' he smiled dreamily.

I can't say no, thought Julie. He can earn much more than I can. And he'll be working for the rest of his active life. Probably I won't.

'And on what they're paying me, you won't need to work,' Bob continued. 'Naturally you can if you want to. But you could also expand your horizons. Study anything that took your fancy. Or laze around. Or...' abruptly he paused, and regarded her tenderly. 'Julie, have you ever thought about us having another kid?'

In answer, she took his hand. She felt too vulnerable and soft to speak.

'Maybe we should talk about that another time,' said Bob, and there was a brief instant when their eyes met in a blazing stare, then switched away hurriedly. 'But Julie, there is something I have to say to you. I'm very aware of how awful I've been. In fact, I'm amazed at myself and I wouldn't've believed it possible. I'm sorry. I guess I'm just no good at being a victim. But now I have a chance here, and it's with my own people and I understand them much better than the people over here. I'm an able guy, I work very hard, I love you, you mean everything to me and I want to take care of you and make your life wonderful. I can't do that over here. I tried, I tried so hard, but I didn't make it. I promise you that won't happen again when I'm back home.'

Julie bit back an impulse to cry.

'I know, love,' she whispered, 'and I love you and I'm going wherever you're going.'

'I know there're things which piss you off, honey,' Bob said, as they drove back home in a blissfully happy state, 'but California's not all bad.' Black rain hammered on the windscreen. 'Would you rather be doing this or sitting out beneath the stars in a hot tub?'

'Oh, I've missed our hot tub,' Julie admitted cheerfully. She was warming to the idea. 'And those great Californian cocktails.'

'God, yes. And Japanese food. The sushi and sashimi's just not the same here.'

'And the Mexican food,' Julie enthused.

'And all the great outdoor sports. Gee!' he exclaimed as though he was a ten-year-old. 'No more warm beer!'

'No more shitty weather.'

'No more people like Charles Haughey!' Bob said with feeling.

'No more surly service!'

The car rolled easily into the driveway. At the top of the house, there was a light shining. Bob and Julie glanced at it and at each other, shook hands and shouted simultaneaously: 'NO MORE HARRY!'

That night, they made love with all the passion and abandon and heat of their honeymoon.

It soon became difficult to believe that the ghastliness of the past had actually taken place. Bob signed the contract and sent it off, and a mere few days later, all arrangements were confirmed via the telephone. The Fosters had three months in which to settle their affairs and move. Julie gave in her notice – which was received with regret – and Bob became a dynamo of purposeful activity. His drinking went right back to normal, as though there'd never been a problem. He exuded enthusiasm; no organisational task was too much for him; he was animated in all he did by his recovered optimism. He was no longer bothered by unthinking slights.

For example, when Michael was told about the move and Daddy's wonderful new job, he didn't appeared terribly pleased at first.

'Will Harry be coming with us?' was one of the first questions he asked. Julie had winced inwardly, expecting Bob to explode, but he'd just laughed good-naturedly.

123

'Hardly surprising,' he told Julie later, 'considering the way I've been acting. A little time and he'll get over it. You'll see.'

And Bob was right. Within a remarkably short space of time, Michael sensed the change in his father and was all over him, often neglecting Harry. Bob welcomed his son's every attention and gave to him. Meanwhile Harry just carried on. He'd risen from his bed the moment he was told the good news.

'Delighted for you,' said Harry. 'Really delighted. And you deserve it. Bob, it couldn't happen to a nicer fella. Not that I'd want to live in California myself. I'm quite happy here, thank you. But, tell you what, I wouldn't mind visiting.' God forbid, Bob and Julie thought behind their smiles. 'And am I glad I started on that basement. Be ready the week after next, you know.' The guy's as fast as the States, Bob thought. 'And I reckon it's lovely when people are so kind to you, as you've been to me, and so you make 'em a present, to wish 'em luck, so to speak, and then along comes a nice, big, fat piece of luck for them.'

'Naturally we'll be putting the house on the market,' Bob said, 'and it seems a shame after all the work you've done – which is so much appreciated – but – uh – Julie and I, we have a proposal. Harry, you've really increased the value of our property. We think you ought to have a share in our profits.'

'No,' Harry retorted firmly, 'absolutely not. That would spoil it all. Please, no money. I'm not interested in money. This,' he held up his hands solemnly, 'this is its own reward.'

There was no persuading him. In the end, Harry carried on secretively working on the basement and the Fosters decided to leave him at it. Things seemed to be returning to the original pattern, with Harry as the cheerful servant whom they didn't have to pay because they were leaving soon.

There was one minor matter which Bob resolved he'd settle before they left – the mystery involving his own father. He'd brooded on that for hour after unproductive hour and, in all honesty, done nothing really practical about solving it. In fact, now that he had a future, he was no longer so interested in the past. There was a duty to be done and that was all.

A week after the breakthrough, Bob announced at dinner that he'd be spending the next day at the Public Record Office.

'The family history, is it?' asked Harry.

'Right,' said Bob, 'but excuse me if I don't talk about it at this stage. What I'm hoping is that there'll be a really interesting story in it.'

'Hope so,' said Julie, who was only mildly curious.

'All right, then, mum's the word,' said Harry, and chuckled. 'But it can be very interesting, family history.'

That night, Harry stayed up late when the Fosters went to bed. Bob and Julie thought nothing of it.

The following day, just after Julie had gone to work, Bob packed a briefcase with papers from the old file of his father's and walked out into the driveway, by which Harry was arranging long planks of wood.

'Going okay?' asked Bob. Harry grinned in answer. 'I'm off on my quest.' Bob opened the door of his BMW.

'Good luck,' said Harry. 'Hope you find out something that's useful.' And Bob drove away looking as though all was well with the world.

He was soon on a fast main road, reminding himself that it was small and slow by Los Angeles standards. On the LA freeways, you could really drive, and driving was one of his greatest pleasures in life.

At least there was a bit of road coming up which had curves and intersections and bridges with neat corners. It wasn't much but it served as a reminder of pleasures to come. One of the first things he'd do when he got back home was take a drive along Sunset until he hit Dead Man's Curve.

Bob accelerated past a Jaguar. The speedometer needle touched seventy-five as he branched off, shooting up towards a bridge, just as he would in Los Angeles. More speed for the first bend, he thought, then he slackened the pressure on the pedal at an imaginary line running through the apex of the curve. The car hurtled round the bend and into the next curve. Bob accelerated again, then realised he'd erred in pumping too much gas. His foot touched the brake pedal lightly. Nothing happened.

In an instant of pure panic, his sole came down hard on the brakes as the car shot relentlessly forward. Bob turned the wheel frantically. The vehicle skidded violently. He spun the wheel in the direction of the skid – and the side of the car smashed into the short, slender barrier, the front wheels lifted, the chassis tilted – and then it was over the little white wall and falling fast upon the busy road beneath.

It landed on its side, bounced slightly once and turned over on its back with a screaming of mangled metal, no longer a vehicle, more an ugly, welded mess – like its driver.

Part Three

15

'He'll be all right,' said Harry. 'You mark my words, he'll be all right in the end.'

Julie said nothing. She just carried on staring at the coffee Harry had made her without feeling the smallest desire to sip it.

It was a week after the crash. To her, it seemed like a week after the end of the world. Nothing mattered much any more except the broken body in the hospital, the tubes that went into it and the tubes that came out. The future was a vague and unpleasant blur and she didn't care about it at all. Like an automaton, she rose and performed essential tasks, then sat around staring blankly into space and feeling hopeless. Sometimes she went to bed at three in the afternoon and stayed there till six thirty, with the covers pulled over her head.

She felt tired and listless all day, and started up and cried at night. She didn't want to see anyone, do anything or make decisions. The most trivial actions required a monumental effort of will on her part. She was often tempted to break down completely. Only the facts that Michael needed her and that Bob might live kept Julie going.

Yes, her husband *might* live. That was what the doctors had said, and they hadn't sounded over-optimistic. Her man lay still, wrapped in plaster as though he were an embalmed corpse, wired to machines and bags of fluid, his mind far from this world. He might live, yes, but no one knew when he might emerge from the coma. By some miracle, it might be the next time Julie visited but it was equally possible that his brain might remain unconscious for over a year. And suppose if, by some act of the God Julie now prayed to daily, Bob did live, there was every chance of some permanent injury which would leave him a maimed and crippled vegetable. It was possible too that the universe would behave with the malice it had shown Julie, and Bob would cling tenuously to life for month after month before expiring.

Every day, she visited the hospital and sat by the bed, willing him to stir and open his eyes, pleading with all the powers that be to intervene for her, trying through some intuitive emotional telepathy to send all her love to him. And each day she spoke with doctors and they told her next to nothing; and each day she returned home with her being numbed by her despair.

It was just as well that Harry was here. He took care of everything. He'd comforted Julie and looked after her during that hideous day when the news came, and he'd appointed himself cook, cleaner, secretary whenever the phone rang, and nursemaid. Whenever Julie wasn't up to being with Michael, Harry was there to console the boy. Most of the time, he didn't say much either – for which Julie was thankful – and when he did speak, it was always to say something kind. Julie didn't want to know about the outside world, so Harry acted as a buffer. He did all the shopping, ran any errands that needed doing and carried on working in the basement.

Julie couldn't stop thinking about Bob, however hard she tried. It was a private torture of the emotions, but she couldn't help herself. Incident after joyful incident sprang back into her mind and love welled up along with her tears. Sometimes she awoke and reached out for her man, still expecting to find him sleeping beside her. Then the truth came down like a heavy hammer on her heart and pounded her being onto the burning coals of her anguish.

She remembered every wounding thing she'd ever said to Bob, every time she'd behaved bitchily, then lashed herself into a state of bitter and bloody remorse. She felt there might never be an end to her grief. *Why* had it happened? And *how* had it happened? Bob was an excellent driver. The car was new and so a mechanical failure was unlikely. However, the bits of vehicle that were left after the collision with the coach were in no state to be examined.

Why me? Why me? Why me? The words drummed inside her brain with the monotonous regularity of a loud, ticking clock.

Another week passed. Slowly Julie realised that she had to go on living. Bob was comatose and she was numb, but there was Michael to be looked after and she had to carry on somehow. She started forcing herself to take an interest in things around her, hard though it was and futile though it seemed. Michael went reluctantly back to school – Harry drove him there and picked him up in Julie's car to spare her the pain of chatter with other mothers. Julie had Angela and Emma over to tea – she still didn't want to go out – and her friends proved warm, sympathetic and supportive.

'Why don't you let Michael come over and play with Pru?' Angela suggested. 'He could spend the night with us. Perhaps a change'd do him good.' Julie saw her point and they arranged it for the following evening.

'The basement'll be ready tomorrow,' Harry told her, on the night that Michael would go to Angela's. 'I know that can't mean much to you now but I still think you'll be quite pleased with it.'

'Sounds really good.' Julie tried to sound as though she meant it. Her fork picked at the casseroled meat with rice he'd made for dinner.

'I imagine,' Harry said, 'that as soon as things're a bit more settled, you'll be selling the house.'

'Right.' Julie nodded. Too many memories, she thought. Can't go on living here.

'Pity about that. It's such a lovely house. But I can see why. Meanwhile, I'll have to find a place for myself. Now the room's done and you seem to be getting back on your feet, it's time I went.'

'Any idea where you'll be going?'

'A rough idea.' Harry drank a little brown ale. 'I want to find myself a cosy little niche somewhere that's comfortable. Quite honestly, I'd like to be in this area. It's a nice area. Better see about that tomorrow.'

'Good luck,' said Julie.

After dinner, Julie wandered into the living room and switched on the TV. Harry put the plates and cutlery in the dishwasher, then joined her. Shortly after eight, he asked her if she minded a switch over to *Dallas*. Julie didn't mind. She didn't really care. But after a while, the soap opera – which Harry was evidently enjoying greatly – began to oppress her. It was all so glossy and unreal. She couldn't bring herself to care about any of the lacquered puppets with their greedy intrigues, so she excused herself and went up to her bedroom.

It was just as well Harry was finally leaving, Julie reflected, as she stretched out on the bed. Otherwise, as she got better and stronger, she'd start taking exception to his domination of the household. Really, it was ridiculous that she should be forced to seek some peace and quiet here whilst he lorded it in front of the television downstairs. It was almost as though she was a guest in *his* house.

She abruptly realised that this burst of irritation was the first strong emotion unconnected with Bob that she'd experienced in quite a while. She must be on the mend.

But, after a while, that feeling faded and the old, weepy lassitude crept back. Julie tried to read a book, then turned the pages of a magazine but the words and the pictures meant nothing to her. Finally, she took two Valium which the doctor had prescribed, switched out the light and buried herself in her bed. She was soon fast asleep.

Some time later, she awoke and was immediately possessed by the horrible suspicion that there was someone else in the room. She stared around but it was too dark to see anything. Julie clenched her teeth and switched on the light.

Harry was sitting at the end of the bed. Julie flinched automatically.

'What're you doing here?' she demanded.

'It's nice, this room,' he answered. 'Cosy, you would call it. Sort of bedroom I wouldn't mind having if I was married.'

'Look, if you don't mind, I'm very tired.' There was a hard edge to Julie's tone. She really did object to his intrusion. He had no right at all to barge into her bedroom and watch her while she slept. It was outrageous. 'I'd like to think my bedroom is a strictly private place and I want to get some sleep, okay?'

'I want a chat,' said Harry. It was as though he hadn't heard her. 'A nice chat. I think it's about time we have a nice chat, don't you?'

'Sure, let's have one tomorrow.' Julie lay back and closed her eyes. Get out, she thought, or I shall scream.

'You know something?' said Harry. 'You look lovely when you're all relaxed like that.' Had he been drinking? He had no right to talk to her like that. It was infuriating. And she was starting to feel very uneasy.

'I'm trying to get some sleep,' Julie retorted sharply. 'I want to be left alone. If there's any talking to be done, let's do it tomorrow.'

'I should've had somebody like you,' Harry continued dreamily. 'Julie, would you consider marrying me?'

'*What?*'

Alarm spread through her body as she sat up stiffly and gaped at him. Had he gone crazy?

'You wouldn't, would you?' Harry said sadly. 'And I don't reckon any woman would, at least not a woman worth having. Although, when all's said and done, I've got a lot to offer.'

'Oh, yes,' Julie humoured him, 'but I don't think this is the time and place to discuss it.' His eyes were all dark and funny now. He was scaring her. She wanted him out – and fast. Out of her room. Out of her house. Out of her life.

'That's where you're wrong,' Harry told her softly. 'Because tonight's the night.'

'What...' Julie shivered inwardly as she stared at him hard. His hands were fiddling with the bedspread, as if impatient to be at work. His mouth was a tight, thin line. His eyes smouldered.

'You don't rate me, do you?' he stated flatly. 'Women don't. You think I'm just some stupid ninny who's useful around the house, don't you?'

'No,' Julie protested fearfully, 'no, not at all. I like to think we've got this nice friendship...'

'Friendship, exactly!' he exclaimed bitterly. 'But I'm not a man to you, am I?'

'Of course you're a man!'

'No. Not in the real sense, according to you. Not in the sense most women mean. And I can't forgive you for that.'

'Harry!' she burst out.

'Yeah?' His response was a cold sneer which chilled her.

'Harry, what's happening? The way you're talking... it's frightening me. What've I ever done to you? We've always got on well. Why're you saying these strange things? Harry!' she squealed, as he rose to his feet and came towards her.

'There'll be plenty of time to explain,' he murmured. 'You'll understand.'

'What're you doing?' she screamed.

In answer, his hands closed around her neck and his thumb pressed down hard on her carotid artery, cutting off her scream and her breath and the passage of her blood to her brain. She writhed and twitched for just a few seconds, then slumped unconscious.

Harry smiled.

16

SOME TIME later, Julie came round to find herself lying on a carpet in a strange, pitch-black room. For an instant, her mind was utterly bewildered, then she recalled her last few moments of consciousness before the blackout, shuddered, moaned softly and wrapped her arms around her naked body, terror gnawing at her guts.

For a few moments, she was wholly petrified. Her mind declined to function. Her body was incapable of moving one muscle. Then she began to shake uncontrollably and small sobs of fear came from her lungs. Michael! The word ran right through her chest like a sharp skewer. He was now alone in the house with Harry, who had done this to her and she was... where? Julie listened hard. There was total silence aside from her own laboured breathing. She'd never felt so frightened and helpless. She'd never been in a place where there wasn't the slightest sound. One always heard passing traffic and sometimes birds in every room in which she'd ever been. But now there was nothing save the oppressive stillness all around her.

She couldn't see anything either. There was only utter blackness. Julie shivered and shook in a paroxysm of horror. She had woken up in her past life from such nightmares as most people occasionally suffer. They were terrible, so terrible that she remembered two or three of them that had oppressed her years before, but they were pure delight to what she now endured, with a weight of sick terror pressing upon her breast.

All she could feel was the carpet's smooth texture. Was she alone? Sight and sound told her nothing, but smell and intuition sensed nobody. She opened her mouth and emitted a squeak. It echoed in the room and mocked her. It was shrill and disturbing, then it died away in the silence and the darkness.

She fought down an overpowering urge to panic utterly, to escape into a semi-conscious seizure of screaming anguish, and with all the will she had left she tried to think things through calmly. Harry had assaulted her – instinctively she touched herself and discovered with relief that she had not been raped – knocked her out and put her somewhere. That much at least was clear, but again the question throbbed within her skull: where? And now she thought of the basement room he'd been building. Hadn't he told her it was ready to show? Julie shook and shivered even though it wasn't at all cold. A wave of nausea surged into her stomach and she wrestled with the impulse to vomit up her loathing and revulsion.

Was there a light? The darkness pressed in relentlessly all around her, enfeebling her hold on her courage. Julie bit her lip hard and crawled cautiously forward on all fours. Suddenly her head collided with a hard, wooden object and she shrieked. Then her hand felt it. It was the leg of a chair. She pressed on, working her way around it, then groping forward with a hand waving slowly before her like a mine detector. At last her fingers felt a wall. Julie edged along it, turned a corner, edged along some more – and detected a door.

Her heart was thumping as she came apprehensively to her feet and her hand traced the line of the door join upwards. At shoulder level, her palm gave the wall an exploratory caress – and landed on a light switch. She pressed it eagerly – and the room was abruptly illuminated by a bright bulb which hung from the ceiling and was surrounded by a dusty red, round shade.

Julie's jaw dropped as she regarded her surroundings. She didn't like the look of them at all. On impulse, she tried the door. It wouldn't move a millimetre. Julie turned again and looked hard at her cell.

It was a medium-sized room. The carpet was beige and the walls and ceiling had been papered with white woodchip. Julie immediately thought of old films of the Fifties. All the furniture was solid and square, even the dull, green three-piece suite. In one corner, there was a woman's brown bureau with foldaway flap and behind it a straight-backed mahogany chair. Some distance away, there was a wind-up gramophone with a pile of 78s. A bulky wireless stood on a plain table by the large, electric three-bar fire.

There were two small, framed pictures hanging on the walls. One showed a wintry scene, the other a vase of flowers. Both looked as though an amateur had done painting by numbers.

Behind that interior, which didn't look at all lived in, was another space which contrasted sharply. Here, everything was contemporary and functional. There was a bed and a chest of drawers. Clothes were lying on the bed. Julie went over and examined them.

She frowned, utterly baffled. For they consisted of a Fifties woman's dress in blue linen with a jacket of the same colour and material, a string of pearls, a bra, a girdle, a suspender belt, black seamed stockings, long, loose white knickers, and a pair of black, high-heeled shoes with pointed toes.

Although she was naked and wanted to be covered, Julie just didn't want to put these unfamiliar garments on. Instead she tossed them onto a chair, took up the blue bedspread and wrapped it around herself. There was a door at the end of the bed. Julie opened it to see two spaces divided by a floor-to-ceiling partition. One was a bathroom and lavatory. The other was a kitchen. Both rooms were small, cramped and rudimentary. The kitchen contained a sink, cabinets, an electric cooker and – perhaps surprisingly – a large deep-freeze in addition to a small fridge. Julie opened everything. There were plates and cutlery, pots and pans and plenty of food. The freezer was crammed with it and tins abounded in the cupboards.

There was fear as well as confusion on Julie's face when she went back into the bed-sitting room. Her eyes darted around the walls, then centred on the walnut table in front of the sofa. A white envelope reposed on the shining surface. She dashed forward and snatched it up. The words 'Mrs

Julie Foster' had been neatly handwritten on the outside. Julie tore the envelope open and extracted a note in the same writing. A strangled gasp came out of her throat as she read it: 'Don't bother screaming. The soundproofing is perfect. You won't be hurt as long as you co-operate. Michael's in safe hands. I'll be down later for a chat.'

Michael wandered disconsolately out of school. Somehow he'd got through another day and at least the teachers had been easy on him. Not that there seemed to be any point in their lessons. Who cared what happened if you divided 121 by 11? Nothing had been anything much since Dad went into a coma.

Every time he pictured Bob or thought about him hard, it brought on tears so he tried not to. He was attacked by waves of guilt for the way he'd behaved when his father was having difficulties and drinking. He'd asked God to give Daddy back and he'd be ever so good – but would it be any use?

Mum was in a bad way. Michael felt he had to help her if he could. There were times when they'd hugged each other hard, then both started crying. Mum always pretended that she wasn't but she was. Yet somehow she'd managed to make her voice sound all strong and hopeful again. 'Don't worry, love, we'll get through this,' she'd say. 'We will, I promise. Just be brave.'

He would be brave. He had to be – because he sensed that his mother needed his love now as much as he needed hers. Thank God Harry was around. Uncle Harry had been fantastic. He seemed as sad about it all as Michael was and he tried so hard to make one feel better. He'd looked after Mum well. And he'd noticed that often Michael didn't want to play the old games, he just wanted to be in his room on his own. Harry didn't force himself upon Michael and the boy was grateful. Yet when Michael needed company and someone to talk to, someone to take his mind off his grief, the man was there. Just like an uncle, Michael often thought. Wish he really was.

His eyes roamed the road until they spotted mum's car with Harry in it.

'Hullo!' he called out, and beamed broadly. 'Had a reasonable day?'

'Same as ever.' Michael clambered into the car.

'Quite nice to see Pru again. She's still a bit too babyish, though.'

'But a nice girl,' said Harry, 'let's not forget that. Oh well, I'm glad you had some fun. School sounds a bit bleak, though. Did they teach you anything today or were they just standing there in front of the blackboard and being boring?'

'They were being boring,' Michael chuckled in spite of himself. 'Although there was one funny thing...' And he started to tell Harry details of his day. Harry was always so interested, almost as though it was all happening to him. Suddenly, Michael found his own attention expanding as Harry laughed at every faintly humorous incident and frowned concernedly at even the most minor, unhappy trivialities.

On reaching home, Harry went straight into the kitchen and made Michael some good, strong, hot chocolate which was given to him along with a plate of four jam doughnuts. Michael munched these eagerly as Harry watched him with pleasure.

'Is Mum in bed?' Michael asked, as he attacked his final doughnut.

'I was waiting for you to ask that. Michael,' Harry's features were etched by troubled concern as he leaned forward earnestly and regarded the boy gravely, 'it's not good news, I'm afraid. Your mum's been taken ill.'

'What d'you mean?' Michael demanded anxiously, and put down the doughnut.

'Well, I'd better tell you straight,' said Harry. 'You know how upset she's been – how upset we've all been. Brace yourself. It all got a bit too much for her. Suddenly she fainted.'

'Fainted?' Michael paled.

'Oh, she didn't hurt herself. I caught her just in time. But she'd passed out with all the strain. It's not too terrible. The doctor says she'll be all right. But – she needs an absolute rest, he said. Complete peace and quiet. So the doctor's had her go to this lovely, special place. Rosy Boughs, it's called. Somewhere in the country. They really look after you there.' Michael was biting his lower lip hard. 'She'll be back with us in no time and fit as a fiddle, you mark my words. But right now – and it's doctor's orders – she isn't allowed to see anybody. Nobody. Not me. Not even you.'

'Oh...' Michael said faintly.

'I know it's upsetting – but don't you see, she can't,' Harry suddenly burst out as if in desperation. 'And you must try and understand that we – I mean you and me – have got to do all we can to make her get well soon. That means we've got to be brave. That means we've got to be men. There,' Harry's hand reached out to ruffle Michael's hair affectionately, 'it'll be all right in the end. We'll get through it. Trust me, Michael.'

Julie wrapped the bedspread more tightly around herself as she gazed forlornly at the door and walls which imprisoned her. How long had she been here? And how long would it be before something new happened?

There wasn't much with which to occupy herself. She had no appetite. She felt too jittery to take a bath, too anxious to concentrate on anything other than her state and Michael's. Playing music was out of the question – and who'd want to play Vera Lynn singing 'We'll meet again, don't know where, don't know when' or Anne Shelton trilling 'Lay down your arms and surrender to mine'? All the records were like that.

And as if anyone could sit down and read. True, there were a few books on a shelf, but they were all for young girls of years ago and had titles like *The Naughtiest Girl In School Gets Made A Monitor*. There was a pile of magazines beneath the coffee table too – old copies of *Country Life, Time and Tide,* a very dull series of the *Tatler* and a stack of copies of the *Lady*. No, Julie threw those down in disgust and despair and chose to pace fitfully around the room.

Suddenly there was sound – a muffled footfall, perhaps? Julie's eyes darted to the door. For the first time, she noticed a spy-hole. She sprang to her feet, crossed the room and pressed her eyes to it. When she realised that it had been positioned so that someone could see in but she couldn't see out, her knees went weak and her stomach sank queasily. Seconds later, the door was flung open.

The sudden impact sent Julie staggering back. As she stumbled into the wall, Harry stepped through and closed the door behind him. There was a click of a lock.

Julie shrank back, alert to his every move. Did he mean to rape her down here? Earlier she'd hunted for a weapon. The knives were all blunt, and short of throwing tins of food at him or heaving the wooden chair, she could use nothing.

'Must be quite a shock for you, this,' he said calmly, as he leaned back against the door and nonchalantly folded his arms.

There was a pause while Julie studied him and became increasingly afraid. His appearance had changed. The hair was still brushed back but it seemed much thicker. His expression had altered from harmless good cheer to a sullen and spiteful brooding. Gone too were the familiar blazer, white shirt, dark tie and grey flannels. Instead he wore a faded leather jacket, an American checkshirt with a bootlace tie and dark, drainpipe trousers.

'Yes,' Julie heard herself reply. 'Yes, it is quite a shock.' He's mad and bad and dangerous, she thought. Be very, very careful. 'I just don't understand.'

'Oh, you will.'

'Harry, why're you doing this?' she appealed.

'You'll find out.' His voice was hard and toneless.

'Have I ever done anything bad to you?'

'You haven't, no. But others like you have.' His stare was cold and pitiless.

'Can't we just sit down and talk about it?' Julie suggested.

'All right.' He came forward to a chair and sank into it contentedly. 'Be my guest.' He pointed to the other one.

'We're in the basement, right?' Julie thought she'd better sit down too.

'Yeah.' Harry smiled proudly. 'Told you it'd be a nice surprise.'

'Harry, honestly, you can't keep me here,' Julie burst out desperately. 'I understand that you're upset about something and I'm happy to listen to you and help you sort it out. But,' she fought to hold her voice steady, 'you must let me go. I mean, it's a crime, what you're doing.'

'Who's going to find out?' asked Harry.

Oh my God, thought Julie. He's flipped and he's a raving loony.

'The police... I don't want to get you into trouble.'

'The police?' he demanded incredulously. 'They don't know anything. Nah. You're not going to get me into trouble,' he snorted scornfully.

'If I disappear, people'll start asking questions,' Julie insisted.

'Not for a while,' he returned complacently. 'You're in mourning and not seeing anyone. You've given in your notice at your job and they won't be expecting you back. Who's going to be asking questions apart from Michael?'

'Michael!' Julie exclaimed fiercely, 'what're you...?'

'Shut up!' Harry snapped. The words were cutting and commanding. 'Shut up and listen. Don't worry about Michael. I wouldn't hurt him for the world. He's safe with me. I promise you, I shan't be laying a finger on him. I'm not some filthy sex pervert like the one they caught yesterday – he ought to have the death penalty for what he did. No, no, Michael's okay with me.'

'He needs me,' Julie insisted. 'He needs his mother.'

'No, he doesn't,' Harry returned instantly. 'That's the last thing he needs.'

'What're you doing?' she demanded shrilly, her voice on the edge of hysteria.

'For once I'm doing what *I* want,' he answered. 'And you're going to do what I want too, for a change. Take those clothes you've gone and put over there. I left them out for you. I was hoping you'd be wearing them but you're not. I reckon you should put them on.'

'But they're not my clothes.'

'They are now.'

'Oh...' Julie moaned as she shook her head from side to side. 'I don't understand!'

'Oh, you will,' he answered casually, but there was a gleam of malignance in his eyes. 'Stop a moment.' His hand darted within his leather jacket and came out holding a photograph which he passed over to Julie. 'Who's that?'

She started the instant she recognised the familiar face. Her tired brain tried to make sense of Harry's action, then drowned in a sea of perplexity.

'Go on,' he demanded, 'who is it?'

'It's Bob's father,' she answered.

'And mine,' said Harry.

17

'No,' JULIE whispered, gazing all the while at the clean-cut, fresh-faced young naval officer in the photograph. 'No, it can't be. You and Bob aren't brothers.'

'Yes, we are,' he replied with quiet certainty. 'Though at first, I didn't believe it myself.'

'But...'

'There's no but about it. It's a fact. Want to know how I know?' He unzipped his jacket, revealing a thick file which had been pressed against his chest. Julie gasped as she recognised it as the one Bob had been studying. 'My dad wrote all this – well, our dad, if you insist. I reckon you should give it a read.' He rose, glanced down at Julie, then handed the file to her.

She opened it up hungrily, desperate for any clue which might explain things. She'd just pulled out the sheaf of papers when she heard a click. Her eyes shot up to see that Harry had opened the door with a small key.

'Take your time,' he murmured. 'There's plenty of that. I'll be back later.'

'Wait!' But before she could cry out in protest, he'd slipped into the narrow passage outside and the door had once more clicked shut.

Julie screamed.

It was a piercing scream of anguish which implored help and tore her throat – but it filled up the room, went no further and died away.

'Let me out!' she shrieked. Throwing down the file, she sprang at the door and beat upon it with her fists, bruising them badly. 'Harry! Please! Let me out!' It was no use. 'Oh, God...' she sighed, slid slowly down the wall and sagged into a heap on the floor.

Minutes passed. She alternated between tormented

imaginings, blind fury and a benumbed emptiness. After a time, she managed to haul herself to her feet, then stumbled back to her chair. There was nothing for it but to open up the file again and read:

> The Statement of Frank H. Foster
> Chicago
> February 3, 1964

Something happened today which shook me up very badly. Right now I'm feeling totally shattered. My past has caught up with me, just as I always feared it might. I've tried so hard to escape it. God knows how hard I've tried. But, in the end, it's beckoned me back and now it's gone and mugged me. I feel old and tired and used up and beat up and washed up.

I'm writing this in a bar. I've already drunk a couple of shots of bourbon. I had to.

The best thing is if I try and write it all down. That way, maybe it'll become clearer. It means I have to be absolutely honest with myself, which everybody finds difficult, and include everything that's to my discredit. So be it – there's no getting away from what I've done.

I was born Francis Harold Foster in Southampton, England, on March 27, 1921. My father was a grocer, like his father before him. He'd inherited what was then considered to be a large store in a good part of town and did pretty well – but I never got to know him. He'd been badly shot up in World War One and he died when I was two, so I was brought up by my mother.

Even today, it's difficult to describe her objectively. Everyone agreed she was pretty and she dressed well. By her lights, she did all she could for me. She was a capable woman too. Although she'd had no business training, after marrying my father in 1918 she took a growing interest in the store as his health gradually failed, held it together while he was dying and made it prosper after his death. I guess she was also lucky in having Mr Thompson there. He was totally honest and he had good ideas for money-making innovations. The business prospered and my mother was wise in leaving the day-to-day running of the enterprise to him while creaming off the profits for herself. Thompson was also in love with her and proposed marriage a few times – but she always said, no, and remained a widow for the rest of her life.

I think she must've decided to invest everything she had in me. Yet I can't honestly say that she gave me much warmth or affection. In retrospect, she was a cold person. But she did have the maternal knack of making her child feel either ten feet tall or one inch small. She also had some very strong values which she tried to inculcate in me. Above all, it was very important to behave 'properly' and it was essential to be 'respectable'. And there were countless things you just didn't talk about because they 'weren't quite nice'.

I guess my childhood was okay. I didn't recall very much about it. I passed some exam at twelve and went to a local private school where I did all right and quite enjoyed it, especially the sports. When it came to studies, I was middling in just about everything except geography, in which I did well. But there was never any suggestion that I go on to university. Not many people did go to college in those days. In my family, nobody ever had.

In my mid-teens, my mother and others started talking about what I was going to be. The teachers at school didn't think I was smart enough to enter a profession like law or accountancy. My mother would've liked that, but there was also another alternative which would content her, and all my relatives on my father's side were keen on that – the grocery store. I should be a grocer like my father and his fathers before him. That way I'd be secure and respectable. The trouble was, though I wasn't exactly sure about what I really wanted to do, I knew I didn't want to be a grocer. I had no interest in the store at all.

Things were happening to me in adolescence – those strange and unfamiliar feelings about which you don't talk to your parents because they'd never understand and they'd only disapprove. As a result, I was coming to hate Southampton with its narrow-mindedness, its smug, dreary people and its obsession with stolid respectability. I wanted to get the hell out of there. I wanted the wide world and travel and adventure, new and fresh experiences – the feeling that I was really living.

But how was I to have that? I remember how I used to go down to the docks and stare longingly at the great steam liners which came and went from every place in the world I'd ever heard of. I wanted so much to run away to sea. But my mother's love and devotion were like a stranglehold on my desire.

Meanwhile, she'd decided that I'd be going into the grocery trade, and when I'd learned the business, I'd be taking over. If I didn't do that, or come up with something she considered to be even better, I'd break her heart. Well, I tried to make her happy and it nearly broke mine. I started work in the store and God how I loathed it! It meant a continual obsession with pennies – and in those days you were expected to fawn before important customers. I hated that too. I could see my life expiring on a long, suburban avenue of neat mediocrity.

I was rescued from month after miserable month of boredom and frustration by an event which brought suffering and death to millions but freedom and joy to me. After years of flabby cowardice and filthy appeasement, Great Britain finally declared war on Hitler's Germany. It may sound strange but that was the greatest day of my life so far. Now I had a way out which nobody could fault. I was a patriot. My country needed me. I volunteered immediately for the Royal Navy.

So much happened to me during the war and I've

bored people with it so often that I shan't repeat it here. But what I've never really talked about is the inner feeling I had. I don't know if anybody understands that nowadays. Yes, the life was hard. There were nights when I was so cold, I could've cried, when I forgot what it felt like to be dry, when I would've signed away my soul for a mug of hot soup and three weeks in a bed on land. All of us knew we could be torpedoed at any moment. It wouldn't be much use getting into the lifeboats because the U-boats often surfaced to machine-gun all survivors. Yet because you lived with death every day, it gave savour to life and I have never felt so alive.

We knew we were in the right. Our commitment was total. We were fighting for a country we loved and believed in against an evil and despicable tyranny. No sacrifice could be too great, yet every trivial action had its meaning in our struggle.

My abilities were recognised. I was promoted through the ranks, becoming a petty officer in late 1940. Then ship after ship went down, men and officers drowned with them, Great Britain shrank to a little, beleaguered bastion of freedom threatened with utter destruction by overwhelming Nazi might – and ability replaced birth and breeding as the yardstick of promotion. I was commissioned gunner in the summer of 1941, made full lieutenant in late 1942 and finished the war as a lieutenant commander.

And of course it's true that the boys had a great time when they came ashore. Nothing mattered except having a great time and getting drunk and whoring because it might be your last chance ever. Those were wonderful times. I'd always been shy with girls and didn't lose my virginity till late 1939 in a Gibraltar brothel. After that, there was no holding me. Later on, I had periods of leave which enabled me to go up to London. There was a lot to be said for the blackout, and for the way in which girls really rated young naval officers. Of course, there wasn't much emotion involved. How could you commit yourself to anyone when you might be dead in a week? At least, that's what I thought until spring 1944: I was up in London once again and an officer friend introduced me to Mary.

She'd just turned twenty-one, she was exquisitely pretty, she was vivacious and flirtatious and, in spite of the wartime restriction, she dressed with incredible style. She came from a respectable family – her father was something in the City and a major in the Home Guard – and she worked in some capacity for the Ministry of Food. She seemed dazzled by me and by my role in the war, and I was captivated by her. She was also the first girl in quite a while with whom I didn't succeed sexually. I went back to sea, a bit disappointed but also enchanted, and found myself dreaming about her.

Many months later, I came ashore in England once again and she was there and waiting for me and all over me in every way except one. I spent a lot of time with her. She still wouldn't sleep with me and that was horribly frustrating but I minded less then than anyone would now. In those days, men still mentally divided women into good girls and bad girls and I was no different. And what I can see from this vantage point is that sexual desire got sublimated into a wild and romantic idealisation. I thought Mary was the finest, noblest, most beautiful and gracious woman in the world.

I went back to sea. We wrote every day, though often agonising weeks crawled by before I could post what I had written or receive her words. Then my luck turned. I can't complain – it had lasted so long. Anyhow, our ship was hit and so was I, and if it hadn't been for the guys I was with and whom I'd grown to love, I would've gone down too. As it was, they brought me back to Britain on a stretcher.

I was in a naval hospital for quite some time. At first

I thought I would die but Mary came to see me at every opportunity she could steal, and maybe that was what gave me my desire to live. Slowly I recovered and I was still in one piece – though I get pains in places even today – and the navy found me a desk job in London.

Naturally I saw much more of Mary. There's no point in going into all the details of our courtship. I'll just describe the things which strike me, after all this time, as being important.

She loved me then. She poured out all her heart in her letters and I thrilled to every word. Above all, she wanted to marry me. I met her parents and they took to me. She met my mother and my mother really liked her. Many times I was tempted to propose to Mary but something held me back. As my health returned, I kept thinking about my future.

The war was just about over and we'd won. What was I to do after that? I think I would've been happy going back to sea if they'd let me. I liked the life and there were still so many places I hadn't seen. Unfortunately, they told me I wasn't fit enough for active duty – I still walk with a limp – and I can't claim I was much good at the safe desk job they'd given me: I got no satisfaction from it. I still wanted travel and adventure and the intoxication of living every moment intensely – but wasn't it about time I settled down and got married like most of my comrades in arms? Mary kept telling me it was time I left the navy. So did my mother.

And oh yes, the temptation to marry Mary was so strong. For me she had real class and style. My mother kept telling me what a great wife she'd make. Yes, I was in love with her. I could take over the grocery store in Southampton and support a wife and children in comfort. I could be a respectable citizen. Or, as Mary often hinted, her father could find me something in the City. Yet, as I say, despite every strong hint – and now Mary was sprinkling those hints with snide comments – I did not propose.

But things got taken out of my hands. One hot summer night in 1945, Mary and I were carried away by our passion and at last she said yes. I wish I could say it was a truly great moment but it was all over so fast, and afterwards she cried and said she felt ashamed. Still, we made love again several times after that, always snatching furtive moments in uncomfortable places. And some weeks later, she told me she thought she was pregnant.

What could I do? What would any decent man do? I thought we'd taken precautions but obviously someone or something had slipped up. Of course I asked her to marry me and she was overjoyed. So were our families. The only person who wasn't delighted was me.

Some people might say that I should've been. After all, I loved the girl and she'd stood by me. Or did I really love her? It was disturbing, you might say it was bad, but I can only describe how I really felt. Screwing her had made her just another pretty woman. All the romantic illusions had gone. I still cared for her, but I was now looking harder and harder at a person to whom I'd be tied for life and who'd enthralled me with a spell so strong, I actually had no idea of her true character.

Well, the moment we were engaged, it was as though my life wasn't mine any more. Her parents and my mother started conferring. A date was set for the wedding. It was decided that I'd be leaving the navy and then 'it would be seen what could be done' for me. I was secretly pleased by the fact that it could take ages to get my discharge, but Mary's dad soon saw to that. He knew somebody very high up and I'd be out soon with no problem. It wasn't long before my commanding officer told me when I'd be going. Three weeks before the wedding.

Meanwhile, Mary's mother had naturally discovered that her daughter was pregnant. That didn't please her at all – but her initial distress was alleviated by the facts that I was being a gentleman and allowances had to be made in wartime, and I showed every sign of turning out to be a good husband. She started looking for a home in which to put the young couple and eventually found something she liked in a respectable London suburb.

I could see my future coming. I knew myself well enough to realise that I could never be the great go-ahead grocer, nor would I be the sensation of the City. I could hold onto that kind of job without screwing up. I'd be regarded as solid and competent and that'd be it. I'd marry and we'd have our child and then we'd probably have more and I would rise slowly and steadily, doing a bit better materially than the previous generation. I'd wash the car and I'd mow the lawn and I'd fix things around the house and I'd probably wind up a leading member of the tennis and Rotary clubs and I'd dream all the time of a past when I'd lived – and that'd be my life for the rest of my life.

There was also the matter of how Mary was behaving. I started feeling that I'd been *got*. I kept feeling that now that she had me, I could do nothing. Before, I'd really liked what struck me as being an attractive, fiery forcefulness which I could handle easily. But as the days went by, I was more and more conscious of her desire to order me around. She kept reminding me of how she'd spent so much time seeing me when I was badly wounded, which made me feel obligated. She persisted with pointing out her pregnancy, as though it was entirely my fault in taking callous advantage of an innocent girl, which made me feel guilty. And she started to dominate me more and more. It was always Harold this and Harold that – I was known by my middle name at that time – as though I was a dog. She expected her cigarettes to be lit and all doors to be opened, and glared at me and cut me down with a comment if I forgot. She wanted me to wait on her, and fetch and carry for her – and her parents and my mother felt that she was absolutely right. In fact, just after she fell ill, my mother told Mary that she was just the woman I needed to straighten me out.

So Mary bossed and bitched. Any time I complained and asserted myself, she drew attention to a pregnancy which excused her, then called me a hard, unfeeling cad. True, there were times when I was just about ready to explode – yet she always sensed those moments and suddenly she'd become sweet and loving and tender and talk of how she adored me, and plead for my understanding at this difficult time and rhapsodise about the glorious life we two would have together. The man who wanted to roar like a lion would soon be purring like a pussy cat.

I started to have nightmares about marriage. And I kept meeting men who'd been married for some years. They were all the same. They preened themselves on their importance at work and then they cringed and said, yes, dear, when they came home. Oh sure, I know there are others who're tyrants – Mary's father, for example – but during that period, I didn't meet any others and I didn't want to be like them anyway.

What did I want? Some kind of loving equality, I guess, but I was too ignorant to see how that could be attained. I wasn't right for marriage then. Like so many men of my generation, I had no understanding of women at all. I still had a lot of things I had to work out.

It didn't seem as though there'd be any chance of that. The great day was approaching fast. I felt as though I'd be walking into a cage. I didn't love Mary any more – but I had to pretend I did. I didn't want dull, steady and remunerative work, but I had to look interested and make intelligent comments whenever the subject was discussed, which was often. I couldn't stand the thought of a lifetime as milady's servile spouse – or one of continuous fighting, for Mary had an iron will whenever she was opposed – yet there it was and coming at me.

Everything I called 'life' was ending, when something happened which changed everything. Six weeks before the wedding, my mother died.

I'd never known just how ill she was. Sure, over the past few years, she'd mentioned that her health was frail and sometimes she'd been in bed with one complaint or another, but she'd always kept the real truth from me. She had a heart condition. I had no idea. One night she had a fatal attack. I was staying with the Parkers at the time.

Let's not spend time on my grief and disorientation. It's enough to say that I'm sure they had their effect upon my subsequent actions. Some might say I acted contemptibly. Probably I did.

There's no helping that now. All I can do is trace the events. I remember how weird I felt when the family solicitor told me that my mother had been a very prudent investor and had left everything to me. The business, the house, the shares and securities – it all came to a hundred and twenty thousand pounds, which was then one hell of a sum.

The evening after that meeting, I got drunk on my own. Then I wandered over to the docks, like I had as a boy and looked at the lights of the great steamships and cried for the vision I had had. Then I thought of my mother and the past and I thought of Mary and the future and I thought of myself now and I cried some more. I couldn't remember when I'd last wept like this – and then a siren sounded in the night and it was as though I was dying right there with all my dreams and might as well be joining my cold mother in her cold grave.

I think that was when it came to me. I mean, the feeling that it didn't have to be like this. I recall one time I talked to a painter in some dive in Chicago – it must've been seven years ago. He told me about how he'd always tried to hold fast to the vision of his youth, but things hadn't worked out for him and now he was broke and old and tired. 'I thought that life would be nice,' he said,

'I really thought that it would be good.' Sad, pitiful, pathetic – but then at that moment, I had the feeling that if only I was brave enough, life would be good again. I believed in life at that moment. I had to be strong and smart and determined, but if I went with what my inner self told me, I wouldn't end with living death.

A plan was planted in my brain then, and though I slumped drunkenly into bed that night and awoke with a hangover which could kill a king, that plan remained. A day passed and my resolution hardened. Another day – and I took action.

According to the values of many people, what I did cannot be excused or forgiven. I did it anyway. I honestly believed I was fighting for my life and for my future integrity. I blotted all doubts and objections out of my mind. I made excuses to Mary about my grief and my need to be alone. I took twenty thousand pounds for myself. The rest of the estate I made over to Mary, with instructions for when she was to receive the news. I spread some money around among men whom I knew and it was all fixed up for me. Three weeks before the wedding, I set sail under an assumed name as a merchant seaman on a tramp steamer bound for America.

I broke totally with my past. None of my relatives ever heard from me again. I entered America illegally and tried to make a new life there for myself. I stopped being 'Harold' and 'Francis', both names I'd never liked, and became 'Frank'.

This isn't the place to put down all that happened to me. Briefly, I went into business, didn't know the ropes and soon lost all my capital. I recovered with some dubious selling jobs where they didn't ask too many questions, made enough to start up on my own again, and once again it didn't work out. There were brief periods of prosperity but they didn't last. I started degenerating into a two-bit hustler.

Throughout I was dogged by bad luck. Just as it seemed I'd finally made it to the major league, something would go wrong for no reason and I'd be back where I started. I began to suspect it was all some kind of punishment for what I'd done. And try as I might, I could not forget how I'd let Mary down and left our child without a father. Sometimes I'd wonder about that child, speculate until my mind went dizzy and my stomach went sick. And always in my head there'd be this image of my mother, revolving with revulsion in her grave.

Eventually, I wound up in Chicago and got married to Darlene. By that time, something vital in me had died, ground into extinction by repeated disappointments. I couldn't cope any longer with the insecurity of adventure. I'd come to accept that my ambition exceeded my talents. There'd always been this dream, of how the world would open out if only I had money but I never attained it. I guess I wasn't precise enough in what I really wanted.

By the time I finally married, I was tired and in search of some safe haven. I took a steady job – which I'm still doing – became a husband and a father and sank into a reasonably comfortable mediocrity. That's been it for years and years.

It's not that I'm very unhappy. I love my wife and she loves me, though we're hardly as impassioned as we were. But we're good friends and companions and I like and respect her. She's a good mother and Bob's a fine young boy. I'm proud of him. I hope to God he'll achieve all I failed to achieve. My life's not so bad, though it's nothing like what I originally wanted – and nothing like the future my mother wanted for me. All the same, I get a lot of pleasure out of my family. There are just those times when I look at photos of me when I was young Harold and wonder whatever happened to him.

To return to what brought this on – I've never been

able to escape the shame of what I did and the nagging of that child in Mary's womb. Was it a boy or a girl? What happened there? And so on.

Over the years, I was often tempted to try and have the child traced. I even thought of visiting England for the purpose. Surely Mary would've forgiven me after all this time? Probably she'd've got married. But somehow it wasn't possible. I didn't have the money or the time. Or I couldn't face Mary, even now. Or I was frightened by what she must've told the kid about me. Or else I simply couldn't face my past. That shows in that I've never said anything about any of this to Darlene. It's the guilt and shame, I suppose. Although the way young people behave nowadays, they'd probably find it impossible to understand the way I feel.

Even so, as the years went by, I got to thinking and couldn't sleep at night and became more and more troubled. Then one day I had an idea. I started a special and secret savings account, just a few bucks each week. Finally, I was able to approach a private investigator with my proposal. It all cost more than I'd expected but the results weren't long in coming.

The investigator went to England as instructed and came back with all the answers. No, Mary hadn't married again. She was alive and well and living a comfortable and leisured life in a reputable London suburb with her teenage son.

I shouldn't've done it. I know now that I shouldn't've done it but I simply couldn't help myself. I sat down and wrote a long letter to Mary in which I tried to explain myself and I asked after our boy. Because I didn't want Darlene involved, I used a PO box as my address.

Mary's reply came today.

(Here, the writing abruptly degenerated and the paper was stained by drink.)

It consisted of the most vicious letter I've ever received and the vilest photograph I've ever seen. I can't believe she could still hate me so much as to do this. I stared at the disgusting things and everything went dizzy. When my head finally cleared, I stared at them again and had to fight down an almost overpowering urge to throw up. I was one throbbing mass of rage and pain. I tore the loathsome things into a thousand pieces. Then I staggered out of the office with tears streaming down my face and I was past caring who saw me.

I feel ultimately responsible for this evil. I am sickened by her, by life and by myself. Existence is a nightmare, a sick joke in bad taste. I can't think and I don't know what to do. I don't know if I can bring myself to write any more. I wish I was dead. How could she...

(The last few lines of the manuscript were wholly illegible. There followed a small sheet of letter paper in a different hand.)

June 11, 1964

My dear husband Frank died tragically within a few hours of writing the foregoing. He was so upset, he had too much to drink and was killed in an auto accident. I wish to testify that he was a fine, hard-working man and I shall always love, honour and treasure his memory and the memory of our years together.

The manuscript was found in a case in the trunk of his car. I was deeply shocked when I read it – as he was when he wrote it – but I cannot understand why he never told me any of this.

I don't want any contact ever with the awful woman who took advantage of Frank when he was young and naïve, and hated him all these years as he says, and then upset him so much one might say that she killed him. I don't care about the child. If the woman writes again,

I'll return her letters unopened. And I just don't want to know about the letter and the photo which Frank destroyed and which destroyed him.

I don't want young Bob to know either.

                                                Darlene Foster

18

MICHAEL CROUCHED excitedly within the dark cupboard beneath the stairs. His grief over his father and his anxiety over his mother were forgotten in the suspense of the game. This was a hiding place he hadn't picked before, and just to make it more difficult for Harry, he was crouching behind the ironing board which leaned against a corner.

Suddenly, he tensed at the tread of approaching footsteps.

'Wonder if he's here...' came a familiar voice. 'Now that'd be a clever place to hide.' Michael held his breath as the cupboard door was wrenched open sharply. 'Is he here? Hmmm. Come out, come out wherever you are!' Though the ironing board blocked his vision, the boy could hear Harry enter. 'He doesn't seem to be here... but I've looked everywhere else so he must be here. Is he here? Mi-chael!'

Michael couldn't suppress a giggle. Instantly Harry seized the ironing board, tossed it aside and stooped to grab him by the throat.

'Gotcha!' he cried triumphantly.

'Aaargh!' Michael screamed. There was an intensity about Harry's grip which frightened him. 'Aaargh!' he screamed again. Harry's hands released his throat.

'Hey,' Harry said gently, 'there's no need to scream like that. Fair frightens the life out of me, that. No, there's no need to scream.' He knelt down and took the boy in his arms, hugging him tenderly. 'I wouldn't hurt you for the world. It's only a game.'

About an hour later, after he'd put Michael to bed and told him a story, Harry slipped out of the house and went down the outside steps which led to the basement. There was a thick oak door there which he unlocked to reveal a small entrance hall. Stepping through, Harry quietly closed the first door behind him, regarded a second door placidly, then peered through its spy-hole for a minute or so. A second key unlocked this second door – and Harry entered the cell he had built, sealed it with a slam and coldly regarded his prisoner.

She was sitting in a chair, the bedspread still wrapped around her, and staring at Harry with fear and loathing.

'Did you read it?' he asked. She glared at him accusingly but said nothing. 'Well?' he persisted.

'Did you try to kill Bob?' she demanded icily.

'What?' He looked baffled, then shrugged as if the matter was irrelevant.

'You did, didn't you,' she snapped. 'You sneaked a look at this,' she tapped the file, 'and you must've read all of it without anybody knowing. You saw that the unbelievable was true – that you and Bob had the same father – and something in you that's twisted and evil made you hate Bob. You planned it all!' she screamed, suddenly beside herself with anger. 'You're expert with cars. You fixed the engine so Bob'd die the same way your father did. You tried to kill your own brother! Murderer!'

She flung herself against her captor and beat against his face with her fists. Harry didn't even flinch. His face took the blows without moving a muscle. Then he picked Julie up as though she was a rag doll and threw her hard at the chair. Julie squealed as her body struck it, then sagged into a shapeless, trembling heap.

'That's enough of that,' said Harry. 'No tantrums.'

'Are you going to kill me too? Are you going to kill Michael? They'll get you. You're crazy but they'll get you.'

'Crazy am I?' he replied slowly. 'Twisted. Evil. Those were the words, weren't they? Well, who made me like that?'

'Not Bob,' she retorted, 'not me, not Michael. Not even your father. You never knew him.'

'Yes, it's funny, that,' said Harry. 'All these years I thought I did. My mum said so, that's why. I thought he was around when I was small. I thought I had dim memories of him. Quite a shock to discover it wasn't like that.'

'Uh?' Julie blinked stupidly. What was he saying?

'See, you still don't understand, do you? You don't comprehend why all this is happening.' She shook her head. 'Well, I've got some more homework for you.' His hand slipped within his jacket and emerged holding a large, blue leather-bound book. 'Here. You must read this.'

'I don't want to read,' she shot back. 'I shan't read it.' Her voice was becoming shrill with hysteria. 'What're you going to do with Michael and me?'

'Tsk, tsk, tsk,' went Harry. 'That's not the right attitude at all. I will tell you why you're here and that's a promise. But,' he held up a warning finger, 'not until you've read what you've got to read. Here.' He tossed it onto her lap, turned and left the room before Julie's numb brain could orchestrate a response.

For a time she just sat and stared straight ahead at the wall. It occurred to her that she hadn't eaten in a while but the thought of food disgusted her – especially food which he had bought. She tried very hard not to look at the blue book, which remained in her lap where he'd flung it but eventually she couldn't avoid doing so. The words DIARY was stamped upon the leather in gold letters. Julie opened the cover to see a photograph of a beautiful young woman. She gave a small gasp of surprise as she recognised the young Mrs Parker. Turning the page, she began to peruse the neat and elegant handwriting.

The Diary of Miss Mary Parker

27 September 1945

I've decided to keep a diary because I've never felt so happy in all my life and I want to keep and treasure every moment if I can. I can hardly believe it but I'm getting married to Harold! I'm so utterly in love with him. He's the most wonderful man I've ever met. And now he'll be mine and I'll be his for ever and ever. Dreams do come true after all.

My heart's overflowing with happiness. Everything seems possible now. The war's over and we've won.

And I'm so proud of what Harold did in the war. Though I often couldn't sleep when he was at sea. I was tortured by worry and having such dreadful nightmares. But Fate's been kind and he's my hero and alive and well and we're engaged and soon he'll be my husband. He'll be so successful too, I just know it.

I don't care about being pregnant now. Mummy was appalled when I first told her and goodness knows what Daddy thought but as I'm getting married, it's all right and in the end Mummy's been so sweet and understanding. Anyway, it happened to Jean Barker too. Just as long as (unlike Jean) I don't look pregnant at the altar.

But I'm so excited. *His* child. *Our* child. Gosh, it gives me goose pimples just thinking about it.

My wedding day will be the greatest day of my life. And Daddy's being so good about it. We won't be on horrid rations either because he knows some people in the black market. We'll be married in our dear, local church which by some miracle escaped being bombed. I shall wear that gorgeous Victorian bridal gown of Granny's.

Oh, I feel so wonderful!

30th September 1945
Every day's a pleasure and it feels so good to be alive. Mummy and I are having such fun planning all the details of the wedding. Especially the guest list. Naturally it'll be quite an event and not everybody who wants to come can come, of course.

Harold to dinner this evening. I can't wait to see my darling and to be with him. But we must have more time alone together.

1st October 1945
Simply super evening with my loved one and we had some time alone together. I could kiss him for ever. And I can kiss him for ever once we're married. Then

there'll be no more problems with parents and privacy and so on and I'll be Mrs Mary Foster. It won't be Miss ever again. And in shops I'd like it to be Madam.

I know I'm being gushy but I just can't help it. He makes me feel that way. I want to tell the world how wonderful my Harold is. He's so much better than all the other men I've known. Handsome. Brave. Strong. And so adoring, loving and considerate. He's the first man I've ever really liked. I've met so many uncouth oafs. Men can be so horribly brutish. It's true that most of them only want one thing, not that they ever succeeded with me (except Harold, but I wanted him so much). Really, there's a lot in the notion that men are beasts who need women to civilise them. Yet even when they're married, some men behave perfectly disgracefully to their wives or they spend all their time with other men, drinking and telling their stupid stories about themselves. Harold won't be like that.

I suppose I love to be envied. After all, don't most people? How I long to sweep into a room with my dashing and adoring husband by my side as I attract the admiration of all! And I admit, I'll still want men to want me – but all they can do is look.

And all the other women will envy my security and my man – handsome, successful and utterly devoted to me. I'll let him brag all he likes, the way men do, but women will know who's really in charge. Isn't that the way it usually is?

I know I'm starting to nag him a bit but it's so important to me that he's a perfect gentleman. Well, he is, but he sometimes forgets these little courtesies which mean so much to a woman.

7th October 1945
I've been so busy these past few days, I haven't had time to write a word.

My fiancé and I went to the zoo on Saturday. In the Lion House, Harold said he felt sorry for this great, big tiger who was pacing angrily about in his cage. To me, it looked the sort of tiger which kills and eats human beings and at one point it looked at me with a repellent savagery in its eyes. I said I was jolly glad that it was behind bars and that a cage was the best place for it. Harold went very quiet for some reason and I wondered what on earth was the matter with him. But afterwards it was fine.

Oh, Harold, my darling, how I love you! How thrilled I am to be your future wedded wife! How I long for our home together and there I shall hug you in my arms till death do us part!

(Julie's attention, which had become fully engaged, slipped somewhat over the succeeding entries, which were all in the same vein. For a time, her face was expressionless. Then, abruptly it assumed a startled expression, she straightened her back and her frown of renewed interest deepened. For the entry before her consisted of a pasted-in letter in the scrawl of Frank Harold Foster.)

My dear Mary,
May heaven forgive me for what I have done. Perhaps you never will.

I love you and I believe I will always love you – but I cannot marry you.

I am not ready to settle down. I feel that there are so many more things I must do with my life. I have acted disgracefully and I am truly sorry. But I have also made sure that you will never have to worry.

Forgive me. I can't express myself any further. Writing this is a torment.

Good luck, Mary. I can't help being what I am, however contemptible others might think it – and they may be right. But I hope that one day you'll understand.

Perhaps you're just too good, pure and noble a woman for me.

By the time you read this, I'll have left the country and I shan't be returning.

Written in shame and sorrow.

Harold Foster

(Mary had dated the letter 2nd December 1945. And over the writing she'd scrawled, in slashing red strokes, the word SWINE. There were then two blank pages before:)

10th January 1946

I think I must be cracking up. I'd vowed never to open this diary of the dead as long as I live, which I hope won't be long, but if I don't say or write something, I'll go completely mad.

My world has collapsed and nothing makes sense. Every effort to trace Harold has been futile. He's vanished altogether and the police can do nothing. I can't believe it! How could he do this to me? I can't write about him or I'll scream and cry.

Daddy wants him horsewhipped. So does Mummy. So do I. Whipped till he screams for mercy and begs my pardon. How could he? And how could he write me such insulting rubbish? And what does he mean by making sure I'll never have to worry? Has he gone mad?

All my dreams are broken. I don't know how I can live.

Everyone in the area is laughing at me behind my back now that we've had to cancel the wedding. I think they're secretly pleased though they all pretend to be so sorry for me. I hate people feeling sorry for me. And I hate you, Harold Parker!

How could I have loved such a worm?

No, no, no, he wasn't that – but he's been so totally stupid, stupid, stupid. Dishonourable. A lying cad. Heartless. Weak and brutish. All men are the same.

And I know what they're saying, the gossips. They're saying, she was such a flirt and a tease, she had it coming to her, the bitch. They're saying he took advantage of me, I was fooled and now he's had his evil way with me, he's left me in the lurch. And some will sneer at me and accuse me of only getting pregnant so I could trap him into wedlock but that's just not true at all.

But maybe he was a brute just out for what he could get. God, I feel so dazed and confused, I can hardly think straight.

And look at what you've done, Harold Parker. You've literally left me holding the baby. I'm jilted and pregnant and unmarried, a disgrace to my parents and the shame of the neighbourhood, only fit to be laughed at, scorned or pitied.

What man's going to want me now? What sort of life have I got left? That's what you've done, you swine, you've ruined my life completely. And why? Because you're so stupid and despicably selfish.

My parents are being so cold to me. I'm no longer a bride, just a cheap hussy who let herself be seduced and abandoned. They know they'll have to keep apologising for me to everyone.

I'm not a person any more, just an object.

7th February 1946

I cry in the day and I can't sleep at night. Everything is an effort. Most of the time I just feel sick. My brain isn't working. Sometimes I can barely speak and all the time I feel short of breath.

My parents are making me feel like a whore without saying anything. But I could die when I see their reproachful looks.

Tummy beginning to swell and swell. I'd like to take a knife and cut it off.

I keep thinking about suicide but all the ways seem so painful and I suppose I haven't got the courage. It'd be nice to lie down and sleep for ever, though.

Harold, I hate you with all my mind and all my heart and all my soul.

14th February 1946
Valentine's Day – and loathsome. Nothing but a reminder of my total misery. Misery, misery, misery.

Now that I'm so obviously pregnant, my mother doesn't want me to go out. She's frightened of what the neighbours will say. It seems I'm to be kept here as a prisoner then sent away to have the baby. There's talk of taking it to an orphanage. I don't care any more.

20th February 1946
Harold Parker, a woman curses you and your life and your kind from here to eternity.

1st March 1946
Nothing but sickness and sorrow. I feel loathing for the little beast kicking inside me. Men are revolting.

10th March 1946
Torment, wretchedness and despair. Nothing interests me. I hate myself and everyone else and especially Harold. All is one throbbing ache of agony.

17th March 1946
I see. So he wants to buy away his guilt. Well, he won't succeed.

Though I must admit I'm shaken. So this was what he meant about my not having to worry.

The letter came from his solicitors this morning. Harold has given me one hundred thousand pounds.

My head's whirling. I feel giddy. It's all happening too fast. I can't think straight.

But if he thinks I'll forgive him because of this, if he thinks he can insult me by trying to purchase my forgiveness, then he is even more stupid than I thought. I shall never forgive him.

Never forgive him.

Never.

20th September 1946

I haven't written in here for ages and ages but feel I must now.

I can't believe how my life has changed again. It's as though I've been through some agonising ordeal then initiated into a new life.

I'm no longer under my parents' supervision and control. I don't need them any more. My money is safely invested and ten thousand of it has been put into the nice, big house in which I'm now living. I feel an entirely different person.

Something within me has been burned out for ever, leaving me with a new and growing part that's all clear and hard and ice-cold but from which I draw increasing strength and satisfaction.

No one can tell me what to do ever again.

I can create my own world.

Harold, thank you for giving me the means by which I can spit on your memory. That's what I do every night.

Oh no, I'm not insane, no matter what anybody thinks.

Harold, I have given birth to the child you callously fathered on me and I'm so pleased it's male. A healthy one too, so they tell me. Tomorrow I'm having him baptised. He'll keep my surname – he won't be besmirched by yours – but I've decided to christen him Harold.

I shall extract retribution. I shall have my revenge.

That's him crying now.

25th September 1946

Thank heavens, I can afford to employ a nurse. I don't see why I should have to cope with all the mess.

The doctor says I'm suffering from 'reactive post-natal depression' which is 'a common condition'. What does he know? Huh! I'm perfectly normal.

I like my new neighbourhood. Lots of trees. It's

quiet and pleasant and eminently respectable. I've cut away from my past and will not see old friends. Here, my neighbours know nothing about me. Yet.

Quite. I'm building an entirely new life.

I feel as though I was a little girl again, playing on my own and making all kinds of magic as I entered a more exciting world in which I ruled as queen. Yes, I can do that again. But I must first convince Dr Stanley that I'm fully recovered and don't need him.

I'm going to tell people whatever I like. Why shouldn't I? I'm going to make up a story just like I used to, and act in it as its heroine. And it's going to be the story of how a beautiful and gracious young lady was shamefully betrayed by a cur of a man and of how she extracted vengeance upon him and upon his entire sex.

But I won't tell that to anyone except me.

What I will tell other people is that I'm a respectable widow whose husband recently died from wounds inflicted in the war. I shall tell that to young Harold, too, when he's older. If he thinks his father's dead, he will never want to see him.

No, I won't be a miserable Miss. I shall be a proud Mrs. Mrs Mary Parker, widow – and Madam in the shops. I can control my present and future. Why shouldn't I control my past too? As a gracious lady, I shall be looked up to as bearing my bereavement so nobly.

I know just how I'm going to be bringing up Harold!

Some day in the future, I'm going to read everything I've written in this book and laugh.

And then – then – I wonder how he'll like what I've done.

No wonder his brat's crying again.

19

'SEE,' SAID Harry, 'that was what happened.'

It was shortly past midnight that same day when he spoke those words to Julie.

'I'm glad you read that,' he continued, leaning casually against a wall. 'It was my mother who wrote that. Can you imagine what it's like,' his voice was toneless, 'having a mother like that?' There was a pause. 'S'pose you can't,' he went on. 'So I'd better tell you. That's why I came down again. To tell you. Because, you see, you need to know. It was so important that you read me mum's diary because otherwise nothing I said would make sense. So I'm glad you've been sensible and well behaved.'

Julie didn't move a muscle in reply. She'd said nothing other than 'yes' when he'd asked her if she'd read the diary. She'd done nothing other than sit still and look at him. She knew she was dealing with madness. Her mind was still unsteady from the shock of absorbing it. But she still didn't have the full picture.

She had to have that before she could plan anything. And now, she couldn't recall ever feeling so frightened and helpless. Yet the lives of Michael and herself depended on her keeping calm. She had to do that no matter how fearful she might feel. Otherwise there was no chance at all.

Listen to him, she told herself. Try and work out the method of his madness.

'And I'm glad you're listening,' he came in again, as though he'd divined her thoughts, 'because I want you to understand. I want you to understand it all better than I did.' He crossed the room and took the chair opposite Julie. She watched him with a horrified fascination she tried not to betray.

'So you're going to listen,' he resumed, 'and I'm going to talk. It's never been like that before,' he added wistfully.

'You can't imagine how I was brought up. Only I never knew why. Or even about my dad. I always thought he died when I was about nine months old. So when I read what you've just read, I was totally shattered by the discovery.

'See, for years there was this photo of my dad in her bedroom. I used to stare at it for hours, really impressed. So that was my dad, I'd think. A real hero. After a time, though, she put it away somewhere. I didn't see it again till the day she died.

'No, I never knew what really happened until now. That's when it all started to become clear. Why. Why she did it.

'See,' Harry leaned forward urgently, 'she didn't want me to be a man. She did all she could to stop that, including cuddling me so I adored her – though really it meant nothing. As a child, I depended on her so much, I was no use at mixing with the other children. Particularly the boys, who seemed so rough – they used to call me a sissy. And whenever I was bullied as a child, which was often, I ran home crying to Mummy. I was very lonely when I was a child. Nobody wanted to play with me. And I couldn't join in the games because if I got dirty and untidy, I got punished.

'Of course, I did everything my mother said. I was so devoted to her. I had no idea that she was anything other than my wonderful mummy who was always right about everything. And when I did something wrong – and for her, just about anything one'd call healthy and masculine was wrong – she...' his face creased into lines of distress, 'she punished me.

'She had this special room where she used to do it too. It looked very much like this one. I'd get spanked and then I'd have to stand in the corner, sometimes for hours. I'd have to wear a dunce's cap too, because she said I was always being stupid. "Stupid! Stupid! Stupid!" – I can still hear her saying that.

'The spanking didn't hurt nearly so much as the disgrace and humiliation. There were times when I wanted to die, I felt so small. And all the while, as I stood there with my nose pressed against the wall, she'd just lie back and lecture me, or else play records...' abruptly he started coughing. Spasm after spasm shook his chest, bringing tears to his eyes, before he could continue.

'But even worse than that was – if I'd been specially bad – then –' he swallowed with difficulty, 'then – I had to wear a dress. A girl's dress. Sometimes I think of that,' there was a manic brightness in his eyes now, 'and it makes me want to scream and maim and kill.

'Anyway,' he continued, his voice rasping with the effort of controlling his emotions, 'I was brought up like that. Whatever she said, I did, like I said. Then when I got older – oh, I would say from about twelve onwards – I started getting these incredibly strong and strange feelings. It's hard to explain, but life out there – as opposed to in the home – suddenly started to seem very exciting.

'The way I see it, windows sort of opened out onto new sounds and sights and all kinds of experiences which I knew my mum didn't want me to have. I started reading a bit too – I'd never read much before, except at school when you had to, and I started questioning things. I suppose you could say that I began to feel a bit rebellious. She must've sensed that.

'Well,' he paused and swallowed, then frowned, coughed and shook his head, 'one day she told me my attitude was all wrong. I argued back and got slapped round the face a few times. Then she took me up to The Room. I was fourteen at the time but I still got spanked. Then she got out these new clothes she'd bought just for me, for this occasion. Girl's clothes. I was stood in a corner. Then I was photographed. But that time I was stronger than her – physically, I mean. And yet I let her do that to me.

'That's what she did to me,' he snarled abruptly. 'Oh yeah, that's what she did to me.' He screwed his eyelids shut as if to block out the memory, then opened his eyes again and stared into some space in the past. 'Oh, and I haven't said anything about the men she saw, have I?

'Ever since I can remember, she was always seeing men. And they were all in love with her too. Sometimes, when I'd be awake at night, I used to hear things. Funny, disturbing things, I thought then. And when I got older, I found out about that and I used to lie there on my bed, squirming with rage.

'Only, you see, I needn't've, 'cos as I realised much later, she never did... you know. She just led them on. She loved leading them on. And, Christ, how I hated some of her tricks. She had this horrible knack of crossing her legs so they could see up her skirt. It was really disgusting. But after a time, when she had them where she wanted them, she always packed them in. I got used to seeing grown men crying as they left.

"Course, *I* didn't have any girlfriends in my teenage years. Hardly surprising. I was terrified of girls. Shy. Tongue-tied. Embarrassed. Didn't know what to say. Wanted them but couldn't get them – not that she would've allowed it. That's the story of my life and we know who was responsible.

'But despite all that, as I grew older I had this feeling that I couldn't stand it. I started having a bit of my own life without telling her. There was this group of blokes at school, you see. Great bunch of guys. All the teachers said they were the worst but for some reason they were really nice to me. They accepted me. They let me spend time hanging around with them, and maybe for the first time in my life I knew what it was like to have friends and be happy.

'I suppose you might call 'em Teds. They liked music – Elvis Presley, Gene Vincent, that sort of thing. They went to coffee bars with good juke boxes. I felt really good when I was with them. Only time I did.

'So I started lying to her so I could spend more time with them. Pretended I was taking extra classes. And I knew all along that I could never introduce them to her. She'd say how common and vulgar they were, among other things. I can hear her saying it.

'Then it was time to leave school. I was never much good at anything there – except woodwork and anything practical with my hands – oh, and I was pretty good at sport only she disapproved of that. Anyway, I had to get a job. I wouldn't've minded some apprenticeship – plumbing, carpentry, something like that, like my mates – but my mum had other ideas. She fixed it up for me to be an assistant in a grocer's shop.

'I told my friends and they said she must be screwy. She was, of course, only at that stage I'd never thought of it like that. Then they said they'd all be leaving home and sharing this place together – a basement somewhere, all very basic but we could have fun together. Yeah, they wanted me to join them and I've never felt so proud. One of them – Terry Halliday, that was his name – said he could get me work helping this painter and decorator.

'Suddenly, everything sort of came welling up inside me. I knew that if I didn't take this chance, I'd never be happy. I'd be... well, I'd be a sort of walking cripple for the rest of my life. So I ran away. Just ran away from home.

'It was wonderful. At first. Absolutely wonderful. I'd never known that life could be so good. Lots of laughs. For the first time ever, I felt free. I loved being with my mates. There was booze. Girls in and out too, not that I ever had any success that way, but I didn't care.

'The trouble was, there were also pills and stuff. Drugs and things which made you feel great for a bit and then messed you up. Also, I wasn't eating well. None of us were. And my friends started nicking things. Bit of burglary too. And dealing in things that'd been stolen. They thought they were so clever. And I thought it was all so exciting. Like a film.

'Well, I suppose that in the end it had to happen. The police caught up with us and it was partly because my mum had them looking for me. So we were all arrested and remanded in custody, and when I was in the cells, it started happening. I had these terrible feelings of shame and guilt and remorse. I wished I'd never been born. I couldn't sleep at night. I had sweats the whole time and it was as though a knife was twisting in my guts. After a while, it got so bad I couldn't think and could hardly speak at all. I just wanted to die.

'Naturally my mum came to see me. I was no match for her in that state. I'd've agreed to anything. I promised her everything, if only she'd take me back. So, she got me a good lawyer and he brought in a good doctor and they built up this evidence. At the trial they said that I was a half-wit. I mean, they didn't actually use those words but that was what they meant. That I was this stupid idiot who'd been led astray. And there was one other thing they made me do too. She insisted on it and I was too destroyed to do anything except agree. I had to shop all my friends, the only people who'd ever been kind to me. I did and all. It's the most disgusting thing I ever did – but she told me if I didn't do that, I'd go to prison for years, and I believed her. Well, my mates went to borstal and I got off with probation.

'I still break into a cold sweat whenever I think of that. It's like I've got a knife twisting around in my stomach whenever that memory comes back. I despise myself for what I did and for the rest of their lives, those mates of mine will be busy despising me too. A little while back, I was in this pub one evening and after all these years, I saw one of them. Phil. Phil Baines. He saw me too, and he recognised me after all these years. And, by God, how he still despised me.

'I saw him, I saw the look he gave me and it's a long time since I felt so sick and ashamed and afraid. It was like seeing a ghost of a man I'd betrayed, and all that time came back to me and I remembered how I was different then – and I ran. I ran away from him. But no, he wasn't letting me get away that easily. He'd always wanted to meet up with me again. He stopped me by the car. I was so choked up, I couldn't speak. He said I was disgusting and I couldn't argue. I said I was sorry but that was nothing like enough. Then he hit me.

'You know what I reckon I should've done? I should've let him give me a hiding. It was all I deserved. But I was all confused and when he hit me, I got angry and then I remembered that he was a coward in the old days and I was always a better fighter than him, so he was the one who got a hiding and I said I'd kill him if he came near me again, because I didn't really want to remember that time – and afterwards I cried and cried, just like a child. Oh yes, I broke down totally and sobbed my heart out over everything I'd lost.

'Because, you see, after the trial and everything, there was talk of putting me in the loony bin. For weeks and weeks I just sat in a chair and stared at the wall. But my mum cared for me. Oh yes, she cared for me. The whole neighbourhood knew how she cared for me. They didn't know that every night I had to get down on my knees and beg her to forgive me or else it'd be electric shocks in the loony bin for ever.

'Something happened to me. I know I was different and better before all this happened but I can't really remember how. I just blocked off all kinds of things and tried to think as little as possible.

'The nice thing, I suppose, the one nice thing, was this probation officer. Mr Thompson, he was called. He was the one who got my mum to let up on me a bit. He encouraged me to work with my hands and he managed to persuade her to let me. And it was him who suggested that I could have my own room how I liked and do what I liked there.

'Apart from that, it was the end of my life, really. At least, that's one way of looking at it. I couldn't fight her any more. I surrendered. Everyone said I couldn't cope with the outside world and couldn't survive on my own. Everyone said I couldn't manage without her. Who was I to argue? I was too stupid, like she said. So at first when they kept telling me how lucky I was to have her, I just agreed with them. I wasn't an independent human being any more. I was just hers, like a poodle.

'No, I didn't want to think any more. I just observed things and felt nothing. My mother got up to her old tricks with men again. I didn't care. She just carried on – and I'm not one for crude language – breaking hearts and busting balls same as ever. I'll never forget her dinner for five, though. Her and five men all competing to please her.

'Meanwhile, I just did whatever she told me. It was simpler and easier that way. I did everything while she told everyone she did everything, but I no longer cared. I couldn't escape. And it wasn't all bad. I had a roof over me, a nice house, a bed, food and no worries about money. Then the handyman bit gave me pleasure and got me out of the house. And there was my room, where I could have my dream world.

'And maybe I wasn't so totally and utterly stupid. Because, you see, I pretended to be worse than I was. I stopped trying to be an individual altogether. When I was in company, I just wanted to pass as reasonably normal. So I always made sure I spoke in old, tried and tested ways. You know. Clichés, I believe they're called, but that's how people speak and no one attacks you if you're the same.

"Course,' Harry continued – and he wasn't talking to Julie so much as talking at her – "course, I did develop my little jokes. It was my own small way of getting some kind of revenge. She was always going on about the importance of speaking proper. Well, as you might've noticed, my accent's not like hers at all. It's very ordinary, like the things it says. Common or vulgar, you might call it. I started speaking that way at school and she hated it. But I carried on speaking that way after – after it all happened, and Mr Thompson said I should be allowed to do that. Let's face it, I'm too stupid to speak any other way than that. I just hope it embarrassed her but I had a feeling it didn't.

'And the other joke – nobody got it but I was laughing up my sleeve the whole time – was always being on about my mum. You probably remember that. Always saying how marvellous she was. Wonderful mum. Best mum in the world. I meant the exact opposite to what I was saying. And not one person, including you, cottoned on to how sarcastic I was being.

'Except for one thing when I wasn't being sarcastic. When I said that everything I am today, I owe to her, you bet I meant every word. Every word.

'I've got used to it, you know. You know, having a useless life. But there's one sense in which it hasn't turned out to be so completely useless after all. I'm talking about the discoveries I've made. And what I'm planning is that maybe and perhaps I can still give some meaning to it.' He moistened his lips.

'Let's look at it,' said Harry. 'Let's look at what happened. First I met you – purely by chance – and through you, I met Bob. Most important of all, I met Michael. I like Michael.' Julie stiffened, every nerve taut. 'Healthy little boy, just like I should've been. He's become a friend too. Lots of people don't appreciate how children can be friends. I've always got on much better with children, especially small boys. You can be natural with them. Only some people think that's peculiar.

'Still, I can't tell you how happy it's made me to be friends with Michael. I was becoming friends with him when my mum died. I don't deny it was a shattering experience. Face it, for all of my life except for one brief escape, she'd ruled my world.

'And as she died, she tore up this photo. I knew that photo. It was a photo of my dad. My father whom I'd thought I'd known. I put it together on the bed as she was lying there and thought of him. A war hero – and me, his son, a poncing ninny in an apron – oh, and I just cried and cried for everything.

'It was weird after that. Suddenly I was free again and I hadn't a clue what to do about it. I had money. And the house was mine – the house where I'd suffered so much. I found myself starting to think again. I didn't want to. It was too painful. But I couldn't stop myself.

'So, one day I forced myself to enter that room again. The room where she'd stopped me from being a man. The room in which she'd broken me. 'Course, it hadn't been used in years. No need. Anyway, I saw it all and I recalled it all. The corner. The girls' clothes. Everything else. And this funny blue book.

'Well, you've read it now, so there's no point in describing it. Let's just say that as I was flicking through it, something caught my eye. The name Foster.

'At first I couldn't believe it. I thought it was all a coincidence. But I had to know the truth. When I read the diary – well, I won't tell you how it affected me. Let's just say that nothing I've read has ever affected me more. 'Cos at last I knew why.

'I wondered if it was possible that Bob Foster was any relation of my dad's. I had to know. So I moved in. I was planning to ask all kinds of questions when I noticed that Bob was studying something to do with his family in this file.

Naturally I got my hands on it as soon as I could.

'It had the same indescribable effect as what my mum had written. I was shattered for days but I managed to disguise it. I'm a dab hand at disguising my true feelings and it should be obvious why.

'But I shan't disguise now what I really felt then. Hatred, pure hatred, that was what I felt. My dad was guilty. My mum was guilty. My dad abandoned me so my mum ruined me. And meanwhile,' now there was quiet venom in his voice, 'my half-brother Bob grew up normally with his dad like I should've done. He had a successful career and a wife and child like I should've had. I mean, that's every man's right – only I didn't have it. I loathed him for that. Loathed him. Oh yeah, I wanted to kill him, all right.

'But I restrained myself,' and now his tone went cold. 'Restraining myself was easy. I'd been restrained all my life. And suddenly, because I knew something no one else knew, I felt in control for the first time ever. Oh yeah, I planned it all. I planned every move. See, I'm not quite so stupid.

'Is it bothering you?' Harry asked, for Julie was gaping at him in a trance of horror. 'Lucky you. It didn't happen to you. I'm the one to whom it all happened. And I'll tell you something else.

'You may have wondered why my dad got so upset when he contacted my mum again and she sent him something which made him get drunk and write what you've read. Well, I'm going to show you. See, she kept a copy of it in her diary and I whipped the stuff so you wouldn't see it till I'd had a chance to talk. Well, now you're going to see what she sent the man who was Harold Foster first and then Frank Foster and my dad all the while. But before I do that, I just want to make one observation. It's very pertinent. It bears very much on why you're here. It might explain something to you.'

There was a pause. Julie stared at Harry as though he were some gross, slime-covered worm with gaping red jaws.

'See,' he said at last, 'you remind me of my mother.'

'But I'm nothing like your mother!'

'I think you are,' said Harry.

20

'ANYWAY,' SAID Harry, 'it's time you saw this.' Julie took the sheet of paper he handed her. Unfolding it with trembling fingers, she saw the familiar handwriting of Mrs Parker:

26th January 1964

Dear Harold,

I acknowledge receipt of your contemptible letter. What a surprise after all these years! So a little worm finally found the courage to wriggle and writhe in an attempt to explain its slimy behaviour? Who would've thought it?

The reasons you give for your despicable conduct are as unimpressive as their author. They do not alter the facts. You deceived me, you exploited me and, like the lying coward you are, you ran away. You proved yourself to be a completely worthless human being.

I do not wish to dwell on the pain and suffering you caused me. Nor do I wish to thank you for the financial bequest with which you tried to atone for your guilt. It was the least you could do and you know it.

You ask after the bastard you fathered on me. I'm glad to say he's nothing like you. I have brought him up to have respect for ladies and done all I can to ensure he would never emulate your own loathsomeness.

I have pleasure in enclosing a photograph of your boy. If you had the slightest sense of decency, things would have been different: but you haven't and they're not.

How do you like what I've done?

Mary

'And here's the photo,' Harry said, as he passed it over.

Julie looked – and drew back in shock and distaste. She recognised the boy in the picture as the young Harry – only he was wearing a girl's party dress in bright pink. His face was flushed with shame and creased with humiliation as he dropped a curtsey to the camera.

'See,' said Harry, 'that's what she did to me. And that was what killed him. So now I'm doing it to you.'

'Doing what...?' Julie's voice emerged as a hoarse whisper.

'Anyway,' Harry responded, as though he hadn't heard her, 'there's Michael to be considered too, isn't there? I mean, you're his mother. And you remind me of my mother. I'm not having you treat my nephew the way I was treated. I'm not having you mess him up. They're dangerous, mothers.'

'Harry, please,' Julie burst out, 'look at me. I'm nothing like your mother. Do I speak like her? Do I act like her? Do I even look like her?'

'Put those clothes on,' he gestured at the navy blue suit on the bed, 'and let's see.'

'Harry, listen just a moment...'

'Put them on.'

'This is...'

'Put them on. That's the third time I've said it. 'Cos if you don't, I'll have to knock you about a bit, same way she did.'

Julie stared despairingly into the eyes of a fanatic. The brain behind them was focused on something very dim and distant. One couldn't reason with him. One couldn't resist. Julie didn't want to be knocked about. He'd cowed all thoughts of physical resistance when he'd picked her up earlier and tossed her into the chair. His strength was alarming. She was terrified of violence. Slowly and sullenly, she rose and pulled on the clothes, wrinkling her nose at their musty smell.

'And the shoes and stockings. She always wore stockings.' Julie complied reluctantly. 'Now walk up and down.' She obeyed, blushing furiously with shame and indignation. 'You know something,' he observed coolly, 'there is a definite resemblance. A very definite resemblance...'

'Harry...'

'Shut up!' he snapped. 'From now on, you speak only when you're spoken to. Oh yeah,' he murmured, as he gazed at her, 'it could almost be my mum standing here in front of me. My mum when she was young. And you know something, Mum,' he continued, as Julie shuddered with revulsion, 'I've a good mind to spank you for what you did. Only I can't, somehow. It wouldn't be decent, really. But I'm very annoyed with you. Very annoyed indeed. Furious!' He spat the word. 'Just like you used to say.

'So, Mum, what I've decided is...' suddenly his lips puckered, as he mimicked the voice of a prissy woman, 'you can jolly well go and stand in the corner.' Julie's jaw sagged in shock. 'Now!' he snarled, raising a large and threatening palm. Julie backed away, tripped on her high heel and staggered into the arm of a chair.

'This instant,' he hissed. Her being felt blasted by his onslaught. She turned.

'Face to the wall. Hands behind your back.'

She obeyed. Moments later, she heard him fumbling for something, then he sighed with satisfaction. She winced inwardly as his footsteps approached. Now she could feel his hot breath on her neck as he fastened an elastic band beneath her chin and a cap upon her head.

'Because you're stupid,' he whispered, then he stepped back and screamed: 'Stupid! Stupid! Stupid!'

Her knees were shaking. There was a sudden, almost overpowering urge to vomit, succeeded by a conviction that she would faint. Yet she kept telling herself she couldn't. She kept upright and conscious through the fear of what Harry might do to her if she passed out. Even so, however hard she fought, she was unable to prevent her body from trembling.

It sounded as though Harry had sat down. He exhaled several long, deep sighs of relief.

'Oh, yes, this is what it used to be like,' he reminisced, 'only I was the one being punished. Now it's you, Mother, and how d'you like it? Eh? Eh? How d'you feel?'

There was silence except for the ticking of a clock. Fantasies rushed through Julie's mind about a hero bursting in through the door, killing Harry and releasing her – but Bob was more dead than alive, and this nightmare was real and without end.

'I'd talk to you more,' said Harry, 'only I'm tired. I want to go to bed. It's time you were in bed too. So I'm going to leave you now but I'll be back tomorrow. At five o'clock exactly.

'And when I come down,' his speech was slurred by the saliva in his mouth, 'at five o'clock, I want you standing there obediently in your corner as I come in. Well,' said Harry, 'I'm going now. As soon as you hear the door close, you're to count to one hundred. When you're done that, you can come out of your corner. But no cheating, 'cos I'll be counting too and who knows, I might be watching you through the spy-hole.

'There's no escape, Mother. This place has got the best soundproofing job I ever did. So you see,' Harry said, 'mum's the word.

'Oh, yeah,' he breathed, just before he left, 'mum's the word, all right.'

'He'll be all right,' said Harry. 'You mark my words, he'll be all right in the end.'

Michael said nothing. He just carried on staring at the body on the bed, hoping that it wasn't his father but knowing that it was. It was pure pain to regard that prone and plastered body, all the while praying for one flicker of an eyelid. Yet the boy felt he had to be there, believed in the possibility of his presence working some primitive and elemental magic which would restore his father to him. Before, he had visited the hospital after school every two days with his mother, and they had sat in silence and held hands for a long and miserable hour. Now Harry came with him. There was no change.

It was at these times that Michael's courage threatened to fail him altogether. For now they'd taken his mother from him too and he was alone and helpless and dreadfully afraid. His chest would start heaving uncontrollably and the tears would start in his eyes as his nose ran. Always he tried to fight it. It wasn't manly to cry. Only small boys cried. But sometimes he knew that he was just a small boy and the weight of his misery overwhelmed him.

Please live, Dad, he begged silently, as tears streamed down his face, then his chest tightened only to explode into a series of sobs.

'Easy,' whispered Harry, and laid a comforting hand on Michael's back, 'easy, easy, it'll be okay.'

Michael swayed back against the comforting strength of Harry's arm. His mother was gone and no one knew for how long – 'If your dad wakes up, we don't tell him that,' Harry had wisely said – and Harry was no substitute for her or for his father, but at least he cared and was comforting and could be trusted like an uncle. Michael gave vent to one final sob, then shook his head and blew his nose and dried his eyes and rose.

The man and the boy left the hospital with Harry's arm still around Michael's shoulders. They climbed into the car and drove away and all the while it was difficult for the man to repress his desire to laugh with joy. He felt happy, terribly happy. And gloriously free to do whatever he wanted, like a spoiled child on the first day out of school.

And why not? he thought. His parents were dead – the bastard and the bitch. And Bob, the brother, who'd had everything Harry should've had but who didn't need much right now – he might as well be dead too. Whether he died or lay in a coma – that was immaterial to Harry. It didn't even matter if he recovered. Harry had plans for that eventuality. Decisive, fatal plans.

Nothing could stop him from being friends with Michael. If Michael's mother dared object, she'd be punished more. As he sped through a succession of green lights, Harry wondered if there was any way he could be appointed Michael's legal guardian. That would bring them really close. How lucky they were to have found one another! It meant an end to those dark, lonely days of hanging around in playgrounds trying to strike up conversations with strange children.

But there was no denying the current, central problem – the woman in The Room, where he'd be going very shortly. It was all fine for the time being, but sooner or later people would start asking awkward questions. They'd want to know why Julie hadn't been seen. So in the end, really, there was only one option.

It'd be difficult to fix, but after all, as everyone admitted, Harry the handyman could fix anything.

Although she was thirty, she stood obediently in a corner with her hands behind her back and a dunce's cap upon her head.

It was five o'clock. There was no one in the room but she never once looked around. She just stood there with her face pressed against the wall, like a little girl in disgrace years and years ago, yet wearing a smart tailored suit in navy blue and with black high heels.

She could not believe this was happening to her, every instinct shrieked out that this was some vile dream. It was impossible that this could be her fate – but the chill of the wall on her nose was real enough, as was the ache in her pressured heels and the excruciating, interminable boredom which tortured her mind into a numbed and catatonic acquiescence on the borderland of sanity.

Time and time again her memory had replayed the sequence of events which had led her to this pitiable state. She saw now all she had missed then. Every incident had been analysed in minute detail and there were moments when she wanted to rend and tear herself for her stupidity – and yet it all had its own horrific and inevitable logic.

Footsteps sounded outside the room. Her body stiffened to attention as her mind went black.

He was coming.

PART FOUR

21

JULIE AWOKE.

Automatically, she reached out for her husband. He wasn't there and there was a sickness in her stomach as she realised why. The bed felt strange too. Where was she? Her eyes were screwed shut. She didn't dare open them for fear of what she might find. Slowly the bitter truth came back to her, her recent memories destroying all attempts at disbelief. She tried burying herself beneath the covers and escaping into fantasy but it was no use. The reality of her situation came down on her like a heavy hammer.

She forced herself to rise, then stared hopelessly around her cell. The dunce's cap was lying at her feet. She had to resist the almost overpowering temptation to crush it. How long had she been here? Long enough for her body to feel cold and utterly empty – yet she still had no appetite at all. Should I go on hunger strike? she thought, as she entered the kitchen and made herself a coffee. But what then? Maybe he wanted her dead. Did he mean to kill her in the end?

Think clearly, girl, she ordered herself, as she sipped the steaming brown liquid. It was difficult. It was all like being in the centre of some dark, mad maze with the Minotaur as captor. Put more plainly, all the pain of a generation ago was now being visited on her.

Be still. Be calm. The words from a meditation class of years ago came back to her. Just be here now, be here now. That was no good and Julie shuddered. The last thing she wanted was to be here now. Yet her only hope lay in quietening her restless mind. Consider it all again, she commanded her wearied brain. Again? her intellect protested. Yes, I might've missed something. Begin with the first fundamental fact. Never mind the motives, they're all too much and I've thought them through before. The fact is that I'm a prisoner and somehow I must escape.

Yes, and being frantic, like yesterday when she'd screamed herself hoarse and bruised and cut her fists in beating on the walls, was just pointless and futile. She'd felt completely freaked and given way to hysteria, but it hadn't helped and it was essential to control herself.

It was thoughts of Michael that had done it. What was happening to him? What had Harry told him? What was Harry doing to him? Those questions had driven her crazy, together with the hideous recollection of yesterday's conversation with Harry.

'Why're you doing this to me?' she'd asked plaintively, as she stood in her corner.

'First, you will ask me for permission to speak,' he'd replied, in that horrible, prissy tone he sometimes adopted.

'May I please have permission to speak?'

'Permission granted.'

'Why're you doing this to me?'

'That's better,' said Harry. 'You really must remember these small courtesies. And in answer to your question, there's lots of reasons I'm doing it. For a start, you interfere too much between me and Michael.'

'But, I'm his mother!'

'You know something?' Harry said. 'I reckon most mothers do more harm than good, that's what I reckon. And I reckon I'm doing the boy a favour by keeping you away from him. Right, that's enough talking. Face to the wall!'

And then, on the old, wind-up gramophone, he'd played Vera Lynn singing 'We'll Meet Again, Don't Know Where, Don't Know When'.

Julie's skin crawled at the memory, then she gritted her teeth. No, she wouldn't let him win. She'd get away somehow. And yes, she'd stop him from perverting Michael, no matter what. If only there weren't these gut-twisting fantasies of what he might be doing to the boy! They made her beside herself with dismay and torment, barely able to endure her own being.

Once more she stared around the room – the replica of The

Room where Harry had been broken – and her nose wrinkled with disgust as she spotted the pile of old magazines beneath the coffee table: *Country Life, Time and Tide,* the *Tatler* and the *Lady.* Inwardly she raged at her captor and riled at the cage of her fate but once more inspiration failed to arrive.

There were no objects which would make convincing weapons – she'd searched the cell thoroughly several times. In any case, violence wasn't a credible option. Harry was too strong and Julie had never been much good at fighting. The only way out was via the door. That door couldn't be sound-proof, since she could always hear Harry arriving outside it – but it led to a little hall and another door, which was almost certainly proof against sound. These doors could not be beaten down. So there was no way out except by getting the key off Harry.

That meant she had to trick him. How? Sure, she was trying to lull him into the proverbial false sense of security by pretending to comply with all his wishes but meanwhile... meanwhile, what? Should she try and talk him out of his mania, as though she was a sympathetic and understanding psychiatrist? But he didn't allow her to talk.

Wouldn't people be asking about her disappearance? Well, which people? Not people at work. As far as they were concerned, she'd given in her notice. What about her friends? They'd assume she was in mourning and wanted to be alone.

What about Michael? What had Harry told him? Again that question stabbed into her heart.

She had to escape.

How could she escape?

The hours ticked by.

'I'm so happy,' Angela told Emma, as she reclined on her new chesterfield in her new Harvey Nichols' dress and sipped lapsang souchong from a Wedgwood cup. From upstairs, there came a sound of drilling: George was putting up shelves. 'Everything's going so well,' she gushed. 'George is so clever, he's had another rise – and Pru's doing so marvellously at her ballet class.'

'I'm so pleased for you.' Emma's voice was strained. So was her face.

'How's Max?'

'He's fine, thanks.' Emma saw no point in admitting that after a whirlwind of glamour, romance and spending, Max was broke again.

'Good' Angela cooed, 'I'm very glad to hear it. Because I think it's up to us to do something for poor Julie.'

'Yes,' said Emma. Of course, Angela was right. Bob's near fatal accident must've been an almost unbearable blow. Julie must still be reeling from the shock and pain. Yet right now, Emma didn't have much to give. There was a thick wad of unpaid bills at home. She was at her wits' end in trying to cope with it all. It was why she hadn't been in touch with Julie.

'Have you see her lately?' she asked.

'No,' Angela put down her cup. 'I had this feeling after the funeral that she wanted to be alone to bear her grief. But you know,' Angela looked thoughtful, 'perhaps we should've made more of an effort. Because something terrible's happened. She's had a complete nervous breakdown.'

'What?'

'Well, Michael told Pru at school that Julie'd gone into a rest home. So I rang up and spoke to Harry – who's still living there, thank goodness – and he told me it's true. It's tragic. She just cracked up all of a sudden. Luckily he was around at the time and called the doctor. They've taken her to a place called Roselands or something. Apparently it's really lovely there. But the awful thing is that her condition must be really serious. The doctors say she can't see anybody.'

'That's terrible!' Emma exclaimed. And I think I've got problems, she thought.

'I suppose I'd probably break down too if something awful happened to George,' Angela commented. 'But we must do something, even if we can't go and see her. What I was thinking is, why don't we both put in a fiver and send her some flowers?'

'All right,' Emma reached for her purse and took out her last five-pound note, the one which was meant to last her for the next three days. Her lips were tight as she passed it over. 'D'you have the address?' she asked. 'I'd like to send a card as well.'

'Harry said he didn't have it to hand, but he'd call back with it and let me know.'

'Why do dreadful things always happen to decent people?' Emma demanded. And why're you so successful and smug about the fact, Angela, she thought. There's no justice in the world. It's not fair. Angela's done nothing to deserve all her comforts. Oh God, why's all this happening to Julie? 'Why?' she burst out, extending her hands helplessly. 'And what about Michael? He's a nice little boy. And there he is suddenly without a father. Now he's without his mother too. I dread to think of how all this could screw him up.'

'Well, at least there's Harry,' Angela declared. 'I always told everyone what a worthwhile person he is. He's so marvellous with Michael too – just like an uncle.' She sipped tea. 'Oh yes, thank heavens Harry's there.'

'You can come out of your corner,' said Harry.

Julie turned, feeling as though she'd been there for hours. In fact, it had only been thirty minutes.

'Sit down,' he commanded her. 'I've got something for you.'

Julie sat down wearily, her face an expressionless mask. All today she'd tortured her brains in quest of some means of escape. She'd even considered writing a note to Michael and pinning it to Harry's back somehow. But that would put Michael in danger. She could see him pointing at the note and shouting before he read it, and then... she didn't want to think about the consequences.

'Right!' Harry's hand delved inside a carrier bag and came out with lipstick and blue eye-shadow. 'No talking.' Sitting on the arm of the chair, he made Julie up, then added a touch of rouge, powder and eyeliner. Finally, he took a curly, blonde wig from the bag and, removing the dunce's cap, placed it carefully on Julie's head. Julie submitted in silence. At last he stepped back and admired his handiwork.

'Mmmm,' he smiled fleetingly, 'oh *yes*. See, I'm very angry with you, Mum.'

'I'm *not* your mum!' Julie burst out in desperation.

'You are now,' said Harry. 'And how dare you speak without my permission! I will not have these tantrums! Back in your corner this instant!'

'When can I see the basement?' Michael asked from his bed that evening.

'When it's ready.' Harry was sitting on the edge.

'When'll that be?'

'When I've done it.'

'It's taking ages,' Michael protested.

'That's because I want to do a proper job. There's still some rubbish I have to clear away. Then add a few finishing touches.' He smiled kindly, and his hand reached out for the boy's head.

'When's Mummy coming back?' Harry's hand froze in mid-air.

'Oh. Soon.'

'Why can't we go and see her?'

''Cos she needs a good, long rest and the doctors say she has to be alone.'

'I miss her.'

''Course you do. That's only natural. I miss her too. But aren't you happy here with me?'

'Yes...' Michael answered cautiously, 'but I want my mum too.'

There was a pause. Then:

'What would you do without her?' Harry asked gently.

'*Without* her?' His eyes widened in horror at the thought. 'How d'you mean?'

'Well, if for example the doctors said she couldn't come back for a while.' That's a possibility, Harry thought. Another one's pretending to take Michael to see her and disappearing somewhere nice.

'That'd be *awful*. I'd hate it. I couldn't stand it. If anything bad happened to her, I'd... I couldn't go on living.'

'But you have me,' said Harry.

'You're not my mum,' Michael retorted. 'You're only an uncle. And you're not really a proper uncle.' Harry flinched.

'How d'you mean?' he demanded suspiciously.

'An uncle's the brother of your dad or your mum.'

'Suppose I was your dad's brother?'

'I wish you were. But you're not.'

There was silence, then Michael began to sniff.

'What's the matter?' Harry asked. Michael shook his head. 'Come on, you can tell me.'

But Michael buried his face in his pillow and began to cry softly. Harry bent forward and put an arm around the boy.

'Daddy...' Michael sobbed. 'Mummy ill...' His body heaved with his anguish. 'I want my mummy,' he whimpered. 'Promise me she'll be all right.'

'I promise,' said Harry, but his voice sounded strangled. 'She'll be all right. It'll all be all right, you'll see.' He clasped the boy to his breast. 'It's okay, Michael, it's okay.' His voice cracked and there were tears in his eyes as he murmured: 'Michael, I love you.'

22

Julie abhorred violence – but she couldn't see any other alternative. Already she sometimes felt as though she'd been imprisoned for an eternity, and that this wretched state might continue for ever.

No, she had to summon up all her last reserves of strength and courage – and strike hard and low for her freedom.

She'd been practising the move all evening.

Michael lay in his bed in the dark and felt lonely. He was also perturbed by a sensation of unease. There was something strange about Harry at present. Michael couldn't really put it into words – he was just acting a bit funny, that was all.

For instance, Michael had written a letter and wanted to send it to his mum. He'd asked Harry for the address. He'd asked him no less than three times – and each time Harry had made some excuse. Why? What was the problem?

Then there were Harry's mysterious trips to the basement. These last few evenings, he'd slipped out of the house after Michael was in bed. Michael had run to the window and seen him going down the steps to the cellar. He hadn't done that before.

Also, it struck Michael that Harry was being uncharacteristically secretive – as though he had something to hide. What did he do in that basement? It wasn't as though you could hear him working. And what did the place look like now? Michael wanted to know.

He was starting to itch with curiosity. There was a growing desire to forestall Harry's promise to surprise him by seeing the basement before he had permission. He'd already observed that Harry used two keys (why two?). He kept one in his jacket and one in his trousers – how could Michael get hold of them?

He started to plot a variety of schemes but his weariness defeated his ingenuity and a few minutes later, he was asleep.

Harry descended the steps to the basement, drew the first key out of his jacket pocket, unlocked the first door, stepped into the hallway, looked through the spy-hole – and drew back in consternation. Taking the second key from his trouser pocket, he let himself into the room and closed the second door behind him, a puzzled frown upon his face.

For Julie, the bedspread wrapped around her, was lying on the floor in a still and silent heap.

'Mum...' Harry called softly, 'Mum...?' There was no response. Harry coughed. 'Julie...' he cooed. 'Julie...?' She remained perfectly still. Harry knelt by her and placed a hand upon her hair.

That was when Julie's fist emerged, clasping a kitchen knife which she drove with all her strength at Harry's groin.

The blade missed his testicles and stabbed into his thigh without piercing the cloth of his trousers – yet Harry screamed in terror and fell back onto the floor. Julie seized the picture on which she'd been lying and smashed the frame down hard on top of Harry's skull. Rage burned up her fear and desperation gave fuel to her strength – but her blow still hadn't been powerful enough to render the man unconscious. He grunted with pain as his foot lashed out to thud against Julie's shins, upsetting her balance and sending her sprawling.

'Do that to me, would you...' he gasped. Panting hard, he swung his arm and smashed Julie across the face. Her head rocked, her senses exploded in a thick fog of pain and confusion. Harry hit her again. 'Cunt,' he breathed, and seized her by the hair. 'Do that to me, would you?'

He flung her back against the floor and collapsed on top of her. His knee came down to force her thighs apart. Julie was sobbing as he unzipped his trousers, thrust himself against her belly – and revealed himself as limp and soft.

'Bitch!' he spat the word. 'I'll teach you!' But even as he

spoke, his phallus shrank. He emitted a high, harsh squawk of rage and frustration, then his thick fingers sought and found an artery at the side of Julie's neck. He squeezed – and Julie was glad to lose consciousness.

When she came to some time later, it was in a haze of discomfort, anguish and despair. She might have vomited had it not been for the fact that some round, hard object had been rammed into her mouth and she was unable to dislodge it. Hammers pounded inside her skull with every breath she took. Her wrists and ankles felt squeezed, sore and lifeless. She tried to move them and could not. Something was biting into her tender flesh. It took a while before she realised that she had been bound and gagged.

She did not want to open her eyes but in the end, she did. He had used a clothes-line to tie her limbs to the legs of the bed. Her thighs were wide apart. She was naked, immobile and utterly helpless. Harry had drawn a chair up to the foot of the bed and was watching her intently.

'You asked for it,' he hissed venomously.

In his right hand, he held a small bottle of pink nail varnish.

23

'You should never have done that,' Harry admonished her. 'You should never have gone for me there with a knife like you did. You really shouldn't've. Because it brought back a memory. I wish it hadn't but it has. I'm going to tell you about that memory. And I've made sure I shan't be having any interruptions from you. You talk too much, anyway.

'I would've been about Michael's age when it happened. See, when I was small, except for when I was at school and she couldn't do nothing about it, I was only allowed to play with girls. She thought that other boys would be a bad influence on me. So I skipped around like a sissy with girls.

'And what she did impress upon me was that because they were girls, they were much better than I was. Superior, so to speak. Whatever happened, they were always in the right.

'Still, there was one girl I really liked. Louise, that was her name. We used to have lots of fun playing together. And she always used to wear these really pretty dresses. She was a year older than me and used to like ordering me around too. We never played the games I wanted, only the games she wanted. But I didn't mind too much. They were quite good games.

'Anyway, one day when we were up in my room, Louise wanted to play this new game and I really wasn't sure about it. It sounded exciting but it also seemed – well – very naughty indeed. I knew my mother wouldn't like it. So I kept saying no and she kept saying yes.'

Harry swallowed and collected his thoughts.

'The game she wanted to play,' he resumed after a pause, 'was a rude one. She wanted to see my bottom and then she'd show me hers. She kept on telling me it would be such fun. Eventually, I agreed. I showed her mine. Then she showed me hers. And while I was looking,' he swallowed again, 'Mum came in.

'Well, she was outraged. Completely disgusted. And she slapped me round the face and knocked me about so I saw stars. Naturally it was all my fault. After all, I was a boy. I was slugs and snails and puppy dogs' tails – that's what little boys are made of, while little girls are sugar and spice and everything nice. I was accused of corrupting Louise in a particularly horrible way and not given a chance to defend myself.

'I was told...' he closed his eyes, and for a few seconds it seemed that the memory was so painful, he could not go on, '... told that I had to be punished. I was taken to The Room and she put a gag in my mouth and took down my trousers and underpants. Then she tied me to a chair. And after that, she took out a bottle of pink nail varnish and painted my privates all over.

'Downstairs, Louise's mother arrived. My mum went and told her what I'd done, though she must've made it sound worse than it was. For the next thing I knew, Mum and she and Louise had come into the room and were pointing at me and calling out comments and laughing... I nearly died... ugh! ugh! ugh! ugh!' he broke down into a fit of coughing. His face was infused by a livid purple hue as tears streamed down his cheeks.

Every muscle in Julie's body ached with tension. Even if her limbs hadn't been tied down, she would've been paralysed by the obscene horror of his story.

'But I'm older and bigger now, so it's not quite the same, is it?' Harry resumed hoarsely. 'Now I'm the one who's doing the punishing – and you deserve it. You went for my privates – just the way she did. And I'm very sensitive about that.'

Julie's eyes widened as he unscrewed the cap of the varnish bottle. She was close to passing out as he leaned forward and proceeded to apply the brush to her labia. It tickled, and she tried to throw her hips around in protest, but he just muttered: 'Keep still, you disgusting thing,' and held her belly down with his free hand. The varnish-soaked brush flicked over her most intimate regions. The liquid was stinging her flesh and she squealed, but he just carried on painting. She closed her eyes to shut out the sight of him and wished herself dead.

'Right,' she heard him say as he stepped back to admire his work, 'now you know what it feels like. And I must say, what a stupid hole you've got there. I've never seen anything so stupid. It's just naughty and silly and because you've got it, it means you're totally inferior. Inferior! Stupid! Disgusting!'

He prodded her with his finger, then exploded in a fit of hysterical, high-pitched peals of laughter.

24

DEAR MUMMY,
I am very sorry indeed that you are not well. I pray every night that you will get well soon. I miss you very much and want to come and see you as soon as the dokters say I can. And I want you back with us at home.

Unkel Harry is being great. He looks after me well.
But I miss you Mum and wish you were here.
Loads and loads of love and hugs and kisses to my darling Mummy.

Michael

The boy's frown of intense concentration relaxed as he placed the letter he'd just written in an envelope and sealed it.

'Uncle Harry!' Michael called out, as he ran into the kitchen early that evening. 'Uncle Harry!'

'Yeah? What is it, son?' Harry looked up from the jam sandwich he was eating.

'I've written to Mum,' Michael displayed the envelope, 'but I don't know the address.'

'Oh, that's not a problem,' Harry answered easily. 'Just leave it with me and I'll post it on to her tomorrow, first thing.'

'But it must be posted tonight,' Michael insisted.

'Why tonight? Why can't it wait till tomorrow?'

"Cos I want it to get there fast as poss.'

'Well, it can't be done now,' said Harry. 'I mean, it needs a stamp. And the post office is shut.'

'But I've got one.' Michael proudly displayed the stamp on

the envelope. 'Mum had one in her top drawer. So can't you post it for me, please?'

'Sure. Tomorrow.'

'Now.'

'Michael, why didn't you tell me this when I picked you up from school?' Harry leaned back in the chair around which his jacket was draped. 'We could've posted it then.'

'But I hadn't written it then,' Michael objected. 'I've only just written it. It's a long letter too. A whole page.'

'Well done,' Harry commented. 'But it doesn't need to be posted now. What's the difference whether it's tonight or tomorrow?'

'A whole night,' said Michael, 'that's the difference. I want it to reach Mum as soon as possible. *Please* post it for me now. Please, please, please...'

'All right.' Harry sighed wearily. 'What a ruddy, little nuisance you can be sometimes. Okay, okay. Just give me the letter and I'll go and find a pen and write the address.' Harry took the envelope and left the room. Michael stared fixedly at his jacket.

'All done!' Harry sang out on his return moments later, then picked up his jacket and put it on. 'And you can jolly well come with me, since you're putting me to all this trouble.'

'Can't.' Michael shook his head.

'What d'you mean, you can't?'

Michael shrugged.

'Come on,' Harry said impatiently. 'What's the matter with you?' Michael looked awkward and stared at his shoes.

'Tummy ache,' he muttered. 'Have to keep going to the bathroom.'

'Oh, I see. Well, it'll be milk of magnesia for you when I get back.' The boy nodded obediently. 'Okay, then. I'll be off.'

As soon as the front door had closed, Michael looked triumphantly at the key concealed in his hand, the one he'd taken from Harry's jacket. Unfortunately, he didn't have the other one, the key Harry kept in his trousers, but perhaps that was just a spare. And he did have the ten minutes or so it would take Harry to walk to the nearest post-box and back – judging by the lack of appropriate sounds, he wasn't taking the car.

Michael darted to the front door and opened it. Outside, it was a cold, hostile and forbidding night. Bare tree branches rustled restlessly in the wind, and moonlight flickered eerily on a dead suburban landscape as dark clouds drifted before the silent satellite. He regarded the steps leading down to the basement and shivered.

Seized suddenly by fear, and also by a succeeding inspiration for overcoming it, he dashed upstairs, grabbed his largest teddy bear and once more went out beneath the threatening sky. His heart thumped hard as he went slowly down the steps, then inserted the stolen key in the lock. He turned it once – and the door swung open silently. Michael took a deep breath and, holding his teddy before him, stepped forward into the dark hallway.

He could just make out the lock in the second door. Again he inserted the key – but this time it refused to turn.

'Bother!' he exclaimed. Then: Wait! he thought. The moon had just come out from behind a cloud and by its light, he could discern a spy-hole. By standing on tiptoe, he could try and see through it. He applied his eye to the glass, stared – then emitted a sharp squeal of shock and reeled back, glassy eyed.

For the room within was brightly lit and within it, he could see his mother. She was naked – and he'd never seen that before. Her legs were apart, and between them, there was hair, and beneath that, a slit that was glossy and shiny and pink.

Her arms and legs had been tied to the bedposts.

'Mummy!' he cried, flung himself back against the door and again looked through the spy-hole, hoping with all his being that this was some foul dream. 'Mummy!' he screamed, for his eyes told him that it wasn't. His fists beat upon the door, then his fingers wrestled vainly with the key. 'Mum–meee!'

His head whirled with shock and terror. His feet lashed

out against the door's stout wood, bruising his toes through his shoes. On the bed, his mother was squirming against her bonds.

'Help!' he bawled. 'He-elp!'

Help? Help from where? Harry?

Harry! Harry had lied to him! Harry had done this!

Harry? Uncle Harry? It wasn't possible, he would not believe it. Yet he could not deny the evidence revealed to the eye he'd placed against the spy-hole.

Then the man was evil, awful and evil. He had done this horrible and disgusting thing to Mummy. He was a monster – and what did Harry mean to do to him? Tears streamed down his face as he shook his head in a daze of shock, bewilderment and fear.

And Harry would be back any minute now.

Michael turned away from the hall, turned and ran up the steps and into the street like one possessed. One thought alone shrieked out from within his skull. He had to call help. But help from whom? From the police? But where were they? From Mummy's friends? Of course – Auntie Angela! She only lived a few streets away.

Michael hared down Kidderpore Avenue, turned into Acacia Grove and ran along it to the crossroads, his lungs heaving with sobs. Which way now? All the streets looked the same. His eyes scoured them in search of some recognisable landmark. Yes! There was the house with the shiny blue Jaguar parked outside it. Michael went left into Denbigh Road – and saw Harry in the far distance.

A blind impulse towards survival made Michael leap frenziedly over the low stone wall to his right, landing in a sprawling heap amongst a cluster of rose bushes. Their thorns tore his flesh and he whimpered with the pain as he crouched by the side of the wall. Blood trickled slowly down his cheek. He tried to control his panting and couldn't. His heart thumped as though bent upon bursting through his ribcage.

He glanced uneasily at the house behind him. Thank God, the curtains on the ground floor were drawn. But suppose someone saw him from an upstairs window? Or suppose someone came out into the front garden and saw him crouching there? Worst nightmare of all – suppose Harry had seen him from the end of the road?

Where was Harry now? Michael compressed himself into a tight, tense ball. Sharp stones in the cold, hard soil bit through his jeans, bruising his body. And now he could hear heavy footfalls in the distance. There was no mistaking the tread. It was Harry.

As the steps came nearer, Michael shoved his fingers into his mouth to try and block the sound of his panting breath. His heart beat so loudly, he was sure Harry could hear it. He held his breath.

Now he could sense Harry's presence. The man had stopped. Panic spread through Michael's body and there was a roaring in his ears. This was abruptly succeeded by the sound of paper being crumpled, then a small, white ball flew over the wall and landed by Michael. Harry began to whistle tunelessly. Michael knew that any second now, his lungs would burst.

Then slowly the footsteps and the whistling receded.

Michael counted to twenty, then the air rushed out of his lungs, leaving him lying on the earth like a burst balloon. As the sounds of Harry died away, the boy gradually recovered his senses. His hand reached out for the crumpled ball of paper, picked it up and opened it out. It was the blank envelope containing his letter to his mother.

He forced himself to count to two hundred, then peered cautiously over the wall. There was nobody on the street. Gritting his teeth with a savage determination, Michael scrambled back into the road and once more broke into a run. Houses and a shopping parade flashed by, he dashed down a crescent, crossed the road into an avenue – and gasped with overwhelming relief as Angela's house came into view.

'Help...' he sobbed, as he pressed the bell. 'Please...'

Yet the door was opened by a big, blonde woman Michael had never seen before.

"Allo,' she said. '*Comment ça va?*'
'Auntie Angela... please...' Michael sobbed.
She shrugged.
'Who is it?' came a small voice from within.
'Pru!' he shouted. 'It's Michael – let me in! – Mummy! – something terrible...!'
'Let him in, Nicole,' said the little girl's voice.

Michael dashed past the strange woman and into the living room, where Pru was drinking a Coke and watching TV.

'Hallo,' she said. 'What're you doing here? And you're all cut and dirty.'

'Please help...' The words tumbled tearfully out of him. 'Need your mummy...'

'Mummy's out,' said Pru. 'There's just me and Nicole. She's our new au pair and she can't speak English. Why're you crying?'

'It's my mummy!' Michael shrieked as Nicole came into the room. He was finding it almost impossible to put a sentence together. 'Harry!... He tied her up... in the basement... naked... help... all tied up...'

'But your mummy's in a rest home,' answered Pru. 'You told me so.'

'Harry told me that... lies... not in home... at home!... basement...'

'I wish you wouldn't make up these tales,' said Pru.

'I'm not making it up!' he screamed.

'Anyway,' Pru told him, 'Mummy should be home fairly soon.'

'That'll be too late,' he sobbed. Then, seized by some inspiration, he ran out to the hall and snatched up the phone – but there was no dialling tone.

'*Le téléphone ne marche pas*,' said Nicole.

Michael threw it down, flung the front door open and ran out into the street once more, ignoring cries of '*Attendez!*' and 'Wait!'. His chest heaved as he wept with frustration and despair, then raindrops spat down on him from the dark sky above and mingled with his tears.

Again, he broke into a run. Emma was now his only hope. How could he get to her from here?

Harry frowned as he approached his home. The front door was ajar – why? He paused by the outside steps and glanced down at the basement, just to make sure everything was all right. His frown deepened when he saw that it wasn't. The basement door was ajar too.

He sprang down the steps, his hand darting into his jacket pocket. The key wasn't there. Panic flickered on his face as he felt within his trousers, then faded as he gripped the second key. But there was nothing at all endearing about the expression on his face when he saw Michael's teddy bear lying on the floor in the hallway.

Within a minute, he'd dashed inside the house, explored every room and picked up Julie's car keys. There was murder in his eyes as he strode swiftly towards the vehicle.

25

'WHAT?' ANGELA gaped at her daughter. 'But you told me Michael said that Julie was in a rest home.'

'But tonight he said that was a lie.'

'This is crazy,' Angela insisted. 'Completely crazy. I've never heard anything like it. It sounds like he was making up stories.'

'That's what I told him,' Pru declared proudly.

'It's not possible. Julie tied up in the basement? By Harry? When did you say Michael arrived?'

'I've told you, Mummy. Just before you came back. He was crying and his clothes were torn and there was blood on his face.'

'Blood...!?' Angela shook her head in bewilderment. 'You've should've made him stay.'

'But I couldn't,' Pru answered promptly. 'He ran away again.'

'Oh, Christ!' her mother groaned. 'That's all I need. I'm absolutely exhausted after a simply hellish day at the shops and now I come home to this. What am I supposed to do?' she asked a picture of herself above the mantelpiece. 'I mean, obviously something's wrong. But I mean...' she faltered, temporarily lost for words. 'I mean... one can't honestly believe that... it's just not possible... it makes no sense... it can't be.' She raised her arms helplessly. 'If only George was here! He'd know what to do. I mean, one can't just call the police, can one? But if Michael's wandering the streets...' She started to pace up and down in a paroxysm of agitation. 'I know. I'll ring Emma.'

'Phone's not working,' said Pru.

'Damn!' Angela squealed. 'Stupid thing. That means I've got to go out to a callbox. And it's raining! My hair'll be ruined! *Double* damn!' She spat the words. 'God! It's all my silly fault, letting George have his night out with the boys. If he was here, there'd be no problem.'

Julie writhed and squirmed within her bonds but utterly failed in her endeavours to loosen them. The stiff cord continued to squeeze her veins and arteries. Her hands and feet had lost all feeling other than a dull and aching numbness.

She'd heard the voice of her son and the frantic rapping of his tiny fists upon the thick door. She'd tried with all her might to free herself. She'd become almost insane with the fear of what might have happened to him. Her anguish had attempted to emerge as a scream which came out of the depths of her being – yet the ball-gag had blocked all but the feeblest of sounds. The sole effect had been a slight shifting of the gag. And as a result of that shift, she was finding it increasingly difficult to breathe.

The ball was now lodged at the back of her throat and impeding the passage of air. Her breath was coming and going in a series of strangled gasps. Her stomach churned and she felt about to retch. She sweated as she strove to suppress the urge which would make her choke on her own bile. Her lungs heaved in a fight for air and drew in a mere pittance.

She coughed – and the gag shifted to block her breath more tightly.

Michael staggered through the dark, wet streets. Black rain pelted down upon him, soaking his hair, running in rivulets down his face and dripping down his neck. His chest was wheezing, his mind wiped out. He was conscious only of a blind need for Auntie Emma as he stumbled along the pavement, lost in a labyrinth of similar suburban roads.

Harry was coughing hard as the car moved through one rain-soaked street after another. His eyes scoured his surroundings for any sign of Michael.

'How could he do it?' he muttered to himself, as droplets drummed on the roof of the car. 'How could he do it to me?' He clenched his teeth. 'Michael...' he whimpered, 'how could you play a nasty trick on Uncle Harry? How?'

His brain raced in a frenzied effort to cope with what had happened. Yes, a plan was forming. No, he wouldn't let anyone shatter his world. Yes, he saw a way in which everything could continue. No, nothing would be allowed to prevent it.

But first he had to find the boy, who had to be around here somewhere.

'Michael, come to me,' Harry wailed. 'I'll be your best friend. Promise.'

Julie's lungs heaved and gasped with every breath she struggled to take. Cold perspiration beaded on her brow then trickled into her eyes, stinging the irises. She choked, caught a tiny intake of breath and choked again.

Let me breathe, let me breathe, let me breathe, she prayed – but this was suffocation and around her she could sense the hideous, brooding presence of her own death.

In his hospital bed not far away, Bob's eyelids began to flicker rapidly, though no one noticed.

He was walking slowly through a dark, narrow passage. He had no idea where it had begun, what he was doing there or where the passageway led, except that it was something to do with Julie and Michael who needed his help. Yes, they were in danger and he had to go to them but it was hard, so hard. A wind was blowing through the tunnel, hitting him with an icy blast which threatened to freeze his limbs. His legs were so weak that it seemed to take hours to progress one step.

Now, on his left, there were bars of steel, and beyond them a cage. Within that cage, a man lay chained. At times he cried out and writhed within his bonds. Bob screamed. The prisoner was himself.

He sank to his knees and crawled along the ground, searching for an entrance to the cage. There were no doors but at the end he was confronted by a thick sheet of glass. He peered through the pane and recoiled in horror.

His car stood outside and within it, Julie was crying out in terror and beating vainly on the doors and windows. At moments, her features were obscurred by a foul, yellow mist which swirled within the vehicle. Bob understood. It was poison gas and she was suffocating.

He tried to smash the glass before him, but all strokes slipped on the polished surface. He shrieked out his helpless fury as his wife implored his aid and then sank from view, gasping and choking – and there, standing by the car, his arm around Michael's shoulders, was Harry. In one hand, he held the car keys. The hand draped round Michael gripped a knife from which blood dripped.

'I can fix anything,' said Harry and laughed, just before Bob sank into the sweet, swooning catacombs of oblivion.

Michael's legs were aching and rubbery as he perceived something vaguely familiar looming in the distance. His eyes widened in hope, then he panted and sobbed out his relief as he recognised the apartment block of Emma and Max.

His will called up his last reserves of strength and he broke into a run. He was vaguely conscious of a car somewhere behind him and the sound of its motor spurred him into a final sprint.

Then someone shouted: 'Michael...!' and he accelerated into a panic-possessed dash for the block of flats, as though the fiend of his foulest nightmares was slavering at his heels.

A hand grasped his shoulder and seized him as another came down hard upon his mouth to choke off his scream.

'Where might you be going?' breathed Harry.

There was a roaring in Julie's ears and a crimson mist about her vision as her starving lungs threatened to burst her ribcage, each cell screaming for air.

She blacked out just before the police broke down the door. And she never would recall the release from her bonds; the giving of the kiss of life; the bewildered, disgusted expressions of the officers Emma had called; and her sudden and hysterical screams for her son.

At the time, though, no one paid much attention to Julie's car, which was travelling south and out of London. Anyone who looked would've seen a nondescript man in his forties, who was driving, and his passenger, who looked pale and exhausted and very much asleep. It could've been a father driving his son.

Or an uncle taking his nephew home after a treat in town.

26

'I'D LIKE to kill him,' Julie said, and drank more brandy. 'I know that's wrong but it's how I feel. I'd like to bloody well kill him.'

It was two evenings later. Julie had been released from hospital this afternoon and was staying with Angela and George. She would've preferred it with Emma and Max but they didn't have a spare room. However, Angela was being a perfect nurse, her house was warm and comforting and Julie never wished to set foot in her own home ever again.

So here she was now, drinking brandy by the fire with Angela and George and Max and Emma – Emma whose prompt and decisive action Julie would never forget – and they were all being so kind and sympathetic, and there'd been an excellent dinner, though she'd been unable to eat more than a few mouthfuls, and she'd been saved from a living hell and death – but she still felt like a walking corpse. Where was Michael?

She'd done her all to answer every question of that nice detective, Inspector MacDonald, as soon as she was able. Now there was a nationwide police hunt. Today, every newspaper carried photos of Harry and Michael. It seemed impossible that they wouldn't be recognised and found – yet so far there was no trace of them at all.

While police combed the country for Harry and Michael, journalists were hounding Julie and offering her rapidly increasing sums for her story. But for her, money was currently meaningless and the persistence of the press disgusted Julie. Nothing mattered except her son's safety. There were no other thoughts in her head at all. It was as though a cassette played relentlessly and continuously inside her skull.

In a moment, she knew she would play it aloud and again

to her friends, who would once more listen sympathetically and try to speak words of comfort. Julie couldn't help herself.

'Where is he now?' she burst out. 'Where?'

'He must be safe.' George reasoned. 'After all, you said Harry liked him...'

The agony continued.

Andrew MacDonald was one of the youngest detective inspectors in London, tough, shrewd and outspoken. This last quality had upset his superiors sufficiently to transfer him from investigating and battling against gangsters and racketeers to pursuing sex offenders, much to his annoyance and disgust. A tall man with penetrating blue eyes and short, dark hair, he now sat in his office chain-smoking unfiltered cigarettes and frowning over a set of reports. All of them were to do with the kidnapping of Michael Foster by Harold Parker.

Since the commencement of the case, he hadn't had much sleep. No doubt about it, this one was coming to obsess him. Why? he wondered. Normally he retained a cold detachment. It was the only way to stay sane in his job. Yet here he felt he was taking it all personally.

Yes, everything he'd learned so far made him loathe and despise the offender. And yes, he was operating under the harsh searchlights of media publicity and catching the criminal would almost certainly boost his career prospects. Yet even these factors were eclipsed by a mental image which kept returning to trouble him. It was of Julie.

MacDonald, who was unmarried, had started out feeling no more for Julie than for any other victim. Gradually, he'd begun to feel sorry for her and then, in the course of watching her while listening to her story, he'd come to like her. She was rather attractive too. Quite a woman, MacDonald thought, and he really didn't want to disappoint her. And that meant that he had reluctantly to stop thinking about Julie and go back to thinking about Harry.

The detective was surprised at the failure of the search so far. National outrage had been aroused, airports, stations and harbours were being watched, every force in the country had men on the alert – yet there'd been nothing but false leads and the futile questioning of innocent fathers and sons.

True, there was some sort of trail. Last night Julie's car had been found, abandoned in a Surrey suburb, with the interior stinking of ether. Three cars had also been stolen from that same suburb and MacDonald had men searching for all of them, but nothing had turned up yet. Drivers of taxis and mini-cabs and lorries were being questioned too, and that was leading nowhere. Where had Harry gone?

After all, MacDonald reasoned, it would be very difficult for a lone man to hide in the company of a terrified and unwilling small boy. And even assuming that Harry had kept the child subdued by administering ether, that would make things equally difficult for him. People would remember the smell and recall a man with a semi-conscious kid. So how come the hunt had so far drawn a blank?

Of course, there was one possibility and it didn't bear thinking about. MacDonald winced as he remembered the twisted swine he'd caught some months back – and oddly enough, his most hideous crime had been committed not far from Julie's home. Yes, it was possible that Harry had killed Michael and the child's molested and mutilated corpse might be lying in a wood somewhere. He pictured himself breaking the news to Julie and shuddered.

But no, it couldn't be. Somehow it didn't fit with all the other bizarre facts, one of which made Harry Michael's half-uncle. MacDonald stubbed out his cigarette and immediately lit another. Again he threw his intelligence and imagination into the exercise which had helped him so often in the past: trying to feel and think like the criminal.

Here he had all the data. Julie had told him all about Frank Foster's statement, Mary Parker's diary and Harry's own story. The picture of the offender was clearer than he'd ever experienced before – MacDonald had even read all the reports relating to Harry's arrest and trial over twenty years ago. Yet try as he might, he couldn't identify with the man. Once more the answer to the question, if I were Harry, where would I go? eluded him.

Common sense told him he'd done all he could today and this evening and he should go to bed, but he suspected that he wouldn't be able to sleep. Again he stared morosely at a photograph of Harry.

I'm going to get you if it bloody kills me, he muttered, then he closed his aching eyes and saw before him the despairing face of Julie.

The female figure sitting by the hospital bed might have been made out of stone. She was as still as the man before her. Her face was impassive. Only her tortured eyes had life in them.

Yes, she had gone back to visiting the hospital daily for one hour. And during that hour, she was continually conscious of the futility of her action, though in a world which seemed devoid of all meaning, no one act was better than any other. She was there because she was there, too drained even to pray.

Earlier today, there'd been more pain. Bob's corporation in California had telephoned to acknowledge receipt of her letter about the accident, to express commiserations, and to say they'd be happy to keep his prospective job open to him for six months. Then Christopher Warnock had rung. He was the managing director of Bob's previous British company. Before Julie had had a chance to explain anything, he'd mentioned that Charles Haughey was 'no longer with us' and had expressed his hope that Bob might be interested in returning to the company in Haughey's place.

Julie had felt like smashing the telephone. The callers might just as well have been soap powder salesmen. Jobs, prospects and the future meant absolutely nothing whatsoever. Only the present was relevant, and it was a present in which her husband and her son might die at any moment, a present in which events conspired to rend and tear her with a pure and concentrated malevolence.

She stared dully at the pale, emaciated face of the man she loved and who had given her the child another had taken. She recalled how she had begged God to let her witness just one momentary tremor of consciousness – and then she gasped because it was possible that an eyelid had flickered; and then she squealed and shot forward with every muscle taut, because it wasn't her imagination and it had definitely fluttered again and now there was a trembling in both lids.

'Bob...' she whispered, 'please... *please*, Bob.'

He opened his eyes.

They were blue and glazed and misty but the light of life was in them. Instantly Julie's arm reached out and the tips of her fingers touched his forehead lightly, though every part of her being willed strength into his. A muscle twitched upon his brow and the eyes fought to focus. As she gazed into them, she saw a gleam of intelligence, then a pure golden dawn of recognition. His lips moved and he strained to say something, though nothing emerged. She had read his lips, though, and she knew the word he was straining to say: *Julie*.

A deep, inarticulate sigh came out of Julie and she had to fight the overpowering desire to take him in her arms and hold him and kiss his mouth and breathe life into him. Her eyes filled with tears as she saw the attempt of his mouth to break into a smile which would announce his will to live, though she took it as done and relaxed his lips with a touch of her forefinger.

'I love you...' she whispered, 'I love you, I love you, I love you.' She knew she should be rousing the doctors and chasing them to the bedside but she could not leave Bob. Again he was straining to speak.

'Hush, it's all right,' she murmured, but his lips had formed the word: *Michael*.

She managed to reply, and Bob managed just the ghost of a smile before sinking back into a sleep in which his face was at peace with his will to live; and Julie ran from the room and to the doctors and nurses with her own face so distraught, they gave her a strong sedative. For what she had forced herself to say with complete conviction was: 'Michael's fine.'

*

'It'll be all right,' Harry was telling Michael somewhere. 'You mark my words, it'll be all right.' The boy regarded him impassively.

They'd been hard, these last few days, but Harry was now feeling more optimistic. He felt that luck was on his side again. It had started coming back at that dreadful instant when Michael had screamed as Harry caught him just outside the block of flats. There'd been no alternative except to gag Michael with one hand and squeeze his carotid artery with the other so he'd pass out – but all the while Harry had sweated with terror in case that hideous scream had been heard.

Please, no, please let us get away, he'd prayed silently and in anguish as he bundled the boy into the car. No one had appeared to raise the alarm. And thank his stars too that the area boasted a chemist who stayed open late. Harry had stopped there for ether, which was easily obtainable if you convinced the pharmacist you were a photographer and asked for the stuff in millilitres. Some people might say it wasn't right to soak a cloth in the substance and clamp it over Michael's face to keep him quiet – but there was no alternative until Harry had a chance to explain things to him.

Another bad bit was when they abandoned Julie's car. It was easy enough for Harry to pick the lock of a vehicle and start it up via the engine, but he'd done so while possessed by the fear that someone might see him. Fortunately, it all happened in a deserted lane at the dead of night and it didn't seem as if there'd been any witnesses.

Since arriving at their hiding place, Harry hadn't made the mistake of going out and so he hadn't seen the papers, but he knew there was a nationwide hunt for him. Not that anyone would ever find him. He felt there was a touch of brilliance about the place he'd chosen, an incontestable proof that he wasn't so stupid after all. In a while, everything would calm down and then he could calmly rebuild the world recently shattered by the abrupt intrusion of reprehensible facts.

'Just trust me, Michael,' Harry urged the boy. Dear Michael, he thought. He'd be all right in the end. Uncle

Harry would look after him. Of course, initially the poor kid had been terrified out of his wits and took a lot of calming down. No wonder, Harry thought sympathetically. He was only a child. He didn't really understand. Although he'd started to understand a fair bit after Harry had explained things.

'I know it's hard for you to accept, Michael,' Harry had told him repeatedly, 'but sad though it is, your mum – whom I really like – really was suffering from this terrible illness in her mind. She felt incredibly guilty about your dad, you see. She felt that maybe she hadn't been nice enough to him during his time of trouble. And strange though it sounds, and I suppose you'll only understand grown-ups when you're one yourself, she wanted to be – well – sort of punished.

'Now I reckoned,' Harry had continued, 'that the best way I could help her was by doing what she wanted, same as I always have done. So I admit I tied her up just like she asked me. She was in quite a bad way but I could see all along how I was doing her good. But naturally we didn't want you or anyone else to know. That was why I had to tell you a few fibs. If other people knew, imagine the disgrace. They'd start saying that she was a bit mental – even though she was getting better all the time – and they'd take her away.

'That's what's happened now,' Harry had concluded sadly. 'The doctors have taken her away. And even though I promise you that she'll be fine in the end, until she's better they'll take you away too if they find you, and put you somewhere terrible. And they'll put me away as well, for ever, 'cos they're cruel and don't understand. But if we lie low for a while, then in time your mum'll be all right and we'll all be together and happy again, I promise you. I swear it on my honour, Michael. You'll see. Everything'll be okay.'

For a long time Michael had stayed silent, morose and extremely thoughtful. Then he'd co-operated quietly though remaining very withdrawn. Harry had failed in his every attempt to make him laugh. Michael wasn't in the mood for games either. Hours passed without anything being said.

Harry told himself to be patient. The boy was probably still suffering from shock. He'd be the old Michael again soon enough and recover his love and belief in Harry. Then they'd be together for ever.

Michael sat still. A clock was ticking loudly. Harry fiddled with a Stanley knife, sliding the razor-sharp blade in and out of its hilt. That was his last weapon if the impossible happened and they found him. One stroke across the throat for Michael and one stroke across the throat for himself. Together in life, together in death, together for all eternity.

'Harry,' Michael spoke up suddenly.

'Yeah, what, son?' Harry leaned forward attentively.

'That knife you're holding...'

'Yes...?'

At last Michael smiled.

'How about a game of Murder In The Dark?' he asked.

'Great!' exclaimed Harry, and laughed with joy.

27

IT WAS a cold, bleak morning when Inspector MacDonald stopped the car outside the neat, suburban house, then glanced anxiously at his passenger.

'Feeling up to it?' he enquired concernedly. Julie nodded. 'I must say how much I appreciate this, Mrs Foster,' MacDonald continued gently. 'It's obviously very, very difficult for you but I'm sure you appreciate the need to consider absolutely every angle.'

Be brave, Julie ordered herself, and once more nodded mechanically. She didn't want to return to the hell where she'd suffered. She felt sickened by the thought of trying to recall every detail she might have missed. But if the process might help with finding Michael, and MacDonald thought it might, then she would have to go back to hell. Julie regarded the house she'd once called home and her body was suffused by a wave of nausea.

MacDonald opened the car door for her and escorted her towards the house.

'Tell me anything about Harry which comes into your head down there,' he said, as they approached the steps. 'Absolutely anything, no matter how trivial. Just one thing we might've missed could be the vital clue.' His hand guided Julie by the elbow as they descended the stairs to the basement; his other hand dipped into his raincoat pocket and came out with the keys.

Julie held her breath. The door opened. MacDonald stepped into the gloomy hallway and pushed aside the second door his men had smashed.

He took three swift strides into the room, stopped, looked around – and then his breath left his body in a half-strangled gasp of shock.

Behind him, Julie screamed. In later years when she was in

bed with Bob beside her, all the money he had earned and all the security they had couldn't dull the memory of what she saw at that moment, for it would always haunt her nightmares.

They saw that Harry had returned to the room he'd proudly built, convinced that no one would ever look for him there.

And Michael, unwittingly brought to a knowledge of evil, had played his last game of Murder In The Dark.

There was a profound sadness on the boy's face as his glassy eyes regarded the sticky Stanley knife he held – and the blood around him which had bubbled from Harry's neatly slit throat – and the crimson wetness which had soaked the dead man's crutch.

'Mum's the word,' said Michael.

ALSO AVAILABLE FROM NEL

GERALD SUSTER
☐	05668 6	Striker	£1.95

THOMAS BLOCK
☐	05839 5	Airship Nine	£2.50
☐	05726 7	Forced Landing	£1.95
☐	05160 9	Mayday	£2.95
☐	05556 6	Orbit	£1.95

NANCY CATO
☐	04400 9	All The Rivers Run	£3.50
☐	05362 8	Brown Sugar	£1.95
☐	05651 1	Forefathers	£3.50
☐	04932 9	North-West By South	£2.50

All these books are available at your local bookshop or newsagent, or can be ordered direct from the publisher. Just tick the titles you want and fill in the form below.

Prices and availability subject to change without notice.

Hodder & Stoughton Paperbacks, P.O. Box 11, Falmouth, Cornwall.

Please send cheque or postal order, and allow the following for postage and packing:

U.K. – 55p for one book, plus 22p for the second book, and 14p for each additional book ordered up to a £1.75 maximum.

B.F.P.O. and EIRE – 55p for the first book, plus 22p for the second book, and 14p per copy for the next 7 books, 8p per book thereafter.

OTHER OVERSEAS CUSTOMERS – £1.00 for the first book, plus 25p per copy for each additional book.

Name ....

Address ....

....